Burke slowly pushed himself up. He walked over and looked at the three men where they lay. None of them moved. He forced himself to look at Reeves' face. Somehow, he felt it to be necessary. In the moonlight the tough face appeared as tough as ever. Burke felt no special sensation at his survival. The odds had been four to one against it, but it just meant four more dead. My brother, my enemy, he thought, and he wondered how many lives his own was worth.

Another Fawcett Book
by Norman Garbo:

TURNER'S WIFE

SPY

NORMAN GARBO

FAWCETT CREST • NEW YORK

A Fawcett Crest Book
Published by Ballantine Books
Copyright © 1980 by Norman Garbo

Library of Congress Catalog Card Number: 80-216

ISBN 0-449-20514-2

This edition published by arrangement with W. W. Norton &
Company

Printed in Canada

First Ballantine Books Edition: January 1985

FOR HARRY LOCKE—

there when needed

Prologue

I

About ten miles east of Beirut, Richard Burke sat near the edge of a forest, his back against a tall cedar, and waited for the daylight that was still an hour away. A rifle lay across his lap, and he fingered its stock, trigger guard, and barrel in ritual order. His rosary, he thought. Except that he had no prayers to recite, only the vague wish that what he had to do would be done quickly and without accident or surprise. He lifted his hands, stared at them in the grey dark and found some comfort in the fact that they were steady.

He was near the crest of a hill that rose steeply above a group of houses a short distance below. Closer to where he sat, another house stood apart from the rest. There were lights in several rooms, but they had been on all night and did not mean anything. Burke could see clearly through the lighted windows with his field glasses, and from time to time had watched the guards talking and moving about. There were four of them and they tended to huddle together for company instead of holding to their posts in and around the house. Arabs, thought Burke. Whatever their merits, disciplined soldiering would never be counted among them. Had they kept the area properly secured, he could never have moved in this close. As it was, he would have a clear shot, from good cover, at an effective range.

Burke watched the sky slowly lighten. He loved this time just before the rising of the sun, with shadows fading to the soft greys of Whistler. All the world seemed to remember Whistler for was that portrait of his mother, but it was his misty watercolors of London that were the best. You just had to look at them to breathe the Thames. Burke was not an especially jealous man, but he had envied Whistler those paintings. There was such purity of purpose there, so clear a knowledge of what was right. He had wondered if the artist had ever been uncertain of anything.

He was growing stiff and shifted to a prone position, careful to keep the rifle muzzle off the ground. The few trees below were clear now. He could see a table and chairs on the second-floor veranda of the solitary house. The veranda was open to the sky, and in the distance behind it the more modern part of Beirut's skyline rose beside ancient minarets. Farther north, the first of the early morning flights took off from the city's international airport and Burke watched the plane's lights until they disappeared. If all went well, he would be up there himself in a few hours. And if it didn't go well? Then he might be delayed. Like forever.

He glanced at his watch, thinking he would rather be just about anyplace but where he was. There was nothing about this assignment that he liked . . . not the killing, not the idea of having to waste a man he knew and respected, and certainly not the fact that he didn't understand anything about it. Up to the time Kreuger had called him to Washington and given him his orders, he had thought Abu Hamaid was high on the State Department's preferred list in the Middle East, a moderate Arab leader with the proper political leanings toward the United States and a genuine interest in a just peace for the area. He had been wrong . . . though not, of course, for the first time. During his more than twenty years with the Service, there had been so many changes in political alignments, so much switching about of friends into enemies and enemies into friends, that it was impossible to know who was on whose side on any given day without a program printed no earlier than that morning.

Ah, I'm getting too old for this, he thought. What I should do is get out of this whole crazy business and go off somewhere and paint. He smiled faintly at this, at what had become a rather wistful dream . . . also, a futile one. One rarely retired from his line of work. It was not a question of loyalty, patriotism, or devotion to duty. It was just that after a certain number of years, you had done too much and knew too much for them to let you go.

His clothes were wet from the dew and he shivered with the morning chill. A bird called from a nearby branch and Burke glanced up at it. The bird had yellow wings and an excited tail that flipped up and down. They looked at each other and Burke wished he could hold the bird and feel the softness of its feathers. He wished he could hold anything that was alive and warm and breathing. You felt alone at many times, he thought, but doing this was the worst of all for feeling alone. Even afterwards, there was no one you could share it with, no one who could understand. When he was still married, he had once tried to tell his wife. They had been much in love and there were moments between them when anything seemed possible. They could almost feel each other's blood, and what one sensed and knew, the other knew also. At one such point he said, "How much do you love me?"

"As much as it's possible."

"No matter what?"

"You should know that by now."

"Yes, but sometimes there are things I have to do. They don't always make me feel very lovable."

"If you do them," she said with the certainty of the young, the foolish, or the very much in love, "then it can't be too wrong."

"Some may think it is."

"Do you?"

"Sometimes. But even then, I believe it has to be done."

3

"Then it's all right," she said, granting him final absolution.

Which was all very lovely and sufficed for his particular needs at that time, but had not held up too well over the long haul. Not for either of them. Besides, he had not been really sharing, only hinting.

The bird flew away and Burke looked down through the cedars again to the house with the open veranda. For a while, he just lay quietly as the sky lightened further and the day came, a shining October morning without clouds and the colors running to soft pinks and purples. To distract himself and help pass the time, he imagined how he would paint it. One had to be careful about the softness because that was the thing in this, not so much the color, but the mood, which was of an absolute serenity.

He painted a great picture in his mind. But how well could he do on canvas? Given the chance, probably not badly. At least that was how he felt for now. At other times, when his work kept him from picking up a brush for weeks or even months at a stretch, he was much less certain of his talents and wondered whether he even had any at all.

He looked at his watch again. Within a half hour, Hamaid, a man of unswervingly regular habits, would be out on the veranda having his usual breakfast of croissants and coffee. Burke had known the Colonel for many years, long before his present rise to prominence, which was one of the reasons Tony Kreuger had thrown him into this job. That, and because Kreuger and he were close enough for trust and honesty in a line of work where both these commodities were in short supply. "I don't like having to stick you with this one," Kreuger had told him, "but there's nobody else I'd want to share it with."

That was all Kreuger had said on the subject, but his face had offered a lot more. He had a wonderful face, with deep-set eyes, high cheekbones, and the look of a born conspirator. If a movie producer were looking for someone to play a high-level intelligence agent, Burke was sure Tony Kreuger's face would get him the part. On that day in Washington, his face had been especially conspiratorial, hiding its nest of secrets behind that great, tough-looking facade, yet showing enough doubt and concern to let Burke know there were forces at work that he did not like and over which he had no control.

But like it or not, Kreuger had put him here and this was what he had to deal with. He knew that thinking was just about the worst thing he could do at a time like this, yet he was oddly unable to control it. Abu Hamaid was awake by now and Burke wondered what he was thinking, what plans he had made that would never be carried out, what love he had saved that would never be spent. Too bad. He was one of the good ones, one of the few who weren't foolish, angry, or corrupt. Which was probably why they had to get rid of him. Only it wasn't they who were getting rid of him. He was doing it. Oh, stop bitching, he told himself. And stop thinking so much too, or you'll really blow it and that won't help anyone.

The sun came up and shone on the house Burke was watching. A cool breeze sighed through the trees and drops of moisture fell. It was almost time and Burke started to get ready. He moved a small rock into position for support, rested the rifle barrel on it and squinted through the telescopic sights. The chair in which Hamaid would soon be sitting showed sharply behind the cross hairs. Burke inserted the clip of special explosive rounds into the magazine, worked one into the firing chamber, released the safety, and waited.

One of the guards came out first, stretched, scratched himself and leaned lazily against a wall of the veranda. A heavy-set woman brought out a well-laden tray and prepared the table with a single place setting, a pot of coffee, a basket of croissants, and a folded newspaper. Then she went back inside. Moments later, Abu Hamaid appeared. He spoke briefly to the guard, who threw back his head and laughed, then went inside also. Hamaid sat alone at the table with the sun shining on him. He poured himself a cup of coffee and looked up at the wooded slope where Burke was lying. Burke saw his face clearly through the telescopic sights. Hamaid seemed to be looking directly at him, his expression thoughtful as he squinted against the sun. Burke dug his elbows into the damp earth, steadying himself, feeling the rifle stock smooth against his cheek, letting the cross hairs drop down from the Colonel's face until they centered on his chest. Then he moved the cross hairs fractionally to the right, took his finger off the trigger guard, touched the trigger and thought, sorry, old friend.

It was the absolutely wrong thought for that specific moment. That is, wrong for dispassionate and efficient killing. Because along with the thought came a minute trembling in the fingers that made it impossible for Burke to keep his sights on target. He breathed deeply and tried again, but the trembling only grew worse and he finally closed his eyes and just lay there.

Easy, he thought. He was making too much of this. Abu Hamaid wasn't really an old friend. They had simply known one another for a long time and spent some nights talking and some days playing tennis and neither of them owed the other a thing. As a matter of fact, the man had just about the silliest serve he had ever seen.

He had to stop being such an ass, Burke told himself. He knew better. Under the right circumstances he knew he could kill anyone. Yes, but he was not convinced these were the right circumstances, and he did not think Kreuger was convinced either. That was the whole problem right there. Never mind the goddamned dialectics, he thought. He had been told to kill Hamaid, not to set Service policy or make fancy judgments. All he had to do was follow orders. The rest was neither his responsibility nor his concern.

Yes? Then where was he when the Nuremburg trials hit the fan?

He was well disciplined and had a long history of performance and control and obedience to orders behind him. So he tried again, and this time the trembling had indeed stopped and the cross-hairs found their target and remained there. But he did not squeeze the trigger. Some kind of psychic bombardment in defense of Hamaid's right to live had begun in his brain. It was suddenly a strange and lonely landscape he saw over the blued steel of his rifle barrel. There was no exhilaration in it, only the knowledge that once this particular place was reached, there was no turning back. It was the most frightening of discoveries. And the worst of it was its finality.

He lay still behind the tree, still held his rifle in firing position as if awaiting a miraculous change, an eleventh hour reprieve that would somehow allow him to carry out his orders and fulfill his mission under totally different circumstances. But there was neither change nor reprieve. Abu Hamaid finished his breakfast and read his morning paper without knowing how close he had come to enjoying neither ever again.

When Hamaid left the veranda and went into the house, Burke also left. He buried his rifle deep in the forest, drove to the Beirut airport in a rented car and boarded the noon flight to Rome that would eventually land him in Washington. There he would face Tony Kreuger and work out whatever terms he could for himself.

II

It was a strange New Year's Eve celebration. Counting himself, there were just the five of them in Pamela's corner room, all patients in the small private New York hospital that was devoted exclusively to the practice of plastic and reconstructive surgery. They drank champagne, sang "Auld Lang

7

Syne," danced the New Year in with Guy Lombardo and wore the silly party hats . . . all in weird contrast to the assortment of bandages, swellings, discolorations, and stitches they wore on their faces. What we must look like, decided Burke, is a coven of witches celebrating the devil's own birthday. Still, considering why they were there, the celebration had a sort of splendor.

Shortly after midnight, Lilly was well enough into it to take off her blouse and show them her new breasts. No one was shocked or even surprised. At that moment it seemed natural and right, an easy, warm sharing among friends. They had going for them by then a rare sense of communion that Burke had seen happen before, but only at moments of extreme stress or physical danger. This was different. And it was especially different for a New Year's Eve, his least favorite of nights. The forced gaiety, the conscious loss of another year, the memory of people and things long gone, invariably combined to depress hell out of him and push him to seek escape alone somewhere at the bottom of a bottle. This New Year's Eve he was neither alone nor terribly drunk, and this was the first of forty-three such nights that he was observing not as Richard Burke. Nor was he observing it from behind Richard Burke's face.

Had he been asked exactly whose face he was wearing tonight, he was not sure how he would have answered. He supposed that his new face belonged to his new identity—a man called Eric Cole. It had been created for that purpose, yet he, as Eric Cole, had had nothing to do with its creation. This was the work of Dr. Obidiah Stern, a major plastic surgeon with the given name of a minor Biblical prophet. And since the flesh, bone, and cartilege still belonged to Richard Burke, their original and longtime owner, the question of true possession was not a simple one. To be absolutely accurate, he thought, he would have to describe the face he had on tonight as a permanent mask, sculpted by Obidiah Stern, out of materials supplied by Richard Burke, and finally accepted, paid for, and worn by Eric Cole.

He had found the concept intriguing and baffling during the weeks since the operation. Day by day he had watched the results emerge from a cocoon of bandages and stitches. Had his parents been alive, he was sure even they would not have been able to recognize him. When he looked into a mirror, a stranger stared back. The only recognizable sign of Richard Burke was the pale, cornflower blue of his eyes . . . nothing more. And even they could be taken care of by colored contact lenses. Gone, the network of tiny squint lines. Gone, the heroic scimitar of a nose that had once earned him the nickname of Beaky. Gone, too, the incipient sagging of neck, chin, and jaw, the scar of an old knife wound, the bags he had acquired over uncounted nights, some pleasurable and some not so pleasurable. The new, synthetic Eric Cole looked at least ten years younger and immeasurably better than Richard Burke had looked when he checked into the hospital. Burke accepted this as a minor fringe benefit. The sole purpose of the surgery had been to give him a new face to go with his new identity. For the present, he cared to think no further.

Celebrating the New Year with Stern's other patients, Burke appeared to be just another accident victim with a surgically reconstructed face . . . the same as David, the youngest of the group. Except that David's auto accident had been real, which made the results of his reconstructive surgery much less positive than Burke's. Apparently there was just so much that could be done with lacerated flesh. Still, it was a face. And, as Obidiah Stern himself had described it to his young patient, a reasonably serviceable one. It was an understandable enough attitude for the surgeon to take. He was a professional who dealt with such things on a proper professional level. But it was David's face to live with, not Stern's, and during their weeks together in the hospital, Burke had glimpsed the doubts and fears that lay behind it.

Yet the kid certainly did cover it well, Burke thought now, sipping champagne from a paper cup and watching him gyrate with Lilly in the frenetic, rock, mating ritual that currently passed for dancing. Lilly had put her blouse back on, but had carefully left the two top buttons undone. She had too much of the natural exhibitionist in her to hide the breasts that STern had made significantly larger. The surgeon had also made her nose significantly smaller, but there she still wore surgical tape.

Pamela and Hank were dancing too, although more sedately than the younger couple. Hank was big, even for a heavyweight, and starting to thicken across the middle, but he moved with the fluid grace of an athlete. Burke remembered seeing him fight. It had been about ten years ago, when he was just starting to come up and he'd had style and a good, solid toughness that could take a lot of punishment. But he had lacked the big punch and never quite made it all the way. Catching Burke's eye, he grinned over Pamela's shoulder. One of the prophet Obidiah's miracles, thought Burke. Fourteen years of ring damage erased in four hours on the operating table.

When the music slowed to what Burke considered a more reasonable beat, he cut in on the ex-fighter. He had once enjoyed dancing, but had not done much since Angela had left him. And that had been about five years ago. My God, he thought, five years! You slid out of one life into another and then out of that one, too, and never even stopped to look back. Then one day you woke up, took a deep breath, and wondered where it all went.

Not concentrating on the music, he stumbled over Pamela's foot and felt her hand tighten across his back as she led him into the beat again. She laughed and teased him, a bright, crisply attractive business executive with a still youthful figure, whose forty-

10

year-old face had betrayed her by finally looking like a forty-year-old face. She had Stern's assurance, however, that when the swelling disappeared, at least ten of those years would also be gone.

By one o'clock, David was drunk and sentimental enough to get out his camera and take some pictures. The walking wounded, thought Burke, rather fuzzy-headed himself by then. What a curious thing they shared. And he had never really been a sharer, neither by nature nor by profession. In fact for twenty years he had led the kind of solitary, secretive life from which even his wife had been barred and from which she had finally abdicated. Yet here, tonight, he had somehow not wanted to remain apart. Maybe the old Burke would have chosen to welcome the new year alone in his room, but apparently not the man who was currently calling himself Cole.

The champagne gave out about two, and much of the euphoria shortly thereafter. Then came the confessionals, with everyone tired and vulnerable.

It was Lilly who slid into it first. Because she was in the theatre and had a fair amount of ham in her, she started off by dramatizing a little too much, by picking up fragments of characters she had once played and taking on some part of their pain as her own. Still, her frustrations were real enough, along with the doubts that might be eased for a while by the new facade Dr. Stern had given her, but would never be cured entirely. She was in the kind of business, she told them, where you either had it or you didn't, and a new nose and boobs weren't about to make that much difference. Look at Streisand's nose, for God's sake! But Streisand had a great and original talent, and finally that was all that mattered. Why kid herself? Second-rate when she walked in here, she'd be second-rate when she walked out.

Hank followed. When it came to second-rate, he claimed seniority. It was all there in his won-lost record. You just had to read it. The ring hung a clear

11

and brutal price tag on a man. So he expected no miracles from his new face. His scars cut a lot deeper than his skin. But even as he spoke, his eyes were dark and hot and held their own secret hope. Never mind the words, said his eyes. They were just a kind of creative suffering, a ritual confession, a necessary pouring on of ashes. His eyes knew better. He was a human creature after all. He owed whatever powers had created him a human life. And without hope, you stopped living.

Pamela picked up the cue next, with the wry, pseudotough, self-mocking approach that was her usual protective style, but which only served to add its own thin glaze to her anguish. She asked questions that did not have any answers. She wanted to know why she had suddenly been made to feel less, when she was not less. What was wrong with people? How could they live out their lives yet learn nothing of what really mattered? All at once, youth seemed to have become the supreme virtue. By merely having failed to live more than a limited number of years, you were automatically judged more desirable physically, and superior professionally than those who had lived a while longer. An utterly insane rationale. Yet she herself had finally surrendered to it and allowed a perfectly decent, serviceable face to be turned into that of a younger and only vaguely familiar stranger.

With David, of course, it was different. His lacerated face had made him the only one of the group who was not there through choice. His reconstructive surgery had been necessary, not elective. Though he had less to laugh about than any of them, he chose to handle it laughingly. He was planning a whole new career, he told them, in horror movies. He'd be a natural. He wouldn't even need any make-up. He was going to speak to Lilly's agent about booking him for a new TV series. They'd call it Monkey Man, he said, and proceeded to demonstrate his talent for the part by scampering about the room, arms dangling, making chattering, simian sounds. Nobody laughed.

Since Burke was allegedly an accident victim also, he had to be doubly careful about how he contributed his own feelings. So he offered what he hoped would be fitting and sympathetic fiction, picturing himself as a man without family or close personal ties, without significant past or visible future, a rather pathetic solitary animal that had chosen to live out life burrowing alone.

It was only afterward that he realized, with a kind of cold amusement, that it had not really been a fiction at all.

At shortly after three, David, the self-proclaimed Monkey Man, lurched towards a window, threw it open, and peered at the pavement far below. Grinning drunkenly, and with his camera still dangling about his neck, he half turned, waved, and called a cheerful, "Happy New Year", to the others. Then he climbed onto the window sill and started to push himself off. Burke leaped forward and grabbed his arm just as he was going over. For a moment, the two figures swayed over the edge. Finally, they fell back into the room and Hank Ryan slammed the window shut.

They all huddled over David, who smiled benignly at them, then wept, then just sat on the floor, looking at nothing. Forming a tight, curiously emotional circle, they held one another close. There was no one else, anywhere. The night and the New Year enclosed them.

Lilly left first with David, taking the now sober and trembling Monkey Man to her room and, Burke hoped, into the at least briefly comforting sanctuary of her bed. When Pamela and Hank began looking at one another with hungry eyes, Burke left also. Still wearing his party hat, he drifted slowly along the corridor to his room and lay down on the bed. It was very late but he was not sleepy and he just lay there, with the lights on, staring at the hospital ceiling.

1

THE BEGINNING   Almost a year after Burke's facial surgery, he saw his former wife, Angela. It was on a Saturday afternoon in late November, in a crowded gallery of New York's Metropolitan Museum of Art. She was standing in front of Monet's *Vetheuil,* which she had always loved for its brightness and color and dazzling illusions of sunlight. She had grown up in a series of gloomy, sunless Brooklyn tenements and had been chasing fragments of sun ever since. She was facing the other way, but he would have known that neck anywhere. Merely the way she held it had once been enough to break his heart.

"My God," he thought. "When am I going to stop loving her?"

His reaction surprised him. Lately, several days at a time would go by without his thinking of her. And it was harder and harder to remember certain details of her face and body. All of which may have made it easier for him to deal with, yet also made him sad. Perhaps you finally did have to bury your dead, but no one said you had to do it happily.

Angela turned and her glance passed over him without recognition, leaving a cold residue. Ah, I'm the one who is dead, Burke thought, and at that instant he began to function professionally.

It took him only moments to survey the gallery and narrow the possibilities to three men and one woman, although choosing the woman was an afterthought. They had begun to use women on surveillances only recently, and Burke had never fully adjusted. He made his final selection more slowly, drifting after Angela through the next few galleries and down the main stairway before settling on a short, plump man in a rumpled tweed jacket as his most likely candidate. To a casual observer, the man would have appeared no different from any number of other art lovers enjoying a weekend visit to one of the world's great museums. He looked at all the paintings, studied some more intently than others, appeared suitably rapt and sat down to rest occasionally. But he also never moved closer than ten feet from where Angela happened to be at any given moment, and to Burke, this was sloppy tradecraft. When Angela left the museum an hour later, the man was still a short distance behind her.

Allowing a safe interval, Burke followed. It was important to know if Angela was actually living in the city or just visiting. He also wondered whether she knew she was being used as bait. There was nothing in his knowledge of his former wife to make him believe she would let them use her this way, but a lot could have happened in the two years since he had last seen her. At that time, she had been living and working in San Francisco. Now, with the Service keeping her under surveillance, there was no way for Burke to accept her presence in New York as an accident.

From a block away, he saw her enter a converted brownstone on Seventy-fourth Street between Park Avenue and Lexington. The small man got into a station wagon, with a two-way radio antenna, parked diagonally across from the house. He sat behind the wheel and read a newspaper. Burke continued on to Second Avenue, found a public telephone, and looked up Angela Burke in the directory. She was not listed. He dialed information, asked for a new listing under her name, and a moment later had her number. Then on the off-chance that someone might be in, working, on a Saturday, he called the San Francisco office of the public relations agency where Angela had been an account executive and learned she had been transferred to New York two months before. There was little doubt that the Service had arranged the move. Two months of dangling bait, he thought, and he had finally stumbled over it. But fortunately, without biting.

He took a taxi home, poured himself half a tumbler of bourbon, and sat down to think.

In retrospect, it had not been a bad year. He had a comfortable apartment in a graceful old building that overlooked the Hudson, a spacious, north-lighted room in which to paint, no money pressures, and enough time to do all the things he had spent most of his working life complaining that he never had time to do. He read. He went to the theatre. He haunted the museums and galleries. He joined an indoor tennis facility and played, with cheerful aggressiveness, at least three times a week. In fact for a period of extreme adjustment, during which he'd had to accommodate himself to a new face, new identity, and new way of life, it had gone far better than he'd had any reasonable right to expect.

Still, he had never tried to fool himself about his future. He was too much of a professional, knew too much about the way these things worked, to believe he would ever be totally in the clear. When he walked along a street, he watched pedestrians, cars, doorways, and windows. In restaurants, he sat with his back to walls, preferably in corners, rear and flanks protected. Before he entered his own apartment, he always listened for a moment at the door, then checked for a tiny, almost invisible splinter of wood he never failed to leave wedged between the door and jamb, about a foot above floor level. He did these things partly from old habit, partly to keep his mind alert, and mostly because a small part of his brain believed that at any given moment his life might depend on them.

Tony Kreuger had stated it with his usual ambiguity at their last meeting. "You're out of it, but you're not out of it. And don't ever forget that."

Kreuger had been no more specific than that. He never was, unless there was an absolute need to know names or details. Which was one of the things that made him so good.

Holding his drink, Burke walked to a window and stared across the Hudson at the Jersey shore. He felt no fear or excitement, only a peculiar apathy, and this bothered him. He considered it a symptom of emotional disintegration. During the past year of his new life and identity, he had been given to frequent reviews of his old life and identity and rarely found them enjoyable. Making a judgment now, he felt forced to admit that he had mismanaged just about everything. His life was a mess. But since it had never really been too great at any time, there was not that much to mourn over.

Taking a long delayed inventory, he wondered whether he was a smart man or a fool. Well, at this point he could hardly claim to be brilliant. Perhaps at one time he might have considered his intelligence to be equal to the top of the line, but not anymore. Intelligence without discipline was like a fast thoroughbred without a rider, and for a long time now his brain had been galloping without true reason or control. Certainly his behavior on that hill outside Beirut, more than a year ago, could be classified as neither reasonable nor controlled. All he had done there was indulge himself in some fancy emotionalism. Had he allowed himself to think the thing through properly, he would have known that if he didn't kill Abu Hamaid as ordered, they would simply have someone else do it. Which was precisely what they had done, and within the week. So much for his concern about Hamaid's life. At best, it had been a futile moral gesture, a belated sop to his own doubts. Had he really cared about Hamaid, he would have found some way to warn him. Which, technically, would have made him, Richard Burke, a traitor, and probably would not have helped Hamaid anyway, but would have at least shown greater sincerity of intention.

So he was a fool.

Kreuger had a stronger word for him. "You're a schmuck!" he had shouted, and Kreuger rarely shouted. "Twenty goddamned years and you can still pull something like this? You can still indulge yourself in what, for us, is the ultimate vice . . . pity? What kind of future do you think you've got now?"

"I don't care about that. I'm getting out."

Kreuger had looked at him with a mixture of disgust and anger. "Okay. Good luck, schmuck." Still, it was Tony Kreuger who had sent him to Obidiah Stern for his facial surgery and stayed with him all the way.

The first hint that he might be in trouble had actually appeared a little more than two months ago. It was nothing dramatic, just a brief, rather cryptic announcement in the *New York Times* to the effect that there had been a personnel shake-up in the State Department's Office for Middle Eastern Affairs, along with several unspecified policy changes. There was also the implication that these changes reflected deep concern all the way up to the Oval Office itself, and carried the threat of further shock waves during the months ahead.

When Burke read it, he called Kreuger from a public booth up in Connecticut, gave him the number there, and waited for him to call back from a safe phone. "What does it mean?" he asked when he heard his friend's voice once more.

"Among other things," said Kreuger, "that it was a serious mistake to have had Abu Hamaid killed."

"So?"

"So you may be in a kind of sticky spot."

"Why?" Burke asked, having a fair idea of the answer but wanting any possible doubt removed. "I was the guy who didn't kill him. Remember?"

"Yes, but you knew about the original order.

Which makes you one of the potentially damaging loose ends. And you know how they are about neatness in these things."

"Lovely."

"You're not badly off yet."

'When will I be?"

"When they find you." said Kreuger.

"You're very funny."

"You know I always make bad jokes when I'm worried. But you're okay for now. At least as long as the agent who actually did the shooting is still walking around."

"How will I know if he's not?"

"Call me at two week intervals."

Burke did, and on the third call Kreuger gave him the news. "They got to him yesterday."

"How?"

"An auto accident."

Burke was silent.

"I'm sorry," said Kreuger.

"I know."

"You realize, of course, that I'm in as bad a spot as you."

"I don't realize anything. You never did tell me the mechanics of it."

"I never had that much to tell," said Kreuger. "I never knew exactly where the order to kill Hamaid originated. It just came down on a need-to-know basis, and I passed it on to you the same way." He laughed, but it had a cold sound. "And I called you a schmuck for cutting out. If you hadn't, you'd be buried right now."

"I may still be."

"Yes, but they've got to find you first, you lucky bastard. If they should ever decide to label me a threat, they know exactly where I am and what I look like."

Well-intentioned hogwash from a friend. Kreuger was, of course, exaggerating the possibility of his own danger to make him feel better. The soothing panacea of a shared threat. Nevertheless, from the moment Burke told him he was getting out, Kreuger had insisted on not knowing any of the details. "I don't want to know where you're living," he said, "what name you're using, what you're doing, or what your goddamned face looks like. It'll be better for both of us that way." It was a basic Service tactic. What you didn't know, no one could ever make you reveal.

Now, sipping his drink, Burke stared blankly out the window at a tug working a string of barges upriver. He was finding it hard to concentrate. Seeing Angela had disturbed him more than he cared to admit. He felt tempted to get out somewhere and call Kreuger, tell him he had seen her, and find out what, if anything, he knew about it. But he put down the urge. It was easy enough to figure out why they had switched her to New York, and there was nothing that Kreuger could add to it. There was also no sense in letting his friend know he was alerted to the bait. It was not lack of trust. Kreuger was probably the only one left he could trust. It was just that it was always better to keep something in reserve.

He broiled a couple of hamburgers for dinner, then went into his studio and fussed with some sketches until well after midnight. When he felt tired enough to sleep, he allowed himself a double brandy as insurance and went to bed.

2

Four days later, on Wednesday, Burke picked up an
early edition of the *New York Times* and discovered
that he was in even greater trouble than he had
feared.

As before, there were no major headlines. It was
just a small, single column notice on the obituary
page to the effect that Anthony Kreuger, an interna-
tionally known geophysicist based in Washington,
D.C., had died of an apparently self-inflicted gunshot
wound. Although no suicide note had been found,
Kreuger was reported to have been despondent and
in poor health for some time, and the coroner's office
as well as the police felt there was little doubt that
he had taken his own life.

Well, Tony . . . thought Burke.

He thought it sadly and with true pain because
Kreuger had been a friend, and Burke had not had
many. But more than friendship was involved. It
was Kreuger himself who had recruited Burke right
out of college, been his chief sponsor and protector,
and taught him pretty much all there was to know of
the trade. Apparently you could never know quite
enough. Even when you were the absolute best. No
one in the Service had ever doubted that Kreuger
was that. And before he had died, Burke was quite
certain he had given them the name of Dr. Obidiah
Stern. There was no condemnation in the thought.
Finally, everyone told what they knew, and it had
nothing to do with any lack of such things as
strength, loyalty, patriotism, love, or courage. It was

21

simply a matter of the vulnerability of flesh and possible levels of pain.

Then Burke put aside for the moment what he chose to consider the idle luxury of grief, and let his mind move into the more practical considerations of survival. On the positive side was the fact that the surgeon's identity was the only potentially damaging piece of information that Kreuger could have given them. Tony had never known where Burke lived or what his new face looked like. Nor had he known the name, Eric Cole, that he had used in the hospital.

All right, Burke thought. So what could they have? To begin with, the name of a New York plastic surgeon. And because Obidiah Stern had done work for the Service through Kreuger for years, he always followed tight security guidelines. No pictures or descriptive records in his files. No questions answered, not for anyone, regardless of official rank or alleged authority. And that included the upper levels of the Service itself, the State Department, both houses of Congress, and the Oval Office. As a further safeguard against possible pressure in that area, Kreuger had even banned himself. "No matter what I ever ask about the identity or appearance of someone I've sent you," he once told the surgeon, "no matter how I may rant, scream, order, or threaten, don't—and I mean don't ever—tell me." And from whatever Burke had observed of Obidiah Stern's nature, he judged the surgeon to be strong and intractable enough to hold to those instructions.

But just as Burke had to assume that Kreuger had finally been forced to give them Stern's name before they shot him, he had to also assume they were now serious enough to use the same methods on the surgeon. Such being the case, Stern would eventually give them the name of Eric Cole (which no longer meant anything since he had switched to the name of Thomas Hutchins immediately on leaving the hospital) and a description of the changes he had made in his face, which would mean little more. Additionally, Stern would give them the precise dates he had entered and left the hospital, as well as the names of other patients who may have been there with him at that time.

Then he remembered their little New Year's Eve celebration. And having recalled this, it didn't take him too much longer to conjure up a champagne-blurred image of David, sentimentally recording the celebration with his camera.

"My God," he thought. "I've been senile for almost a year."

It was necessary to see Obidiah Stern alone. Burke waited until late that night. The surgeon was unmarried and lived with a housekeeper in an East Sixty-fourth Street townhouse that also contained his office. Burke walked down the block shortly after eleven and stood in a doorway across the street from the house, watching it. The house was dark except for a light in a third-floor window. Burke had no way of knowing whether the housekeeper slept in; that was a chance he would have to take. At three minutes to midnight, he put on a pair of thin, leather gloves, crossed the street, and tried the front door. He had it open in less than a minute.

A small night light was on in the foyer and he stood there for a moment, listening. Muted traffic noises came from outside, but the house was quiet. He breathed in the mingled odors of a doctor's office, that night's cooking, and a piney disinfectant. He had hoped to be free of all this, had hoped to be able to ring doorbells and enter houses as normal people entered them, but here he was again, breaking and entering, stealing into a man's home just to talk to him.

He had to tell this gentle, eminent man: you've done a lovely job on my face and I'm quite pleased with it, but I'm afraid there are complications. You see, Obidiah, there are some people who would like to see me dead. I don't know their names or what they look like, so we're faced with a bit of a problem. And unfortunately, you're included. Because very shortly now, I expect them to pay you a visit to get your help in identifying me. And whoever they are, they don't fool around. They've already killed Tony Kreuger and they're not likely to treat you any better. So I'm breaking into your house tonight like a thief, because I couldn't risk the phone, or your housekeeper seeing me, and I had to warn you.

A foolish dialogue, he thought, climbing the stairs slowly, planting his feet with care and listening after each step. What good would a warning do? Stern could hardly run away and hide. Short of surrounding himself with armed guards, what possible action could he take? Still, he had to be warned and this seemed the fastest and best way to go about it. Burke liked Obidiah Stern. At a time when the word physician was increasingly coming to mean equal portions of greed and callousness, Stern still clung to the heart of his Hippocratic Oath. "It's our liferaft," he had once said. "Without it we'd drown in a sea of avarice." Unhappily, many of his colleagues seemed to have already done their drowning.

On the second floor landing, Burke breathed the air again, consciously and deeply. He had a difficult nose to live with. It was too sensitive. It told him too much. Obidiah may have changed its size and shape, but not its capabilities. He went up the stairs and did not stop again until he had reached and entered the lighted third-floor room.

The room was half bedroom, half study, with books lining two walls, an old-fashioned double bed, a few scattered chairs, and a large mahogany desk covered with papers, assorted memorabilia, and the body of Dr. Obidiah Stern.

The surgeon lay with his head on the desk, dark hair rumpled as if from sleep. His left shirtsleeve was rolled up and there was a hypodermic syringe in his right hand. His eyes were open, glinting in the light, eyes perfectly clear and blue. He was quite dead.

Richard Burke—Eric Cole for a short time and currently Tom Hutchins—stood looking at Obidiah Stern's face. Every instinct told him to get out of there, fast, but a peculiar apathy was upon him. They had moved a lot faster than he had expected, which meant he was high priority—probably Code-One. Very flattering.

There was a handwritten note near the body. Scribbled on a prescription blank, it read "I'm sorry . . ." and was unsigned. They were apparently big on suicides these days. Everything all neat and accounted for. No loose ends. And apart from whatever else he felt, it suddenly made him angry. Of all those he had ever known, none had less reason to take their own lives than Tony Kreuger and Obidiah Stern. To have them stamped as suicides, was insult added to the ultimate injury. There was nothing he could do anymore about Tony, but Obidiah was something else.

Carefully thinking it through, Burke rolled down and buttoned the dead man's sleeve, removed the hypodermic from his hand, and put it and the suicide note into his own pocket. Then in a short, vicious, cutting blow, he drove the side of his hand into the back of Stern's neck and heard that awful cracking sound. Ah, Obidiah. Even dead, it hurt. But all right. Let the bastards worry a little about that. It would also give the locals something to do besides chase whores up and down Eighth Avenue. It was a small victory and the satisfaction was brief. A decent man with the unfashionable given name of a minor prophet was still very much dead, and unless he himself was willing to join him soon, there was a lot to do.

He left the surgeon at his desk, a murder turned into suicide and then into a murder once more. The broken neck would confuse them for a while. The autopsy would later reveal the murder as drug-induced, but it would never be a suicide again.

On his way downstairs Burke checked the rest of the house for the housekeeper, not really expecting to find her. They could not have done what they did, had she been around. They would not have had any qualms about killing her along with her employer, but a second murder would have ruined their neatly plotted suicide script.

Using a small flashlight, Burke went through Stern's first floor offices until he found the cabinet that held his patient's files. He had to assume that before they allowed Obidiah the privilege of dying, they had drained him of all pertinent information. And this would have included the name Eric Cole, the dates he entered and left the surgeon's private hospital, and the names of other patients who had been there at the same time and might be of help in identifying and locating Cole. First, he looked for his own file under the name Cole. It was not here. Then in quick alphabetical order, he looked for the folders of Pamela Bailey, Lilly Moraine, Hank Ryan, and David Tomschin. Without surprise, he found them gone.

He left the front door locked behind him and walked west on 66th Street. When he reached the entrance to Central Park, he went in and continued for a while on the east-west transverse. Then he cut north on a pedestrian path, walking slowly because he did not want to get home too soon, and letting the anger build until it felt cold and solid in his chest. Lost in it, he did not see the two men until they were almost in front of him.

"Hey, man! Got any bread?"

He stopped and looked at them. The one who had spoken was big, with a flowering Afro that made him look even bigger. His companion was shorter, but wide-shouldered and well set up. Standing together, they blocked the path. The shorter one, Burke saw, was carrying an open switchblade. There was no one else in sight.

"Sure," he said. "I'm loaded, man!" He grinned as he mimicked the man's speech, certain he had somehow dreamed these two up because they fitted his mood so perfectly.

His response and grin threw them off. Finally the big one said, "Okay, man, give it here."

"Screw you, man." Burke said.

This drew another long moment. "Hey, don't go messin' 'round," said the one with the blade. "Hand it over or you gonna get cut."

"Come and get it."

Feet scraped nervously. Burke could not see their eyes, but could feel the uncertainty. Maybe they thought he was a police decoy or had a gun. The park was getting tougher all the time for hard-working dudes. The silence stretched and Burke was afraid they were going to back off entirely.

Then grunting, the big one came at him with a wide, looping right. Burke stepped inside, drove his fist into the man's middle, and knee'd him as he doubled over. He dropped and his partner lunged. The blade glinted as Burke turned to let it go past. He grabbed the arm with the knife and twisted until he heard it go. The blade fell, the man screamed, and Burke sent him down with a cold chop to the throat.

He walked away without glancing back.

He couldn't sleep, so he spent the night trying to work it through. Here he was, he thought, an invisible prey for equally invisible hunters. Yet there was a particular irony even in this. Somewhere high up, there were those who wanted him dead because they feared he could tie them to a political murder that had begun to stink. He had no idea who they were.

By the end of the night he found himself no closer to a useful answer than when he had started. The more he thought, the more bleak his prospects seemed. Seeking respite, his mind drifted to the tiny

27

group in the hospital on New Year's Eve, to the warmth, the *gemütlichkeit,* the good feeling of sharing. Now they were about to share something different, he thought. But this time, there was going to be damned little good in it for any of them.

3

Burke stood in the narrow hallway outside David Tomschin's apartment and felt himself sweat with frustration. He could make out two voices beside David's. They had locked the door behind them and there was nothing Burke could do until they came out. Burke had resigned himself to that. Now he just hoped the kid was smart enough to give them what they wanted as quickly as possible and not get himself hurt.

They had been waiting outside in a car when Burke first strolled past the building. David arrived home and went upstairs about an hour later. The two men followed close behind, and after a short interval, Burke did the same. He had not recognized either of the men. He had been calling David's number since early morning, but had received no answer, and it was late evening now. Too bad he had not been able to get to David first. It would have saved them all a lot of trouble.

The self-service elevator opened and a couple came out and walked down the corridor, talking. Burke fumbled through his pockets, as if searching for keys or cigarettes, and hurried towards the elevator. When the couple disappeared into one of the apartments, he went back to David's door. The voices were still going. Then he heard a sharp cry and the sound of something heavy falling. He put his ear against the door. A moment later he tied a handkerchief across his face below his eyes and took out a pistol. It had a silencer attached. As the door opened, he levelled the gun.

"Back inside," he said.

Silently, the two men backed up. One was tall, with a gaunt, ascetic face, the other was chunky, and they both stared at the pistol with total fascination. Burke closed the door behind him and took a quick inventory. Books were strewn about, drawers were open and emptied, and David was stretched out on the floor. His face was white and his mouth was bleeding. He looked dazed but not badly hurt.

"Okay, give me the pictures," said Burke.

"What pictures?" asked the one with the ascetic face.

Burke's eyes held him. "Don't sweat it."

"Sure. They're all yours."

But the man did not move and the three of them stood there like figures in a tableau.

"Now," said Burke.

"You got it, friend." said the chunky man, which must have been some sort of pre-arranged signal because both of them lunged forward at precisely the same instant, arms extended and fingers reaching. In fact it all happened so fast that Burke never saw whose hand reached the gun first and ripped it free. He knew only that it hit the floor with a clatter, and he made a dive for it. But the tall man kicked it across the floor where it struck a chairleg, bounced off, and came to rest against David's thigh.

Seeming to react out of pure instinct, David reached for it, picked it up, and pointed it at Burke and the two men, frozen again in another tableau. Burke's handkerchief-mask had fallen during the struggle and David stared. "Eric," he whispered.

Then the moment broke and the two men went for the pistol. They went for it with no more apparent thought or concern than if it had been lying loose on the floor and not pointing at them from David's hand.

"I'm not shit!" David yelled and showed them he wasn't, showed them pointblank as they came, with the silencer cutting the explosions to a soft *whoosh . . . whoosh . . . whoosh* and the bullets going in without any sound at all.

The gun was empty long before he finally stopped squeezing the trigger. Then he got up and started to kick the two bodies where they lay. He kicked and kicked until Burke dragged him away and sat him down in a chair. He started to sob then, and Burke took some ice from the refrigerator, wrapped it in a towel and pressed it to the back of his neck. "Oh, my God," he wept. "Oh, my God, my God."

Burke found some brandy in a cabinet and forced him to drink. After awhile he stopped crying. "Now pay attention." Burke said. "Are you okay? Can you understand me?"

David stared through him for a moment. Then his eyes focused and he nodded.

"Good," said Burke. "Now tell me everything those two men said and did from the moment they walked in here. And take your time. Think carefully."

David blew his nose a few times, but the hysteria seemed to be over. "The dirty sons-of-bitches. They pushed me around like I was shit . . . like I wasn't even human. Even at the end, even when I was pointing a gun at them. You saw? You saw how they just came at me?"

Burke nodded. "Who did they say they were?"

"Cops. They said they were cops investigating Dr. Stern's murder. They showed me their shields and said they just wanted to ask me a few questions." He started to weep again. "Oh, Jesus. I've gone and killed two fucking cops. I don't believe it. I . . ."

"What kind of questions?"

David took a deep breath. "Questions like, 'When did I last see or talk to you and the others from the hospital? When did I last see Dr. Stern?' Things like that. Then when they found out I'd taken some pictures during our New Year's Eve party, they went kind of crazy. They said you'd killed Dr. Stern and they needed a picture of you because otherwise they'd never find you with your new face. But I didn't believe that shit. I knew you couldn't have killed Stern. So I made like I'd forgotten where the pictures were. But they just tore the place apart until they found them. When I picked up the phone to call the D.A.—because they had no search warrants or anything—they just slapped me down. Just put me down like I was nothing." He sipped his drink and the glass rattled against his teeth.

"What else?" said Burke.

David stared blankly at him.

"Do you remember anything else?"

"No."

"You're sure?"

"Yeah." David shook his head. "No. I mean one of the bastards made a phone call. He told someone that pictures were taken at the hospital."

"Did you hear who he called? Did he use any name?"

"No."

"Did he say where he was calling from, or who took the pictures?"

"I . . . I don't think so."

"We've got to be sure of that. No thinking. *Sure.*"

"Oh, God," David whispered.

"Are you sure?" Burke repeated.

"I'm sure. I'm sure. He didn't say any names."

"Okay," said Burke. "Now listen to me. To begin with, those two men weren't cops. They were a couple of hard-nosed, less-than-blessed intelligence agents, and they had absolutely no right to come in here, pass themselves off as police officers, ransack your apartment, and abuse you. Which doesn't mean you can just shoot them at will. But at least morally and legally, you're in a hell of a lot better shape than if you had shot a couple of honest-to-God cops acting in the line of duty."

David shook his head. "You don't understand. I shot those two guys because I wanted to, because I hated their guts. I didn't care what they were." He stared bleakly at the bodies on the floor. "And you know something else? I'm not sorry, even now."

You will be, thought Burke, but said nothing.

"Why were they after you?" David asked. "I knew what they said was crap, but what did they really want you for?"

For a long moment Burke stared silently at the younger man. From old habit, the thought of killing the kid did briefly cross his mind. It sickened him; once you shared something like this, it was out of control. The kid had saved his life. There were the two bodies. They changed everything—David's future as well as his own. Which meant that from this moment on, the kid was inextricably involved. But he was not about to kill him.

He gave few specifics, but even in vague outline it came across as a chillingly gothic tale, although this was precisely the world he had functioned and survived in all his working life, now hoping he had accumulated enough knowledge and skill to help him survive retirement. Still, this accident-damaged young man, acting out of pure emotion, had just saved both their lives. And how did you go about making rational judgments about that?

When Burke finished, David sat staring into the remains of his brandy. "Jesus," he said.

"How do you feel?"

"I'm not sure yet. Kind of numb, I guess."

"We've got a long, hard night ahead. Are you up to it?"

David turned and forced himself to look at the two

bodies. It was a sort of litmus test. He swallowed once, then nodded. "Just tell me what to do."

Once they were into it and functioning, it was better for them both. Burke could almost feel some of the old gears grinding into place. David kept his car garaged just a few blocks away, which would at least simplify moving the bodies. But there were details to be taken care of first and they were not pleasant. They stripped the bodies and Burke searched their clothing. He found David's pictures. There was nothing else of importance. Nor was there anything on the men to tell him who they were. Then he and David scrubbed all traces of blood from the floor. Sometime during the next few days, the entire apartment might be gone over by experts. Finally, they crammed the bodies into two old footlockers that David had used for storage.

Shortly after eleven they used the elevator to get the footlockers down into the basement. David brought his car around to the service entrance and they loaded up. A few people were passing on the street, but no one paid any particular attention to them. Burke glanced at David. There was a controlled, calm expression on his face that looked as though it might disintegrate at any second.

"Better let me drive," Burke said.

They rode for almost two hours, until they reached the beginnings of the Catskills. There was a low moon and the night was warm for November, with strands of mist hanging over the roads and fields. A dirt track ran off into the woods, and it was here that they scraped into the soft earth, buried the bodies, and covered the grave with leaves and rocks. Then leaving the two unblessed souls to fend for themselves, they drove back towards New York with the empty footlockers.

It was after four when they crossed the city line. David was driving now. Sprawled beside him, Burke felt drained and saddened because of what he had inadvertantly gotten this decent, already afflicted kid into.

"You're an incredible young man," he said.

"Sure. I'm terrific. They slapped me around a little back there and I vomited on the rug."

"You also saved both our lives."

"You mean those two apes really would have killed us?"

"It was their job to find and kill me. And since you would have been a witness, they'd have had to kill you."

David drove on in silence.

"How have things been going for you?"

"Stinking."

"Why?"

"You kidding? With this face? I'm lucky the city doesn't pay to keep me off the streets."

"It's really not that bad."

"Ah, come on. I've been living with it for almost a year now. I don't need any of that bullshit."

Burke said nothing.

"The thing is, nobody can really look at me. Not my parents, not women, not anybody. When they try, their eyes just kind of slide off my face and ease around it." David laughed coldly. "So I make it easy on them and keep to myself. The only one who can actually put up with me is this little hooker I found on Eighth Avenue. I figured with someone like her, it's strictly a cash deal. Her name is Dolores. She's nineteen years old and looks like sixteen. Imagine. I couldn't even get it up with her the first time because she reminded me of my kid sister. But I got over that." He glanced at Burke as he drove. "Anyway, you asked, so I'm telling you. Though I shouldn't bitch. At least I got enough insurance dough out of the accident so I don't have to worry about money. And I'm writing. It's probably not much good, but I'm finally getting stuff down on paper." David grinned shyly, self-consciously. "And

35

that's the story of the short, terrible life of David Tomschin, Jew-boy killer."

"You did okay tonight."

David stared thoughtfully at the road ahead. "I think tonight's the first time since my accident that I've forgotten about my face for a few hours. But Jesus, what a way to have to do it."

4

Pamela Bailey left her office at 2:10 P.M. for a late lunch and walked up Madison Avenue towards Fifty-second Street. She did not see Burke, watching her from a tan Plymouth parked diagonally across from where she worked. Burke started the car and drove slowly after her, the crawling midtown traffic allowing him to keep pace. He studied the people on the sidewalk, but saw nothing to disturb him. At up to a hundred yards, he could spot a tail as easily as he could pick out a bad hairpiece, and assumed it was just too soon for them to have missed and replaced the two agents David had shot. Still, he took nothing for granted. He had found that for survival, fear usually offered you a lot more protection than assurance.

Pamela was waiting for the traffic signal to change at 54th Street and Park, when he drew up to the curb and stopped beside her. "Pamela!" he called.

It took her a few seconds to bend, peer into the car, and recognize him as Eric Cole. "Hey! Look who's here!"

He reached over and opened the door for her. "Please get in, quickly."

Pamela was sitting beside Burke and they were starting across Park Avenue only an instant after the light had turned green and the driver behind had blown his horn.

"You really don't have to kidnap me," she said. "All you have to do is smile nicely and ask."

Burke grinned. He was sure Pamela had not been

37

followed, but his eyes kept watching the rearview mirror anyway. "You look great," he said. "Twenty-five years old and beautiful."

"Look who's talking! That nose of yours is an absolute masterpiece."

"We were lucky. We had a good man. They don't come any better than Obidiah." Burke paused. "You heard about him?"

"It was awful. Animals are loose in the city."

"Has anyone been questioning you?"

"What do you mean?"

Burke turned onto Third Avenue and headed uptown to avoid a traffic tie-up ahead. "The police?" he said. "Detectives? Anyone like that?"

"Why should they want to question me?" Then seeing where they were heading, "Listen, if we're really leaving town I'd like to pick up a toothbrush."

"I need about an hour. It's important."

"You mean this wasn't just a happy accident?"

"I've been parked across from your office for more than two hours."

She sighed. "I have this terrible feeling you're not lusting for my body."

Burke drove up the East River Drive, then across the Triborough Bridge and north on the Major Deegan Expressway. He talked as he drove, finding the telling easier this time. Spilling the seed, was what Tony Kreuger had called it, believing that the more people there were who knew about you in this work, the shorter your life expectancy. But Burke felt he did owe these people at least a warning and a chance to make their own decisions. Though how much good any of it would finally do them, he did not know.

Pamela sat shaking her head. "Poor David. What a thing for the kid to have to go through. How is he?"

"He's okay. How are you?"

"Why me?"

"Haven't you been listening?"

"You said those two men were dead."

"Yes, but there'll be others. Also, when they called in to report the existence of those pictures, they apparently never said who had them. Which means it could be any one of you four. And when they fail to make their next scheduled contact, a replacement team will be trying to find out which one of you it is."

"I don't understand. Can't we just call the police?"

"I'm afraid it wouldn't do much good. Washington can easily smother any local interference in national security matters. And right now there are apparently those who consider me an outright threat to our national security."

"But this is America, for God's sake!"

"So it is. And that's how they're trying to keep it."

She was indignant. "But aren't you even angry?"

"If I thought it would help, I'd happily be angry."

"How can you be so controlled?"

"You learn."

Burke exited at Van Cortlandt and parked near the lake. "None of us are really villains," he said. "Not even those two we buried last night. We've just had to learn history more thoroughly than people who do other things. We've learned that virtue doesn't matter to history and that crimes go unpunished, but that every mistake by people in government is paid for in blood. So we do our best to avoid mistakes. When we can't avoid them, we try to wipe out any signs they ever existed. Unfortunately, I'm currently labelled as one of those signs."

She sat absolutely still, staring at a crow in the top branches of a naked tree. "I don't understand much of that. But I don't suppose that really matters, does it?"

Burke said nothing.

"So what am I supposed to do now?" she asked.

"It's hard for me to tell you that."

"Why?"

"I can't ask you to take risks because of me."

"Why not?"

He laughed. "You do ask the damnedest questions."

"Well, you do come up with the damnedest situations. Just tell me my options and let me decide about the risks."

"It's not that simple."

"Just tell me."

Burke took a moment. He was unsure of himself, of the situation, and of this woman. But he still trusted his instincts, and these favored what she had so far shown him of herself.

"There are three things you can do," he said at last. "You can just disappear for a long vacation until this is settled one way or another . . ."

"What does settled mean?" she cut in.

"They identify and eliminate me, or I identify and eliminate them, or him, or whatever."

"Lovely," she said and made a face. "Go on."

"Do you still have the picture of me that David sent you with the others?"

She was staring up at the crow again. It had now been joined by another on the branch below. "Of course. I keep it beside my bed. With the Bible."

"Well, then you can wait and give it to whoever appears and asks for it. That is, if they come at all. They may go to Lilly or Hank first and get the pictures from one of them. I haven't spoken with either of them yet, so I don't know how they're going to react to all of this. Naturally, that would be the simplest and safest way for you to keep from getting involved."

"Naturally," she said. "All right. Now that you've gotten all the bull out of the way, let's hear what you really want me to do."

"You're a very funny lady."

"Sure. I'm a panic. But since I'm obviously not going to get laid this afternoon, I may as well reach for another kind of truth. So tell me my third option."

"I can't really be sure of that until I find out what

their next moves are going to be. But to begin with, it would mean doing nothing any different than you're doing now. Just go on leading your usual day to day life. Except that I'd like you to burn my picture."

"Burn that beautiful thing? Then what am I supposed to use for my fantasies?"

Burke grinned and handed her the snapshot that he had composed and printed in David's darkroom early that morning. "You can try using this. The face belongs to an uncle of David's who died a few years ago, but the gorgeous body is still mine. If they should ever press you for my picture, it could save you a lot of trouble if you give them this."

Pamela studied the photograph. "I like your face better. But it's a cute idea. Do you think they'll go for it?"

"It might buy me some time."

"Time for what?"

"To find out who it is who considers me enough of a threat to want me dead. Because that's about the only chance I'm ever going to have to walk around like a human being again."

They sat without speaking.

The two crows suddenly flew away from the tree, cawing loudly, and Pamela watched them until they were out of sight. "I don't know why," she said, "but I've always felt terribly sorry for crows. There's something so lonely and sad about them. Maybe it's that mournful black they have to wear, or that poor, awful sound they make." She looked at Burke. "Do you have any particular feeling about crows?"

"Just that they're the only birds my father ever said it was okay for me to shoot with my air rifle."

"You see? The poor things are pariahs, absolutely friendless. Everyone is after them."

Burke half smiled. "You mean like me?"

She thought about it. Far off and faint now, the crows could still be heard.

"Well," she said at last. "Maybe a little."

41

"It's all right. I don't mind you feeling sorry for me."

"If I do feel that way," she said, picking her way carefully, "it's not for you alone."

"Who else?"

She shrugged. "Probably for myself. And for David. And for Lilly and Hank, too. When I think of us all back there on New Year's Eve, hoping and expecting so much, yet going through those fake confessionals, pouring ashes on our heads, and making believe we didn't really hope and expect . . ." She hesitated. "It takes a long time and a lot of practice to become a human being. It's obscene, that having finally done so, you find you no longer seem to be of any value to other human beings." She was about to say something more, but changed her mind. She was breathing heavily, not perhaps from any one emotion but from a whole mixture. She tried to smile, but it never came off.

"Have you seen Lilly or Hank at all?" he asked.

"I saw Lilly in a show, off-Broadway, about six months ago, and I stopped by her dressing room. It was a terrible mob scene. We barely said hello. She seemed to be doing great. She had a good part in a hit show. But there was a kind of wild look to her. I don't know. Maybe she was just stoned." Absently, Pamela's fingers polished the rough fabric of Burke's sleeve. "And Hank?" she said. "Hank called me and we saw each other a few times. But it was so sad. He couldn't find work and we never really had that much to say to one another. I think he kind of resented me finally. You know . . . my job and the big salary and all. I suppose he found me a threat or something. Anyway, he stopped calling after awhile. I called him a few times, but he always made some excuse. And that was pretty much it."

Burke drove her back to midtown Manhattan at about four o'clock. They did not talk much on the return trip. Once, she looked at him and smiled. "My poor crow," she said, and leaned over and kissed his cheek.

"Caw . . . caw . . ." said Burke.

5

The Orange Lantern was an Eighth Avenue massage parlor with a flickering neon sign over the entrance describing it as an oriental health spa for men. Burke walked past it twice, once from each direction, before he finally climbed the wooden stairs to the second floor reception area and presented himself to a motherly-looking Chinese woman, sitting at a desk.

Ten minutes later he lay naked on a rubbing table in a private cubicle, while a not-so-motherly-looking Chinese girl, in pale blue bra and panties, ran practiced hands over his body.

It was the first time he had ever been in such a place and he thought, curiously, that what it really made him feel like, was the keyboard of an old, out-of-tune piano. It also made him feel vaguely decadent. Being an essentially spartan type, it went against his usual concept of things merely to lie there while another person labored to bring him pleasure. Still, it was all quite pleasant and happily erotic, and since he was there and part of it, he relaxed like a king lion in the sun and let those ten, pre-paid fingers romp. The girl had a gift, and he was off on the nicest dream of oriental palaces with their scents and spices, of slant-eyed, nubile maidens breathing rosy pictures into his brain.

"Lovely," he said when both he and she were finished. "Absolutely lovely."

Being one who took pride in her work, she beamed.

"You're really much too much," he told her. "There should be some kind of law against you."

"I believe," she said with gentle innocence, "that in some places there is."

He laughed and started to dress. "Now, I'd like you to do me just one more small favor, child. Would you please ask the manager to come in."

He was just putting on his jacket when there was a knock on the door and Hank Ryan came in. "You asked to see the manager?" he said to Burke's back.

"Funny," said Burke, turning then so that Ryan was able to see his face, "you don't look Chinese."

"Oh, Jesus Christ!" said the fighter.

"Shhh . . . I'm here incognito."

They embraced. And feeling those great, heavily muscled arms across his back, Burke thought, with some surprise, my God, I'm glad to see this guy.

"Where the devil you been hiding?" said Ryan. "You're not in the damn phone book and information never even heard of you."

"You mean you missed me?"

"Hell, I was broke and figured you for an easy touch."

Still grinning, they automatically checked out each other's face, members of a secret fraternity exchanging high signs. We must be worldwide, thought Burke; a vast undercover network of anonymous face jobs, hidden hopes, and invisible nightmares.

"Hey, you know about Doc?" said Ryan, no longer grinning.

Burke nodded. "Too bad. He was a helluva guy."

"You could puke, I swear. What a town this is

45

getting to be. Full of hopheads and creeps. A man like that."

"Have any cops been asking you questions?"

Ryan shook his head. Then he frowned. "Hey, how'd you ever find me in this joint? I thought no one even knew I was working here."

"You keeping it a secret?"

"Damned right, you think I'm proud of it?"

Burke did not answer.

"Listen," said Ryan. "I was right up there, with three good shots at the title. And how do I wind up? As house pimp in a goddamned Chink jerk off joint." He laughed but it was not a happy sound and Burke could feel the pressure underneath. "What a year."

Burke remembered what Pamela had said that afternoon. "It was that bad?"

Ryan laughed again. It was a conditioned reflex. You took a belt in the gut and you either cried, vomited, or laughed. He had found laughing better suited to his style. "You kidding? In eight months of pounding pavement, I got exactly three job offers. Know what they were?" He counted them off, one finger at a time. "Collector for a Greek loan shark, bouncer in a waterfront gin mill, night manager in this slant-eyed pussy parlor. And that's even with my beautiful new puss."

Burke sat down on a rubbing table and lit a cigarette. When he offered the pack to Ryan, the fighter shook his head. Then suddenly aware that Burke had never answered his original question, he asked it again. "So how did you find me here?"

"It was easy. I just found out where you lived from the phone book, waited for you to come out tonight, and followed you here. Then I called up the Orange Lantern, asked if Hank Ryan worked there, and was told you were the night manager. And other than for that relaxing little fringe benefit with Lotus Lee, the rest is, as they say, history."

Ryan stared at him with the same mixture of confusion and concern he might have shown for an escaped mental patient.

"And to answer the other questions you're about to ask," Burke went on, "I didn't speak with you on the phone because I had no way of knowing if your wire was tapped. And I didn't approach you at home or on the street because I wasn't sure if you were being watched."

Ryan frowned, "You stoned, or something?"

"I wish it were that simple."

"Then would you mind telling me what the hell this is all about?"

"That's exactly why I'm here." Burke slid off the rubbing table. "Do you have an office somewhere? I don't want Lotus Lee to think I've gone queer for the manager."

Ryan led him along an empty hall to a small, windowless office that held a desk, two chairs, a file cabinet and a great deal of dust.

It was different, spilling to Ryan. David and Pamela had been awestruck enough to listen without interruption. While whatever it was that Hank Ryan felt on hearing Burke's saga, awe was clearly no part of it, and he kept cutting in with questions.

"You mean you've been a goddamned spy all these years?" he said at one point.

"No. I did use different covers, but I wasn't really a spy. At least not in the accepted sense. Although sometimes I did that too."

"Then what the hell were you?"

"Whatever I had to be. Or whatever I was ordered to be. The Service took a very loose view of job guidelines. In fact, officially, none of us even existed. We were considered illegal, unconstitutional and immoral. We never had any real funding. Our operat-

47

ing money was scavenged from assorted catch-all military appropriations and never showed up on budgetary listings."

"You keep talking about the Service," said Ryan. "I never heard about anything with that name."

"Neither has anyone else, outside of a chosen few in the executive branch." Burke suddenly noticed a change in the fighter's speech. Absorbed, taken out of himself, he seemed to lose the New York colloquialisms and street slurrings he usually used. Burke filed the fact mentally. "I told you," he said. "Officially, no one in government will even admit there is such a thing. Yet we've always had a twenty-four hour hotline into the Oval Office itself."

Ryan's eyes were flat. He stood up and leaned against a wall that suddenly looked too small and weak to hold him. "And now they want to bury you?" he said.

"Something like that."

"Christ! And I've been bitching to you."

Burke shrugged. "We're not exactly famous for our retirement benefits. Someone can always get nervous about what we know. It's one of our occupational hazards." He smiled faintly. "Like busted noses are yours."

"But isn't there someone back there who can help you? A friend, for Christ's sake?"

"There was. But not anymore."

"Why not?"

"They killed him a few days ago."

"Just like that?"

"Not exactly. They took a little trouble with it. They put a gun in his hand and made him a suicide."

"Holy shit. The Mafia are kids next to your boys."

"But we're more polite. We've always been very proud of our good manners."

"And he was the only friend you had there?"

"I was lucky to have him," Burke said, and thought this was true and was glad he had never treated it lightly or taken it for granted. Which happened between friends, but never with Kreuger. Not that they ever spoke much about it. They never had to. Still, there probably were some things he might have said that he never had.

Ryan was looking at him curiously. "You must be one pretty tough boy yourself. I mean, you're still alive, aren't you?"

It almost sounded like an indictment. And how often, Burke thought, had he indicted himself over the years? Kreuger had lectured him about it early in his career. "I'm warning you," he once told him. "If you don't stop punishing yourself every time you have to do something unpleasant to someone, you're simply not going to last. Just remember this. There are only two concepts of human ethics and they're diametrically opposed. One is humane and considers the individual sacred and inviolable. The other believes any sacrifice of the individual that advances the common good is not only justified, but necessary. Since governments must function according to the second concept, and since we're committed to work for our government, we must either work according to that ethic or not work at all." Finally, of course, he had chosen not to work at all.

"Yes," he admitted almost apologetically to Ryan, "I'm still alive."

"Okay, so tell me what I have to do to keep you that way."

"You don't have to do anything, Hank."

Ryan straightened against the soiled and dusty wall. Burke had the feeling that this was pretty much the way he must have looked in the last minutes of a bad fifteen-rounder, when he knew it was all gone anyway and he had nothing left but will and a hatred for his own failing body. "Listen," he said softly. "You're one real bright boy and you know an awful lot. But one thing you sure as hell don't know, is how much I have to do this."

"Well," Burke said, feeling curiously awkward and touched, "I want you to know I appreciate it."

"If you dare kiss me, you sonofabitch, I swear I'll scream."

6

It was nearly 3:00 A.M. when Lilly Moraine left the tall, Greenwich Village apartment building Burke had seen her enter several hours before, and started walking briskly towards Fifth Avenue. A few moments later, Burke drew up beside her in the tan Plymouth. "How about a lift from an old friend?"

She was able to recognize him in the light of a nearby streetlamp. "Well I'll be damned!"

"Don't be damned. Just get in and be blessed."

"If this isn't crazy," she said when they were moving. "I almost feel I conjured you up. I've been thinking of poor Obidiah so much lately. Then of course I'd start thinking of you and the others and all the rest of it. Then *shazamm!* Here you are."

"Well, all that thinking didn't hurt your performance tonight. You were great."

She was indignant. "You bum! You were at the theatre and you didn't even stop back to say hello?"

"I'm saying hello now. There were too many people around before. I wanted to see you alone."

"But how did you know where I'd . . ." Then it broke through and she grinned. "You're kidding! You've been following me ever since I left the theatre?"

Burke nodded. There was little traffic and he drove slowly east, past high-stooped tenements and darkened loft buildings.

"But what if I hadn't come out for hours and hours?"

"Then I'd have waited for hour and hours."

"It's that serious?"

"It's that serious," he said. Then after learning she had not yet been questioned by anyone, he launched into it for the fourth time in twenty-four hours, feeling almost as though he were one of the performers in that night's play, routinely mouthing someone else's words. If you repeated something often enough, he thought, it finally lost its passion and meaning. With his first recital to David, he'd had to yank each word out like a bad tooth. Now, with Lilly, he actually felt bored with the telling. Still, the facts remained the same, and their impact was just as strong on her as on the others.

She lit a cigarette, and in the flare of the lighter the shadows beneath her eyes looked back at Burke with a rare fatigue. "I knew this was going to be a really special night. Do you believe in omens?"

"Only when I'm drunk or desperate."

"Not fifteen minutes ago," she said, "I left the bed of a man whose last name I didn't even know and whom I suddenly decided I hated. It took me a long time to get to that point, but I got there tonight. Then as soon as I walked out, you came along and hit me with this." She paused and tried to peer up through the windshield. "Hey what sort of moon we got up there anyway?"

"A full one, I think."

"It figures." She laughed and, throwing back her head, howled. When they came to a break in the skyline, the view opened up and the moon was there, all right, full and radiant. Lilly blew it a kiss. "You know something? I've never met a real live spy before."

Burke did not bother with denials. It was simpler to just be a spy. "Am I a disappointment?"

"You're perfect. Just the right air of reserve, of quiet control, of strength and courage under pressure."

"That's just the new look Obidiah gave me. Underneath, I'm pure jelly."

"No, not you." Touched by an occasional street

52

light, her face looked half grave, half mocking. "You see, I'm not easily fooled. I'm an orphan, which gives me strange mystic powers. It's nature's way of compensating. Instead of parents, I got a small private angel to look after me."

"As protection against omens and full moons?"

"Exactly. And against the evil enemies of good spies."

"You only have my word for that. I might be the evil one."

"My little angel tells me different."

"Is your angel always so dependable?"

"When I find she isn't," Lilly said, "then I'll know I'll soon be dead."

Whatever mockery may have been in her face before was gone now. And suddenly primitive feathers of doubt stirred in Burke's brain and he wondered if he was driving a hearse. "It may be best if you could just manage to disappear for a while," he said.

"Why?"

"Then you wouldn't have to lie or answer any questions. And it would certainly be a lot safer for you."

She was silent for a moment. "Have you spoken to any of the others yet?"

"Yes."

"Who?"

"All three of them."

"Are they going to disappear?"

Knowing what was coming, he hesitated. "No."

"Then what makes you think I'd be the one to run off and hide?"

"I gave Pamela and Hank the same option. There was no reason to treat you any differently." He smiled. "I certainly didn't intend it as an insult. If it came out that way, I'm sorry."

"Okay," she said, "but you may as well know the truth of it. I'd take to the hills in a minute if I didn't have a sensational part in the best play of the season. And ain't nothin' gonna make me run out on that. So since I'm stuck here anyway, you may as well tell me what I'm supposed to do if any of the baddies come 'round."

Burke told her pretty much the same things he had told the others. Yet somewhere in the middle, out of fatigue and tension and exhaustion of every lie and subterfuge, every possible disaster that might lie ahead, like a bonus he did not truly deserve, a vague hope began in him, sweet and subtle and impossible to follow, and he thought, I've just finished putting my life in the hands of four people I don't really know at all, yet I feel better about it than anything I've done in years.

Then with a faint smile, he wondered what Tony Kreuger, who had lived through a solitary lifetime of nondependency and nontrust, and had died the same way, would have thought about that.

If I'm insane, thought Burke, then so is the rest of the species. But he had to admit that the evidence against him at this particular moment was pretty specific and personal. For there he stood, alone in a midtown New York garden in the dark of a late autumn night, peering through the lighted bedroom window of his ex-wife like an over-aged peeping-Tom. Having discovered that the surveillance on her was lifted at midnight and kept off until 8:00 A.M., he had arrived at 12:15 through a connecting basement and alley, and established his beachhead.

The window was protected by steel bars, offering Burke the sensation that he was watching Angela in a comfortably furnished, private prison cell. Good, he thought. A just and fitting punishment. For the sin of abandonment, for the heinous crime of walking out on a devoted and loving husband, you, Angela Burke, are hereby sentenced to a life of solitary confinement within your own bedroom.

Ah, Angela . . . I never blamed you for leaving.

Yet she was there now, no more than five yards from where he stood, his feet on a pair of oversized clay pots, emptied of their summer flowers and turned upside down. Breathing carefully, fearful she might hear him, Burke watched her. She was wearing a white quilted robe and the same kind of fuzzy slippers she had always enjoyed at home. Her blonde hair, still fine and smooth even with the years of touching up, hung loose as she moved between the dresser and a pile of laundry she was putting away. Burke studied the curved, delicate line of her profile, the soft flesh under her chin as she stood for a moment, folding some towels. He could see the color in her cheeks and the green of her eyes. He had painted her portrait often over the years, and the eyes were probably the only feature of her face he had ever gotten right.

What he was not able to see was her tender and vulnerable heart. If she were aware of the state of his life right now, he was sure she would cry. Instant tears. Her eyes had a way of filling and drowning without any of the usual preliminaries. Yet she was not by nature an unhappy person. Quite the contrary. When Burke thought of her, she was usually smiling or laughing. And she loved to sing—sweet songs usually unfamiliar to Burke. Angela adored baths. She believed in them as a cure for all ailments, and insisted that Burke believe in them too. They were her penicillin, her infallible chicken soup. They were also her psychiatrist's couch. Whatever the problem to be faced or worked through, it never failed to come out better in the tub.

Burke's foot slipped off the edge of one of the pots, tipping it over with a clatter. He grimaced in the dark. Terrific. Now just let some paranoic neighbor look out the window and scream for the police. What in God's name was he doing here? Was this really possible? Had a lifetime of service to his country, to the democratic ideal, to all its passions, virtues, and traditions finally brought him to this? As if anyone cared. As if the irrational behavior of Richard Burke affected the fate of the nation. What he felt for Angela was his own business.

Gazing through the barred window, he ached with tenderness for her. Yet what did he hope to accomplish with this silliness? She had looked at his face in the museum and had not recognized him. As far as she was concerned, he had been dead for more than a year anyway. With Kreuger's help, he had managed to change her from a divorced wife to a divorced widow. So when her alimony payments stopped with his alleged death, Tony was able to work a substantial lump-sum settlement for her out of the contingency funds. Good old Tony. But good old Tony had not been happy about the whole thing. "You bastard!" he complained afterward. "That was one hell of a job you handed me." Burke wanted to hear all about it of course. How many men, after all, were ever in the unique position of being able to learn how a loved one was affected by the news of their death?

Kreuger had flown to San Francisco to tell her in person, but had been given no thanks for his trouble. "I swear she came at me with both hands," he told Burke. "I was the villain of the piece. I was the one who got you into this ugly business in the first place. I was the one who made it impossible for her to live with you. And naturally I was the one who finally sent you out to be buried in some anonymous grave." Kreuger paused. "And if I want to be absolutely honest about it," he said more softly, "I have to admit she was right." This once, at least, something seemed to have gotten through to him.

Angela finished with the laundry and stood for a moment, unmoving, in the center of the room, her face pensive as she considered a far wall, or some problem, or perhaps just the life about her. Then she sat down at a dressing table and brushed her hair, moving the brush slowly, lazily, and causing Burke to remember all the other times he had watched her do the same thing. Usually, then, he had been waiting for her in bed, enjoying the intimacy of the small ritual, along with the knowledge that he would soon be holding her. The perfume, he thought, next came the perfume, which was invariably Arpége and which, even now, when carried faintly to him by some passing woman, never failed to bring her back. In bed, as elsewhere, she had wanted only to add joy and richness to his life and bring him the fulfillment he chased in all the wrong places.

She had once thought him a man who cared about the highest things. Had she loved him any less at the

57

end? She claimed not. She had simply been unable to go on living with him. She had asked for no great sacrifices. She did not want him to shower her with material luxuries, or to appear regularly at meals, or to acquire memberships in exclusive clubs, or even to be more tolerant of her utterly intolerable mother. She asked only that he be with her from time to time and stop risking his life by doing what the passing years had caused her to understand and approve of less and less. For a logical woman, she seemed curiously blind to the fact that she was being illogical.

At one point near the end, she said, "I can't take any more of this."

"Any more of what?"

"Of what you're part of. Of what you're doing."

"But you don't really know what I'm doing."

"I don't have to know."

He took a deep breath and let it out in a sigh.

"I read the papers," she said, her voice calm and oddly remote. "I listen to the news on the radio and watch it on television. Do you think I'm an idiot?"

"No, darling."

"Don't call me darling. I'm not your darling."

"All right."

She stared at him in silence, as if she had exhausted a small, precious supply of argument. Then she began to cry. "Goddamn them! Goddamn them! Why can't they leave you alone?"

Since he was able to give her no answer, he just held her and stroked her hair as though trying to memorize it. And he thought, if there is such a thing as a distant garden somewhere, in which loving objects grow, the heart of Angela Burke must surely be one of its more delicate blossoms.

But that had been more than three years ago.

Now, leaving her dressing table, Angela switched off all lights except a bedside lamp, took a book from a shelf, and lay down to read. Burke strained to see the title of the dust jacket, but could not make it out. And if he could? What would he do then? Run out and buy the book for the shared reading experience? Probably, he thought, and wondered to what other ridiculous ends this new foolishness would finally lead him.

Angela suddenly rose and left the room, and Burke carefully adjusted his feet on the clay pot upon which he was balanced. Flattened to the wall, his fingers grasping the smooth cold brick of the window ledge, he stared at the empty bed. Softly, he hummed an old tune. And like a computer with a smoothly functioning memorybank, his brain recalled the heroically maudlin lyrics:

> Are you lonesome tonight?
> Do you miss me tonight?
> Are you sorry we drifted apart?
> Does your memory stray, to a bright summer day,
> When I kissed you and called you sweetheart?
> Do the chairs in your parlor seem empty and bare?
> Do you gaze at your doorstep and picture me there?
> Is your heart filled with pain?
> Shall I come back again?
> Tell me dear, are you lonesome tonight?

Burke laughed silently. At last count there were about three billion human beings in the world, each with some love, some secret pain, each believing that their particular feelings represented the true center of life and living. And here he stood, surely knowing better, yet balancing himself on an upside-down flower pot, silently serenading a lost wife with the mushy lyrics of an old-fashioned lover's lament.

Then he stopped laughing.

Angela had come back into the bedroom, but not alone. A man was with her, a tall, dark-haired man with a heavy moustache who was smiling at something Angela had evidently just said. He seemed relaxed and comfortable, as if he had been with her in this room many times before, and Burke thought, Oh, Christ, I've got to get out of here.

But he did not go. Instead, he looked at Angela. She was talking brightly, animatedly, using her eyes and hands in a way she had when she was going all-out. The man lit a cigarette and stood leaning against the dresser as he listened. Occasionally he grinned and nodded and Burke had the feeling he was someone Angela worked for or with, and that she was describing something that had happened in the office that day. When she had apparently finished her story, they laughed together and the man reached out and touched her hair where the lamplight caught it. Then he put out his cigarette, drew her close, and kissed her. Angela's arms went around him and the fingers of one hand toyed with his earlobe. Of course, thought Burke, and felt much the same sensation he had once experienced in Buenos Aires, when he had briefly been in the hands of the wrong people and was about to have an electric current applied to his testicles. No switch had yet been touched and there was no current, but he had felt it tear through him nevertheless.

Still, he did not leave. And watching what came next, he was able to recall a discovery he had once made about pain. He had found that regardless of how bad it may be while it lasts, it is impossible to fully remember it afterward. So those fingers to an earlobe, those few anticipatory touches, caused nothing in him to match the kind of raw hurt that came with what followed. Because he saw it all, saw a body he knew as well as his own, responding to the touch of flesh that had absolutely nothing to do with all their years together, with all the sharing and the feeling and the rest of it that had made them what they were, separately and together. Finally, he thought, none of it made any difference. Flesh was flesh and they were all interchangeable. At the end of a life, a man, any man, surely had the right to expect something more than this. But to whom could he appeal? God? And what was he supposed to say? Listen, God, I've got a little complaint? Regardless of the name I'm using now or may have used in the past, I'm still Richard Burke, with all the good, bad, and in-between stuff that being Richard Burke has meant for forty-two years, and that I don't like feeling that this never really mattered?

Another foolish dialogue.

Silently, Burke stepped down from the inverted flower pot, righted it, and placed it and the one he had knocked over earlier back where he had found them. Then leaving his former wife lying naked in the arms of an equally naked stranger, he walked home through the streets of the city.

8

It was exactly the sort of college that Burke, as a boy, had once dreamed of attending—graceful old buildings, tree-shaded walks, an aura of high academic tradition set among Maryland's gently rolling hills. But money had been tight and he had ended up, more practically, riding the subway each morning to C.C.N.Y.'s grimy, downtown highrise. Almost a quarter century later, he still felt cheated.

It was dark now, but he had arrived on campus while there was still some light and had driven around to check for possible watchers. He had been here twice before for holidays with Tony and his parents and the Kreuger house had left a lasting impression. The shrubs were taller and thicker now, but half the front gate was still missing and the stone head of Rousseau stood above the doorway, looking as incongruous and formidable as ever. Driving past, Burke had not actually been able to read the philosopher's words carved below his head, but remembered them well. *Man is born free, and everywhere he is in chains.* And he thought, if I have to take a chance on anyone, what better choice than a man who had chosen to live beneath these words.

Parked a short distance from the house, Burke watched two students leave, then saw the kitchen light go on as the professor went in to prepare a solitary dinner. There were few things quite as alone, he thought, as a man alone in a kitchen. He had written Tony's father a deeply felt note of condolence when his wife died a few years back, starting a warm correspondence that Burke had to end without explanation upon leaving the Service. Now the old man had lost his only son to a bullet in the head, and what sort of condolences could you offer for that?

Burke waited, wanted to let Professor Kreuger finish his meal without interruption. Routine was important to the elderly, and at best his visit would be a shocker. In fact, deciding to come here at all had not been easy for him. Contacting anyone related to Tony or himself was a risk, but he had to start somewhere and knew of no better place. Or was coming here mostly a sentimental need to share his own mourning? Tony himself would have had little patience with any such concept, having believed that if nothing else killed in their line of work, sentiment would. Still, thought Burke, he was the one finally dead.

When the kitchen went dark and a light appeared in the living room, Burke left his car, walked past the wrought iron half-gate and knocked on the door beneath Rousseau's head. At once a dog started barking and a voice called, "Quiet, Casey! It's only a student, you dummy."

The door opened and Walter Kreuger peered out, a tall, thin man with long, white hair that blew in the night wind. "Yes?" He stared at Burke without recognition, his floating white hair making him look like an ancient musician, too lost in cantatas to remember to have his hair cut.

"It's all right, Professor. It's me . . . Richard . . . Richard Burke." He gave the old man a moment to remember his voice, then smiled as further encouragement. "I'm okay and you're not going blind or crazy. They've just done some work on my face. Don't worry. It's still me under here."

Kreuger squinted, took off his glasses, put them on again and squinted once more. "Good Lord." He seemed unable to move. "Richard?"

Burke's smile was beginning to stiffen. "I'm sorry I had to hit you with it like this."

The old man's fingers slowly opened the door

63

wider. Moving as though in a trance, he stepped back
to let Burke in. His dog, a shaggy, moplike mutt, was
all over Burke, licking his hands and yelping until
he picked him up. The air in the room was close and
faintly sour with furniture polish. The remembered
luster was there, in the cabinets and tables. His
wife's legacy, thought Burke, and he was faithfully
keeping it up. The rest of the house could go to pot,
but the cabinets and tables would glow like the vigil
light in a memorial. Walter Kreuger himself had
aged since Burke had seen him. His face was deeply
lined, his hands lumpy with arthritis, his move-
ments labored and painful. Still, his dark eyes were
luminous, bright and wet as a baby's as they struggled with what they saw.

"Richard . . . Richard . . ." He closed the door and
touched Burke's arm. The flesh was solid but anonymous. "What in God's name have they done to you?"

Burke had forgotten the old man's voice. Deep,
resonant, oddly young, it belied the way he looked.
Burke put down the dog, forced something extra into
his smile and handed Walter Kreuger a bottle of Na-
poleon. "Get out the glasses, Professor. It's a long
story."

"I wondered." The old man floated around the
room, searching out the snifters, fussing with the
foil, the bottle, the whole ritual. "You weren't at
Tony's services. I assumed you were away somewhere, out of the country. I knew if you weren't
there, you had a good reason."

His voice faded off as he poured the brandy, carefully measuring equal levels in two plump snifters.
He handed one to Burke. His face was a staging of
masks, a collapsing of flesh until the bones stood out.
There was a private war going on.

"I don't understand," he said with another voice,
this one far off, anguished. "He never even let me
know he was sick, never told me a thing, never gave
me a chance to talk to him, then he put a bullet in his
head." He looked at the surgically altered face of

Richard Burke. "It was bad enough to have to bury him, but that way was the absolute worst."

Burke took a moment. "It wasn't that way," he said. "Tony wasn't sick. And he didn't shoot himself."

"I don't understand."

"He was murdered."

The old man stared at Burke. Then his hand began trembling so violently he had to put down his glass. "What are you talking about?"

"It's part of the same long story."

So Burke carefully went over it all once more, but this time with Tony's portion added. And Tony's father silently listened, his eyes steady and clear once the first blow had been handled. He was not like some elderly people, Burke thought, watching him as he spoke, who finally became hardened toward their own and other's suffering and death. No, his response was sharp and deeply felt, and Burke was touched with pain for him.

He nodded when Burke had finished and looked vaguely around at him, at the worn couch and chairs upon which his wife and son had once sat, at the polished tables and cabinets. He seemed disoriented, as if unable to remember where he was or what he was doing there. Then it passed. "Thank you for telling me," he said. "I know you took a chance in coming here."

"It wasn't only for you. I also need help."

"From me?"

"You were closer to Tony than anyone. He talked to you. He may have said things."

"Not about his work—never about what he was doing. Until you just told me, I never even knew about you, not all these years."

"Yes," said Burke, "but sometimes things creep in anyway. We're all human. We still give off unconscious signals. Especially when we're relaxed with those we love. And Tony knew he was in trouble for a while. When did you last see him?"

"About a month ago. He was on his way some-where and stayed over." The old man picked up his glass and stared at it. "He didn't sleep much that night. I heard him walking around and found him poking through a couple of old picture albums. We had a drink and talked."

"What about?"

"Everything and nothing. He seemed nostalgic and kept looking through these old albums. We also had a go at some of our regular political battles. We rarely agreed there, so that was nothing unusual. I claimed we were trying too hard to carve the whole world in our own image, and Tony laughed at me for being lost somewhere among Rousseau's archaic mo-ralities."

"May I see them?"

"What?"

"The picture albums."

Professor Kreuger rose. "What do you expect to find?"

"Probably nothing. It's just that I've never known Tony to be nostalgic about anything."

There were two large albums and they held the usual assortment of faded snapshots: of outings, holi-days and family occasions, of the Kreugers and their friends posing self-consciously, of Tony, smiling and laughing from infancy up through middle age. They should outlaw these things, thought Burke, peering at a shot of the three Kreugers, frozen forever in a moment of youth, health, and summer sun. No one should ever have to be reminded of how they and those they loved looked twenty years ago.

Burke pointed to an empty space surrounded by four stripped mounting corners. "What was here?"

The old man looked. "One of Tony's college pic-tures, I suppose. At least that's what is on the rest of the page."

Burke flipped through the remainder of the al-bum. There were no other empty places. He went back to the college page and studied the assortment of young men and women posing with and without Tony. Then he carefully removed every snapshot on the page. "I'd like to borrow these."

"Do you believe Tony took out that missing picture?"

Burke shrugged. "I'm just poking around." He stroked the dog, lying serenely beside him on the couch. "How did you find out about Tony? Not from the newspapers, I hope."

"No, I received a phone call. It was very early in the morning. It woke me." In the yellow lamplight the old man's face relived the call. "Every time the phone rings now I shake inside. I don't know why. What else can they tell me?"

"Do you remember who called?"

"Some man. I think he said his name was Needham. Or maybe it was Naidham. Something like that. I'm afraid I wasn't hearing too well."

"Could it have been Beecham?"

"I suppose so. Do you know someone with that name?"

Burke nodded.

Walter Kreuger's eyes seemed to cloud over. They went through Burke to the wall beyond, then past that too. "The bastards," he whispered softly, "the filthy, murdering bastards. What did they want? He gave them everything—heart, brain, soul, all he had. He lived and breathed his work, his country. He cared about nothing else. He would never even marry, never risk having children, for God's sake, because his loyalty might have been divided. He abstained from the most natural of impulses, stayed permanently isolated. And how did they finally pay him? With a bullet in the head. I thank God his mother didn't live to see it."

His eyes returned to the album, to a picture of his son in a Boy Scout uniform complete with merit badges. "Look at him, an Eagle Scout at the age of fifteen. Even then he was a patriot. How that boy loved his country." He began to cry. The tears ran

67

down into his mouth and he swallowed them. "Forgive me. I thought I was all through with that."

Burke was silent, feeling his face rigid and aching.

Professor Kreuger shook his head and closed the album. "They wouldn't let me look at him. They said there was too much damage, that it was better that I didn't see him. Even so . . . even so I see him." He stared off again. "My son, the patriot."

Burke sipped his brandy and was aware of a faint nausea, very like the depression with which he had been waking lately. Ah, why don't I just go away and leave him in peace? he thought. But he knew there would be no peace for his friend's father no matter what he did, and that this way there might at least be some hope of repayment.

"I don't know how you'll feel about this," Burke said slowly, "but if you want to, there may be a way you can help."

Kreuger had control again. "You mean help you stay alive?"

"Yes, and maybe get to whoever was to blame for Tony."

"My God," whispered the old man.

9

Burke decided that about the only thing Tony Kreuger had failed to adequately prepare him for in recruiting him, twenty years ago, was the waiting. He had warned him about all the other, more obvious joys of the profession, such as the loneliness, the danger, the absence of material reward or even of appreciation. And once he had even lectured him on the proper philosophical approach to the Service. "You don't have to believe in it as a creation of high moral purpose." he said. "And certainly don't expect any of the more common forms of justice from it. At best, all you can reasonably hope for is that it will take care of you up to a certain point, and do its utmost to preserve our form of government." All proven true and accurate enough over the years, thought Burke, but never a word about the damned waiting.

The waiting was what he was doing now, although in a very different cause. It was nearly midnight and he had been waiting for more than two hours. He stood in a dark cluster of bushes and trees, standing the way professional waiters and watchers stand all over the world—legs straight, weight balanced equally on both feet. From here he could see the college's administration building, the roads and walks approaching it, and the security guard making his rounds. Burke had clocked the guard twice and had him pegged at about fifty-minute intervals. The campus was quiet. A chapel bell tolled the hours and an occasional car or pedestrian drifted by. That was all. It was a small but old and very prestigious college, (not unlike the one at which Professor Kreuger taught) its growth deliberately stunted in the belief that in education, bigger had nothing to do with better. And from the fall of '52 to the spring of '56, Tony Kreuger had been a student there.

Burke watched the lighted, first-floor windows of the registrar's office. With the rest of the building dark around him, a man worked alone at a desk. Burke sent him a telepathic message. Go home and go to sleep. The man rumpled his hair tiredly, but remained bent over whatever problem was holding him there this late. Burke shifted his feet in the soft earth and settled in to wait some more.

Burke's thoughts drifted to Angela. In a sunlit haze, he recalled one of the few vacations they had ever taken together, a single week on Martha's Vineyard which, in retrospect, seemed to stretch through the summer, through the year, and through every summer he had known since. They had eaten lots of clam chowder, lain on the warm sand, and gone to the movies almost every night. In bed their flesh smelled fresh and clean from the sun and they could not seem to get enough of each other. I love you, she told him, I'll always love you. He told her the same. Then the week was over and he was sent to Peru for a long, hard, bad time from which he almost did not return. Some of the things that happened there were in the papers, and although not all of it was true, a lot of it was. And he had not been able to explain any part to her.

Did she ever think of those few days on the island? It was so brief, gone so fast. Everything they'd ever had was brief. Still, he was lucky to have had that much, he thought. You could go through fifty years with someone, and the good might not add up to as much as they'd had. So he had no right to complain—at least, not about that. Then about what? About being dead, he thought. He had plenty of right to complain about that. He smiled sourly in the dark. At best, it was unnatural.

He had arranged to see her twice more since the

night he had stood outside her bedroom window.
Once, he had gotten on the same rush-hour bus as
she rode to work, brushing past her in the crowded
aisle, actually touching her, breathing her perfume.
How could she not have known he was there? Surely
she should have felt something on the back of her
neck. What exquisite torture. At that moment he
was able to understand some hint of the sweet pleasures of martyrdom experienced by the early saints.
When the soul passed a certain threshold, a condition approaching nirvana was apparently reached.
Burke's nirvana ended when Angela left the bus at
Fifty-fourth and Madison, followed, an instant later,
by the inevitable watcher at her back.

The second time, she was having lunch in a restaurant and he watched her from a table across the
room. She had a particular way of eating, of using
her knife and fork, that lent a rare grace to an essentially graceless act. "All people but you," he had
once told her, "should eat in private, should be shut
from public view. Only you can make eating seem
lovely." She had laughed. "That's just because you
love me." Which was how she thought. She believed
that love, or lack of it, was at the center of everything. The good was good because love was there,
and the bad was bad because it was not. You needed
a brave and true heart to live with such a concept.
He never doubted that she had it. While he, evidently, did not. So that looking at her that afternoon
from across the restaurant, (carefully, since the
watcher was watching) he thought of this as her
eyes, passing his, seemed to hesitate and hang there
for one . . . two . . . three beats, a few split seconds,
no more, before they moved on. But only to come
back and go through it again. And he had felt all of
her there in those well-loved eyes, and all of himself
too, along with an insane need to whisper, 'Ah, love,
sure, it's me,' an urge so strong that he could almost
feel himself leaving his chair, crossing the length of
the restaurant, taking her hand and leading her out

71

as the watcher followed, until he got him off alone somewhere and put him away. Lovely. Then the insanity passed and he hurriedly paid his check and left, not daring to risk so much as another glance in her direction.

It was shortly after midnight when the light finally went out in the registrar's office, and the man who had been working there left the building, got into his car, and drove off. Burke waited until the security guard came through and completed his next round. Then he slipped around to the rear of the building, picked the lock on the basement door, and let himself in.

The air held the same stale, bookish, overheated smell of every school building, kindergarten through college, that Burke had ever been in. They must use some sort of special academic spray, he thought. He had a small flashlight in his pocket but did not have to use it. The glow from the exit lights was enough to show him the way to the registrar's office and the record room behind it. It was a large, shelf-lined storage area and since there were no windows, he was able to turn on a desklight without fear of being seen from outside. Still, he found himself sweating and his heart beating like that of a sparrow held in the hand. Which bothered him. Was he really that far gone?

More than a century of files and records were arranged in long, dusty rows. He chose the 1953 through 1956 yearbooks and sat down with them at the desk. Then he spread out the college photographs he had taken from the Kreuger family album and went to work. Without knowing exactly what he was looking for, he understood the value of following routine investigative procedures when there was little else to go on. "Take care of the small details," had been Tony's early advice, "and the big breakthroughs will take care of themselves."

He began trying to match up the faces in Tony's album photographs with those in the yearbooks. Then he tried to identify them by name and background data. A few faces were too small or too faded to recognize, but after half an hour Burke did have a list of eleven names. He went over each one slowly, scraping his memory, trying to reach back for possible points of recognition. He came up empty. Not one face or name meant anything to him. But he had not really expected much here. These were the faces left in the Kreuger album. The single photograph taken out was more likely to hold some connection to something.

At about the time he expected the security guard on his next round, Burke switched off the desklamp to avoid showing any light under the corridor door. Waiting again, he sat there in the silent dark, wishing he had a drink, and hating the smell of the past around him. He felt as though he had fallen asleep in a fire and was silently burning. He could not even scream. And if he could, who would hear him? He thought of those he had involved . . . David, Pamela, Hank, Lilly, his four changeling innocents, and wished there were some way to wipe them clean of him. If he never came out of this room, he thought, if he somehow quietly burned in here, it would be the best gift he could offer them. Except that some notice would have to be left, or those who wanted him dead would have no way of knowing their hunt was over. In his mind, he composed a properly formal note: To-Whom-It-May-Concern . . . Please let it be known that I, as you find me, am the man once known as Richard Burke, and that although I still have no clear or reasonable idea of why you want me dead, I am nevertheless doing my dying here, in this place, as well as I know how. In return, I ask only that those whom I have inadvertently implicated be held blameless in this entire matter and that they be allowed to live out in peace those new lives they so naively hoped would offer them a change for the better.

Amen, thought Burke.

But he was not yet dead, and his problems, and

those of the others, remained the very real affliction of the living. During the past days he had learned what was happening to all four of them. He had heard first from David. Following Burke's prearranged procedures, David had called from an outside line, given a message and a false name to an answering service operator, then gone back to the same booth exactly three hours later to take Burke's return call. "They're following me," he said and there was obvious panic in his voice. "They're all over the damn place."

"How do you know?"

"I've seen this same blue Ford in three different places, there's a pink-faced bald man I've noticed at the library and the counter where I eat, and a blonde woman is walking her dog past my house at all kinds of crazy hours."

"It's okay," Burke told him, "You're supposed to know you're being watched."

"What do you mean?"

"If they didn't want you to know, you wouldn't know. This is just another way of putting on the pressure, of trying to scare you into making some kind of move."

"Oh, Jesus!"

"Don't worry," Burke assured him. "So far they haven't a thing."

There was a pause. "I did something stupid. I told Dolores about shooting those two guys."

"Who's Dolores?"

"That little hooker—that girl I told you about. I guess I had to brag. You know. Play big macho. I'm sure she won't say anything. She . . . she cares about me. I'm even asking her to move in. I didn't tell her your name, or anything like that, but I know it was stupid."

Burke said nothing.

"Listen," David said, "I know it sounds crazy—her being a hooker and all—but I swear I'd trust this kid with my life."

74

"You already have," Burke said.

Pamela and Hank were getting their own share of the heat. Hank reported coming home from work and finding his place totalled—drawers and closets emptied, upholstery ripped, furniture smashed, clothing shredded. It was more than just a thorough search. It was a wasting. Fearing Pamela had gotten the same treatment, Hank had rushed over to her place at six in the morning. "But she was okay," he told Burke. "Just scared."

"I'm glad you went over," Burke said. "She's a woman alone. Keep an eye on her if you can."

"Damned right I will. Those sons of bitches. I'd like to tear their balls out by the roots."

"I'm sorry, Hank."

"Shit, it's not your fault. But Christ, there are some real dolls around. This stuff been going on long?"

"Long enough."

"And they can get away with it?"

"I'm afraid so."

"And that's your lousy government?"

"It's yours too." How sad to see that sort of old-fashioned faith destroyed, thought Burke.

"Hell, I ain't voted in fifteen years." He thought about it. "So maybe I got no real right to bitch, huh? All this time . . . all this time and the only things I cared about were fighting, eating, taking a crap, and getting laid. But that don't stop me from being sore as hell anyway. What's happening to the fucking country?"

"Just take it easy." Burke told him.

"Shit!" said Hank.

But it turned out that Lilly was the one actually approached next. Reporting it to Burke through their usual telephone procedures, she said it had happened very much as it had with David, except that there was only one of them, not two. He was waiting for her as she left the theatre after an evening performance, a big man, thick through the shoulders and chest, who introduced himself as Detective Frank Harkevy of Homicide and said he was investigating Obidiah Stern's murder. He drove her home from the theatre and was so pleasant, so friendly and flattering about her performance, that she invited him up for a drink. When he finally got down to the questions, they were essentially the same as those asked David and she answered them without problem. In response to the question of what Burke looked like, she told Harkevy she believed she did have a snapshot somewhere, taken at the hospital, and after a suitable period of rummaging through drawers, produced Burke's composite of his own body crowned with the head of David's late uncle.

"And that was all?" Burke said when she had finished her recital.

"Pretty much. Except for having a few more drinks. Actually, the guy was kind of cute."

"I'm sure."

"I mean it. He looked like an All-American linebacker from about ten years ago. And I think he really went for me."

"Why not? You're very easy to go for."

"He wants to see me again. He invited me out to his beach house in Amagansett on Sunday."

"In November?"

"He said November's the best month for the beach."

"This is no game, Lilly."

"Maybe I can find out a few things for you. I think I might be able to really help."

"You've already helped, and I appreciate it. Now please, just leave it alone."

"I've already accepted the invitation."

"Then cancel it."

She giggled and it had a light, girlish sound over the wire. "I really think I like being a spy. It's exciting. And stop worrying so much. I'm a big girl. Besides, you've forgotten. I've still got my private angel to watch over me."

"Lilly!"

"I'll let you know how I make out."

Now, Burke sat in the dark, college storeroom and waited for the security guard to go by. After he finally heard his steps approach, pass, and fade away, he turned on the desklight and went back to work once more. This time he started through the yearbooks page by page, studying every photograph, name, and caption. Nothing. Then, as he was looking at a picture of Tony taken with other members of the 1954 debating team, he suddenly whispered a soft, "I'll be damned," and bent closer.

Alongside Kreuger, at the very center of the picture, was the team's faculty adviser. He stood straight-backed and tall above the others, his leonine head and sweeping mane of hair unmistakable even in the quarter-of-a-century-old photograph. The hair had been grey, not dark, when Burke had last seen it, and the face beneath had grown lined and puffy. But he did not even have to look at the name in the caption to know it was Arthur Montgomery Millang.

He checked through the other three yearbooks. Tony had been on the debating team through all four of his undergraduate years, but Millang had apparently been his faculty adviser for only three. A different faculty member was pictured with the team in '56. Looking through other records for that period, Burke found that Millang had taught political science for five years, but had left the faculty in 1956 to become a Washington political pollster. Which was the only professional capacity in which Burke had ever known him. He had also known him, through Tony, as an occasional bridge, tennis, and drinking companion. But this was Burke's first awareness that the two men went back more than twenty-five years together. And for no reason other than it was his first awareness of it, the fact was suddenly important.

Burke put everything back in order and left the room, the building, and the campus.

Driving home through a pale pink sunrise, he tried to make some sense of it. He had taken a wild shot in the dark because it was the only shot he had, and he may just have hit something. He had no way of knowing whether Millang had been in the picture missing from the Kreuger album, or whether it was even Tony who had removed it. But that part no longer mattered very much. What did matter was that Tony and Millang had known one another for more than a quarter of a century, that Millang had left an academic career to start a business in Washington, and that Tony had followed him there immediately upon graduating. And it was additionally significant that in all the years Burke had known Tony, and as close as they had been, Tony had somehow failed to mention these facts.

All of which meant what?

Perhaps nothing, thought Burke. But he did not really believe that. Again, he refused to trust coincidence. He preferred his own suppositions. And it was working at these that helped him keep awake during the long drive back to New York.

10

Richard Burke was indulging himself. He was taking a break. After days of driving, thinking, digging, plotting, and just plain worrying, he was rewarding himself by spending at least part of that day, a Saturday, with Angela at the Metropolitan Museum. Angela, of course, did not know he was with her. Just as he himself had not known an hour ago, that they would again be at the museum together. He had simply awakened that morning, decided he wanted to see her, waited unseen down the block until she left her house, and followed her and her watcher (a different one this time) as they walked their separate sides of the street to Fifth Avenue, then uptown to the museum. Taking foolish chances? Sure, he thought. But they were at least controlled foolish chances, and he had finally learned to accept them as part of his needs.

She was wearing a dress today, not slacks, so he was able to see her legs, which were not simply good but great.

She had gone directly to the Rembrandt section, so he knew her mood at once. She was abstracted, troubled, in need of solace. Angela went to museums as other people went to churches, synagogues, or shrinks. What's wrong, love?, he thought. They giving you a hard time at the office? You find a new wrinkle on your face last night? The guy with the moustache not turning out quite as you hoped? Or maybe—just maybe—you woke up missing and wanting me a little this morning? Well, I'm here, Angie. And it's going to be all right. So just sit down for a while in front of Remmy's Old Woman and let it soak in.

And she did sit down, right there in front of the painting, while Burke settled comfortably in the next gallery. From here he was able to watch safely both her and the new watcher, a thin, balding, constipated-looking man in an oversized turtleneck. Tense and exhausted for days, Burke began to feel a bit better now. He had been in extreme states like this before, sometimes alone on extended assignments in alien places, where there was no one he could talk to and not a single burrow for him to crawl into for warmth. But it was different this time. This was not just another assignment. This was his life.

He had gone through a frenetic few days. From the moment he had stumbled over Millang in Tony's old college yearbooks he had not stopped going. And the fact that he still had only assumption to go on had in no way slowed him. Clutching the august name of Arthur Montgomery Millang like a coveted blue ribbon, he carried what he hoped would be his first real prize straight to Tony's father.

He had arranged to meet the professor at a small motel just off Route 95, but had first warned him to make certain he was not followed. "You still want to help?" he asked the old man when they were at last in the room together.

"You still have to ask?"

"It could be dangerous."

"Just tell me what you want me to do."

In the dingy motel room, yellow plasterboard walls shook from the turnpike traffic. Next door on their left a TV was going. Earlier Burke had prepared instant coffee with an electric wall gadget. Pouring it now into two plastic cups, he tasted one, made a face, and handed the other to Kreuger.

"Do you know Arthur Montgomery Millang?" he asked.

"Who doesn't know Millang? Presidents don't go

80

to the bathroom without first having him run a poll on the possible results."

"I mean do you know him personally?"

"Yes. Rather well, in fact."

"How do you know him?"

"We've met often enough around Washington over the years. He had also consulted me professionally on various political issues."

"How did you meet him originally?"

The professor frowned at his coffee. "It's been so long. I'm not quite sure anymore."

"Could it have been through Tony?"

"I suppose so." Kreuger thought for a moment, then nodded slowly. "As a matter of fact it was. I remember now. We did meet at Tony's place the first few times."

"Did Tony ever tell you he knew him at college, that Millang was actually his debating team faculty advisor for three years?"

"No. I never knew that."

"I never did either," said Burke. "At least not until the other night, when I was digging through some old yearbooks."

"Which means what?"

"Maybe nothing. But I don't think so. Because it's the kind of fact that would have somehow come out over the years—to either one of us—unless it was being deliberately concealed."

"I don't understand. Why would Tony and Millang have wanted to conceal it?"

A couple of car doors slammed outside and footsteps approached and entered the room on their right. Burke sat listening to muffled voices and laughter for a moment . . . recognizably male and female. Then he asked, "How much do you know about the Service?"

"Practically nothing. All Tony ever told me was that it existed and that he believed it performed a vital national function." Gently the old man rubbed the top of his scalp, as if probing for hidden facts.

"He also said no one but me was ever to know he was part of it, not even his mother. He could die of a few careless words. As I've told you, I never even knew you were part of it. I had a vague notion you had something to do with nonferrous metals and did a lot of traveling as a consultant." He looked at Burke. "But what has this to do with Millang?"

"I think he may be part of the Service too."

"You think? Wouldn't you know?"

"It doesn't work that way. I knew only whom and what I had to know for any given assignment. And in the Service hierarchy, I've never known any name higher than Tony's. He was my division chief. Which is why I can make only an educated guess about Millang. Because if he's in at all, he's in somewhere over Tony's level."

Burke rose, walked over to the wall on his right and stood listening for a moment. The male-female sounds from the next room had quieted, but now began again along with the splashing of a shower. Burke sighed. "Anyway," he said, "here's some of my thinking about Millang. I think the main reason Millang Polls come out of nowhere and grew as meteorically as they did, was because of the government contracts the Service quietly nudged its way. Since their new boy in town needed a prestigious cover, fast—one that would provide free access to the top echelons of government, industry and communications—this was how they gave it to him. I've checked back. In less than two years' time important contracts had somehow filtered in to lift an unknown ex-college professor to national prominence in a tough, highly competitive business. The man may be good, but nobody is that good. Next, we know that Tony came directly to Washington to join the Service right from college, and never once mentioned to either of us that he had even known Millang there."

"But if they're pictured together in those yearbooks," the professor cut in, "surely it couldn't be any great secret."

"You're right. And there's no real threat to the Service in their having known one another in college. In fact that's how many of our people come in, with former professors or classmates recruiting them. I came in that way myself when a college friend told Tony to get in touch with me. All I'm saying is that when what should have been a casually revealed piece of background information is somehow not revealed over a period of years, it automatically takes on significance. And I'm also saying that Tony never mentioned it to me because he knew I'd immediately assume Millang had, indeed, recruited him, and therefore was probably somewhere above him in the Service ranks. And I'm guessing he didn't mention it to you, because a basic Service tenet says to never volunteer any piece of personal information unless there's a reason."

The professor looked at Burke with a mixture of confusion and indictment. "I'm beginning to think you're all a bit mad. Is this really what's needed for national survival? If it is, then maybe I'm just as lucky to be standing with one foot in the grave."

Burke said nothing and they sat with their bad coffee. The couple next door had left the shower and begun to make love.

Listening, the old man shook his head sadly. "Even in that . . ." he mourned. "Even in that, there's no evidence of grace and love anymore." He blinked, as if to clear away old visions, then said, "Tell me. What's to be my part in all this?"

"If you'd rather not . . ."

"Please. Just tell me."

Burke nodded. "All right. When was the last time you saw Millang?"

"At Tony's funeral."

"What did he say to you?"

"Just the usual condolences."

"And you haven't spoken with him since?"

"He did call once to ask if there was anything he

could do. I thanked him and said there was nothing. That was all."

"Okay," said Burke. "Then I'd like you to call him this evening and tell him there is something he may be able to do for you. Make an appointment to meet with him. Let him know it's urgent, but don't say anything more than that on the phone."

They met again two days later. This time, because Burke was almost sure Professor Kreuger would be under surveillance if his idea had any validity at all, he slipped into the old man's house at 1:00 A.M. through a rear, basement door.

"No lights," he said as the professor reached for the switch. "I didn't see anyone out there, but there's no point taking chances."

They went upstairs to the study and sat down in the dark. The smell of old leather, dust, and books hung like a dry mist, and Burke had the feeling of being in some chapel of the intellect, with invisible relics hidden away in small boxes.

Kreuger found Burke's hand and pressed a snifter of brandy into it. "All ready for you," he said. "I'm well into my third. If I have to start playing spy at my age, I may as well do it as painlessly as possible."

"Why not?"

"I shouldn't need an excuse to drink, but it's hard to break old habits. Especially foolish ones. I'm lately convinced we're all just ingenious machines for turning alcohol into urine." He raised his glass in the dark. "To Tony . . . and to finding whoever did him in and wants you done next."

"Amen," said Burke.

This makes five, he thought. Although with the others their involvement had been more the luck of the draw than his own initiative. They had simply been at the wrong place at the wrong time.

"What is it you intelligence people call this process?" said Kreuger. "The debriefing?"

"Exactly," said Burke, not able to see the old man's face in the dark, but imagining it and knowing precisely how he would paint it, with all that classic strength, stubbornness, and lively youth trapped among the wrinkles. He would use a strong side-light that left half the face in shadow and brought out the rest in strong relief. How much better certain faces became as they grew older. Which was about as close as he would come to finding anything good in the aging process.

"Is there a proper procedure?"

"Just tell it as it happened. When I have any comments or questions, I'll cut in."

"Well, I called Millang as you told me to," Professor Kreuger began, "and made an appointment to meet him for lunch at his club the next day. My last class was over at noon and it was only a forty-minute drive, so it worked out conveniently."

"How did he seem when you met?"

"Pleasant, warm, a trifle subdued and deferential. As befitted my position as a recently bereaved father. Quite frankly, I've never made any judgments about Arthur on the personal level. I've always pretty much accepted his charm and intelligence at face value. But I must say I was impressed with his feeling when he spoke of Tony. He apparently cared about him a great deal. And I don't believe it was put on for my benefit. I was paying particular attention and it rang true."

"It probably was true. He knew Tony a long time."

"Then I got down to it," the professor went on. "I told him I knew Tony had worked for a top-secret, government agency called the Service. I said I was the only one he had ever confided in about this, and that I had respected the confidence for as long as he lived. But while going through his things the other day, I had come across some information that looked official and important and I didn't know what to do about it."

"What was his reaction?"

"None. He just went right on eating his caesar salad. Then after a moment he asked why I had

85

picked him to tell this to. I told him I had several rea sons. For one thing, he had been Tony's friend for a long time and I had a feeling he may have suspected something of what Tony was doing. For another, because I trusted and respected him as a man who cared about what happened to this country. And finally, I said because if anyone in Washington knew the right person to contact about this, and could do it discreetly, he could."

"What did he say then?"

"Nothing. He just nodded and kept working on his salad. I was too nervous to do much eating myself, so I just sat there watching him go at that goddamned, double-sized caesar salad as though it were the single most important thing in the world."

"How was he sitting?" Burke asked.

"What do you mean?"

"What was his position in the room? How was he sitting in relation to you, the walls, and the exits?"

"What has that to do with anything?"

"Please, professor."

Kreuger breathed deeply. "He sat opposite me on a banquette. He was facing a stairway and two exits. One wall was behind him and the other was on his right."

"He was sitting in a corner?"

"Yes."

"And you're sure the wall was on his right?"

"Yes."

"Think carefully, professor. Was he eating with his left hand? Was he left-handed?"

Kreuger took a moment. "Yes. I believe he was. Which means what, for heaven's sake?"

"He was sitting the way a professional would. Rear and weaker flank protected by walls, gun hand on the exposed side, and a clear view of the room, exits, and entrances. The way I myself would sit, and the way Tony spent his life sitting in restaurants."

"Marvelous," said the old man coldly. "So they

didn't kill Tony in a restaurant. They killed him somewhere else."

Burke palmed his brandy, feeling the snifter round and smooth in his hand. Somewhere off in the darkness, a locomotive whistled.

"Who spoke first after that?" Burke asked.

"I did. For a normally big talker, Arthur showed a remarkable capacity for silence at that moment. It seemed to stretch forever. I finally had to ask whether he could be of any help and he shrugged and said he wasn't sure. He wanted to know how I was so certain this information was important or top-secret or whatever, and I told him I wasn't certain, that I was just guessing, but that there were some markings that might mean something to someone who understood these things."

"Did he ask what the markings were?"

"Not at first. In fact he spoke of other things for a while and I was afraid he was going to ignore it entirely. Then very casually, over coffee and a rich dessert—my God, that man loves to eat—he asked if I remembered what the markings were."

"Good. Great!"

"I told him they were just hieroglyphics to me, a bunch of numbers and letters like, Code I . . . dash . . . zero . . . M . . . E . . . dash . . . zero . . ."

Burke was leaning forward in his chair. "How did he react then?"

"It was interesting. He was just in the process of eating a spoonful of chocolate mousse when I went into my little recital, and so-help-me if that mousse didn't seem to turn sour in his mouth. But all he actually did was nod slightly, and I'm sure I wouldn't have noticed anything at all if I hadn't been watching for it. Yet the reaction was definitely there. From then on he avoided the subject and we just spoke of politics in general until lunch was over and we were ready to part. Then again, very casually, he said he didn't know whether he could be of any help, but was pleased and flattered that I had come to him and

87

would certainly do his best. His final words were that he would get back to me as soon as possible, and that it might be wiser not to mention this to anyone else until he did."

"Terrific," said Burke. "You were absolutely beautiful, professor."

"Then you think he'll get back to me with something?"

"I know he will."

The old man slowly got up, walked to a window of the darkened study, and stood looking out at a black row of pine. "It's a curious thing, Richard, but this whole thing, all this skulking about and secret mumbo-jumbo still doesn't seem real to me, still doesn't seem like anything more than a lot of childish play-acting. Yet it represents what Tony believed in, dedicated his life to, and finally died of."

Burke sat between walls of books and said nothing. His brief moment of elation had passed, leaving only a cold residue. There was so much that lay ahead—by far, the worst of it.

"A lifetime," said Kreuger. "All these years and I never even shared it with his mother. Tony said no one else was to know, and no one else knew. But there was never a moment when I did not resent it, did not despise having to shut my wife out of so important a thing. I knew that woman for more than fifty years, Richard, and this was the only thing I ever kept from her. There were times when I almost hated Tony for doing this to me, to us, but I respected his needs and his integrity. I know that in the world's scheme of things my son's needs and integrity were only very minor considerations, but they were never minor to me." He laughed softly. "The unavoidable hazard of spending your life at the front of classrooms. It finally becomes impossible to say anything briefly or simply. All I'm really trying to say, Richard, is thank you."

"For what?"

Professor Kreuger turned around. "For letting me be part of this in some small way."

Now, a day and a half later, he was back in New York, enjoying his Saturday of Angela-watching. He had given the professor instructions on how to reach him when he heard from Millang and could do nothing but wait until then.

Watching from the next gallery, he saw Angela get up and leave Rembrandt's *Old Woman* and stop in front of his *Noble Slav.* Ah, she's feeling better, he thought, recalling the delight she had once taken in that marvelously dignified old man in the shimmering turban of a fake, Eastern potentate. "What fun Remmy must have had dressing the old boy up," she had laughed, "making a street beggar more regal, more kingly-looking than any real king. That's what I call an artist." And as if trying to prove herself equally creative, she had hustled Burke straight down Fifth Avenue to Saks and outfitted him from top to bottom in the latest designer fashions. At home, she considered the results. "How do I look?" he asked. Sadly, she shook her head. "Like a spy in Saks' clothing," she said and pulled everything right off. "Can you love me this way?" he asked, naked. "I'm trying," she said. "Lordy, I am trying."

But evidently not hard enough, thought Burke, and felt the remembered warmth drain off.

11

Burke picked up two messages from his answering service: one from Hank, the other from Lilly. The arrangements were for him to return all calls either three, six, nine or twelve hours from the exact time they were clocked in, depending on his own situation and when the messages were picked up. If he was unable to call back at any of these times, the next twelve hours would then be skipped entirely and the original schedule repeated. In this particular case, Burke was able to call Hank on the six-hour-spot at his designated booth on Forty-eighth Street and Third Avenue.

"I'm afraid I fucked up," the ex-fighter said without preliminary.

At a public phone in Bloomingdales, Burke felt a familiar coldness in his gut. "How?"

"You're not going to believe this, but I killed a guy. An agent. He said his name was Bishop . . . Tom Bishop. I didn't mean to. The damn thing just got away from me."

"What happened?"

"I was only trying to help, damn it. Pam said it was stupid, and I guess it was. But I was sore as a sonofabitch and had to do something. And I thought I had a terrific idea, I really did. But Max, my old manager, always said I was okay til I started thinking, and the fucker was right. Shit, I don't believe how it turned out."

"Just tell me what happened."

"I even got Pam into it. I been seeing her a lot, even staying over at her place. I mean, she being scared and all. But it's more than that. We've got something going. I don't know what she sees in a dummy like me, but . . ." He took a long breath. "Christ, listen to me run off at the mouth. I'm nervous as a cat. You should see my goddamned hands shaking."

"It's okay. Take your time."

"What time? I suddenly feel I got no time. Anyway, I got this real bright idea to find out who's after you and why. I knew Pam had a tail on her, so one night I had her lead the guy past this empty, burned-out building where I was waiting, and I cold-cocked him and dragged him inside. Then I tied him up and blindfolded him. When he came to, I told him I was you and started asking questions."

The operator came on the line to ask for more money and Burke threw in the change. "Go on," he said.

"At first I had him fooled. He really believed I was you. And when I slapped him around a little, he said they wanted you for selling out to some people in Beirut. Does that make any damned sense?"

"It makes sense. It's just not true. But that must be the story they're passing around."

"I asked where he got the story and he said it came from his division chief. But when I asked where he got it, and kept pushing for an answer, he figured out I wasn't you because he said you would have known he didn't have that kind of info. Is that right?"

"Yeah."

"Christ, am I a dummy! I should have had my goddamned brains fixed instead of my face. Who the hell did I think I was, trying to pull something like that—James Bond?"

Burke stared vacantly out at the Bloomingdale shoppers and waited.

"Anyway it didn't take him long to figure out who I was after that. Even blindfolded. Since Pam led him into the trap, and I was close to Pam, it had

91

to be me. So there I was, right square in the shit-house. But the guy swore he'd forget the whole thing if I cut him loose, and I had to take his word. The only other choice I had was to kill him right there and I wasn't about to go that route. I've played rough all my life but never killed nobody. So I cut him loose. And the second I do, he picks up a brick and swings it at my fucking head. If he'd hit me solid, I'd have been dead right then . . . brained! But he's a little off target and just knocks me dizzy. Then he comes at me again and I get lucky in the dark and he misses and I hook an arm around his throat. I'm bleeding like a pig now and close to passing out. And if I go out, I know for sure I don't wake up. Because this fucker's out to finish me. So I hang on and hang on while he fights to bust loose. When he finally stops fighting, I go out cold. And when I come to, my arm's still around the bugger's throat and he's dead."

Burke's mouth was dry. "Does anyone but Pam know about this?"

"No."

"You're sure no one saw you?"

"Yeah."

"What did you do with the body?"

"I left it right there."

Burke sighed over the wire.

"Some fuck-up, huh?" Hank said flatly.

"You may be all right. When they find the body, they'll probably just hang it on me. In fact I'm sure they will. Just as I'm sure they blame me for the disappearance of those two men David shot. It's too bad it happened, but it could be worse."

"I'll tell that to Bishop."

"Stop punishing yourself. It's done. And from what you told me, you acted in self-defense. Better him than you."

Hank said nothing.

"Just do me one small favor," Burke said.

"Yeah?"

"Don't help me anymore."

Two hours later, Burke answered Lilly's call from a booth on West Seventy-second Street. "What's doing?" he said.

"Nothing. I was just hungry to hear your voice."

"I'll bet."

"Is it so impossible?"

"With you, yes."

"Are all spies so smart?"

"No. Just me. That's why I'm in such great shape."

She laughed. "I'll bet you could be fun if so many people weren't trying to kill you."

He waited.

"I went out to Amagansett with Frank on Sunday."

"Frank, is it? I can see how much my warnings mean."

"Aren't you curious about what happened?"

"I know what happened. You fell madly in love and got laid in front of an open fire."

"Jesus, what a smartass spy." She giggled. "But you got the order reversed."

"Only because I'm old-fashioned. I'm still saddled with the crazy notion that love should come at least fifteen minutes before lovemaking. But what the hell. At least you remembered his name."

"Why are you being so nasty?"

"Because you scare hell out of me with what you're trying to do and I don't know how to stop you."

"I told you not to worry."

"That only makes me worry more."

"Listen," she said and her voice changed slightly. "Just listen a minute. Frank told me some things. He said he's not really a detective investigating Stern's murder, but an intelligence agent looking for

93

you. He also said he has no idea why you're wanted, but that it happens all the time when politics change, and he even feels kind of sorry for you."

"And he told you all this because you're such a terrific lay?"

"God, you can be a miserable bastard."

"Lilly, this is heavy stuff. Don't fool with it."

"He told me this because he believes I don't know where you are, he cares about me a little, and he hates the idea of having lied to me. Is that really so impossible to believe?"

Burke left that one alone.

"But something else happened last night," she said. "When I came home from the theatre, there were two other men waiting for me in my apartment. One was black, the other white, and they called each other Waldo and Kevin. They said they didn't believe any of the answers I'd given Frank and wanted to question me themselves. They made like a real comedy team, except they weren't very funny and got even less funny as they went along."

"What did they ask?"

"When did I last see you? And how I get in touch with you when I want to talk?"

"How did you answer?"

"According to the script. I said I hadn't seen you since the hospital, and wouldn't know how to reach you even if I wanted to—which I don't."

"And then?"

"Then they really started getting nasty. First they made me take off my blouse because they said they wanted to see my beautiful new tits. Then they showed me a darling little electric-shock machine they had in an attaché case."

"Oh, Christ," said Burke and ground out his cigarette against the glass of the booth.

"At first I was scared half to death. But then I figured if they really meant to use that thing they'd have bound and gagged me, which they hadn't. There are very thin walls in my building, and one scream can bring half the tenants out into the halls. But I was real pleased with myself for staying cool enough to think that clearly. Anyway, it was around this time that Frank came in like the Seventh Cavalry and really gave it to those apes. When he finally finished with them, there was blood all over my carpet, but it was all theirs and I loved every drop." She paused and the wire hung dead for a moment. "So what do you think of that, Mr. Smartass Spy?"

"I'm sorry you had to go through it all."

"Never mind that. What do you think of my Franky now?"

Burke hesitated, but had no choice. "Maybe you can get him a part in your play. He seems to be an exceptional actor."

"You cynical son of a bitch! Don't you believe in anything?"

"I'm afraid it's an old ploy, Lilly. Every security outfit in the world uses it. It even has a name. It's called the Good Cop and the Bad Cop. The bad cop abuses the suspect, and the good cop rescues and protects him. Then the suspect feels he has a friend in the good cop and confides in him. It's all a performance. You're an actress, Lilly. You know how convincing a good performance can be."

"I know this was no performance. And you don't know Frank Harkevy. If you did, you'd realize how idiotic you sound."

Burke was silent.

"I'm telling you I saw him knock them down then kick their heads in. There was real blood on the carpet. You can't fake real blood."

"Please. Try not to take this so personally. Your Frank is just doing his job. It probably has nothing to do with how he feels about you. You're beautiful and lovable and I'm sure he's crazy about you. I just want you to know that things are rarely as they seem in this business."

"Oh, fuck you!" she said and hung up.

There were no messages from David.

12

It was late, after 1:00 A.M., but Burke was still in the studio, working at his easel. This was not his usual hour for painting, but tonight he was very much in need of the composure he never failed to find in simply working a brush on canvas. The touch, the feel, the smells, the sense of dominion over at least this small, two-dimensional illusion were inevitably soothing. Once he had fantasized, had even expected much more from his painting, had felt it nourish a hard core of integrity within him that believed regardless of whatever else he did, his paintings would add to his worth, would demonstrate what he had learned of life and living, would move people with his insights, exalt them with his visions of beauty. His paintings, he had hoped, would scream of the injustices of society, the anguish of loneliness, the futility of hate, the need for love, the tragedy of the loss of wonder. But that had been a long time ago. At moments like this, he was willing to settle for it as a tranquilizer.

Three days had passed since his last meeting with the old man. He had heard nothing and it was beginning to disturb him. He had set out a beautiful piece of bait, dangled an authentic, top-priority code number in front of them, and had not even got a nibble. In their place he would have responded within twenty-four hours. It made no sense. Unless, he had been wrong about Millang being involved.

He left the apartment at exactly 2:00 A.M., took a crosstown bus through Central Park, and got off at

Lexington Avenue and Seventy-second Street. He walked up Lexington and turned west on Seventy-fourth Street, past the converted brownstone where Angela lived, to Park Avenue. He knew there would be no watchers at this hour, but old habit made him check anyway. Then walking back to Angela's house, he quickly picked open the locks on the iron-grilled front door and the glass vestibule door behind it.

A short hallway led to the rear apartment; he moved silently down it, listening for possible sounds. He heard none. Along with his other concerns, he feared frightening her half to death. At the moment his own pulsebeat was much too fast and none too steady, bringing a pain that stabbed him exactly between the shoulder blades. It climaxed, faded, and went away, leaving him breathing heavily in the red-papered-hallway in front of Angela's door.

In preparation he had been here for a dry run late that afternoon while Angela was at work. He wanted no fumbling at the locks, no sound that might waken her. And he had taken still another precaution. He had made certain the tall man with the moustache would not be spending the night. That was one contingency he was not about to gamble on. As far as it was possible to prepare for such things, he had prepared. Burke drew air into his lungs and let it out in a burning exhaust. No surprises here. He had expected to feel no differently. The thing was, it made no sense, was totally without logic. There was absolutely no reason for him to be here, other than the single reason that had finally brought him. He wanted to be here. He was tired of being sensible, tired of acting rationally, tired of hours, days, and months based solely on the logic of survival. Finally, there had to be something more—even if it was only the ability of the soul to take foolish risks in the pursuit of love.

So just let me love her, he thought, and he put his hands to work on the more practical matter of unsealing her locks.

The door swung open and he carefully closed it behind him. Inside, it was totally black, but he knew the apartment's layout from his afternoon visit and felt his way toward the bedroom. For an instant, he had the impression of moving through a dark, airless tunnel and sensed a remembered brightness go out of him, much as the death of a friend carried off some small piece of you. Then he touched the edge of an open door and was in the same room with her.

Pausing, he heard her breathing and recalled a thousand nights he had lain beside her, hearing the same soft, regular sound. A faint, almost phosphorescent glow came through the barred rear window and he saw the outlines of her body on the bed. But then all the old uncertainties rallied and came back to hit him; he was afraid to make a move. What he might want was one thing, but this sort of romantic foolishness was beyond belief. She thinks you're dead, man—dead. And even when you were alive to her, she left you. Remember? What in God's name makes you think she'll care for you any more as a latter-day Lazarus? And then, of course, there was always that other possibility, the one that said she did not really believe him dead and was letting them use her as bait. Which, if true, would be the ultimate irony. Cupid's poisoned arrows. But he knew if he allowed himself to believe that, there would be little good left for him in anything and he would be tasting bile for the rest of his days. Nevertheless, there were any number of lies they might have told her about him, and everyone, even she, carried their own small demons.

He knelt on the rug beside her bed.

She slept curled on her right side, facing him, her arms under the covers. As gently as possible, he slipped one hand behind her head on the pillow, placed his other hand over her mouth and leaned lightly across her body. Her eyes opened and her body stirred, then stiffened as she came out of sleep in a rush. She managed a muffled gasp. That was all.

"Don't be frightened," he said, not whispering, but wanting her to hear and recognize his natural voice. "It's me, Richard. I'm not dead. Please. Don't be frightened."

Above his hand, her eyes stared wildly. Not knowing how much she was able to see in the darkness, he said, "My face is different. I had to change my face. But I'm not dead. It's still me. My voice is still the same. Don't you recognize my voice?"

Slowly, he removed his hand from her mouth. His throat ached and his palms felt clammy. Her mouth was open but she made no sound. She just lay there, staring up at him. Not knowing what to do, how to reassure her, he stroked her hair, her face. Emotion blinded him. Wiping his eyes, he said "It's me," and kept saying it. "It's me . . . it's me . . ."

Her mouth moved. She tried twice to speak and could not.

"Richard?" It was the faintest of whispers, as if she feared that anything louder would awaken her if she were asleep and dreaming, or get her committed if she were awake and overheard.

"It's me . . . it's me."

"Is it really you?"

"Don't you know my voice?"

"But you're dead," she said. Then she gasped a little and began to weep. She covered her face with her hands and wept silently, her body shaking beneath the covers.

Burke knelt on the rug and watched her. The last time we were together, he thought, we fought and she was also crying. Now here we are three years later, with all sorts of things behind us, including my own death and resurrection, and she's crying again.

"Tony told me you were dead," she wept.

"He had to."

"How could you let him do that to me?"

"Things happened. I was in trouble. It was the only reasonably safe way for me to go on living." He was silent for a moment. "Besides . . . considering . . . I didn't think it would really matter that much to you."

"You didn't think . . . ?" She gasped again, working for control. "I loved you."

"You also left and divorced me."

"That had nothing to do with loving you. I just couldn't live with you."

"I know."

"No you don't. If you did, you couldn't have done that to me. Do you know what it's like to lose someone you love?"

"Yes."

She realized what she had said. "I'm sorry. But at least you didn't think I was dead."

"Do you think that made it any easier? It made it worse. Dead is dead and once you accept it you can go on from there. But I couldn't go anywhere. I was stuck all the way back there, loving you. I couldn't have you and I didn't want anyone else. Do you know what that's like?"

She did not say anything and they stayed that way in the darkened room, she, still lying beneath the covers, he, kneeling on the floor beside her bed. Outside, a police siren wailed as it went by.

Angela reached out and touched his shoulder. "I know it's your voice: I hear it. I recognize it. I'd know it anywhere. But I still can't believe it's really you."

"Believe it."

"May I . . . ?" She hesitated. "May I see your face?"

"It's not important. It's just a face."

"Please."

Moving heavily, he got up and closed the blinds. Then he turned on a small lamp and knelt beside the bed once more. Watching her eyes, he could tell nothing. What if she had come to him with another face? he wondered. How would he feel? But it was impossible for him to even imagine her looking any differently than she did.

"I think I've seen you," she said and was back to whispering again. "I think I've seen you somewhere."

"You have."

"Where?"

"At the museum. On a bus. In a restaurant."

"Oh, God," she whispered. "Yes. The restaurant. I remember the restaurant. This man was looking at me from across the room, and for a moment his eyes—I swear I had this crazy feeling about his eyes. I didn't know why or what, but I kept thinking about them for the rest of the day. And that night I dreamed about you. It was awful."

He smiled. "Thanks."

"I cried all night in my sleep. I was a mess in the morning. In my dream I kept calling you, but you were running and wouldn't stop."

"I have been running."

She sat up in bed and touched his face. "You look so young. You look thirty years old."

"I feel sixty."

"And that big, beautiful sword of a nose. It's *gone.*"

"I had to pay double for that."

She suddenly lay back and pulled the covers over the lower part of her face. "My God! I must look like your mother."

"You look like you, beautiful," he said softly, and again felt his throat clotted with emotion.

"Please don't look at me."

"There's nothing else I want to do."

"Not yet. I'm not ready for that yet. Give me a little time. Please, Richard. Turn out the light."

He did as she asked and they were in the dark once more. She found his hand and held it, pressing hard, searching out bones, knuckles, tendons, all his. "I'm not just dreaming?"

"No."

"Swear it."

"I swear you're not dreaming."

She sighed. "You don't know how often I have."

"I love you."

"You shouldn't." She wept softly. "When Tony came and told me you were dead, I hated him. Later, I hated myself. I was like a character in a soap opera. I had left you for all the wrong reasons and now you were dead."

"You weren't wrong."

"Please. Please let me say this. I've thought and dreamed about saying it for so long, but who expected this kind of miracle? So please."

He felt her hand, warming him in the darkness. A wind had come up and it rattled the blinds at the barred window. Tonight, at least, he was on the right side of the bars. "All right," he said, and waited for her to go on.

It took her a moment. "When someone you love dies," she said, "it makes you think. So I thought. I thought about our life together and saw what a fool I'd been. It wasn't enough that I had love, I had to have everything else, too. I loved and married you for what you were, then tried to change you because it was hard to live with. And because you refused to change, I left." She shook her head tiredly. "It wasn't easy for me to learn, but I've learned."

He heard her crying again.

"Why did you wait so long?" She wept. "Were you punishing me?"

"No. Just myself. I wasn't sure how you felt, anyway. And you were being watched. You still are. They had you transferred here from the Coast just for bait. And they were right. Finally, I had to come."

He leaned forward, felt her wet cheeks and kissed her. It was their first kiss.

"I read about Tony," she said. "I'm sorry. I know how close you were. Was he sick very long?"

"He wasn't sick at all."

"But it said in the papers . . ."

"It says a lot of things in the papers." He did not really want to talk about it now but it had to be done. "Tony was murdered."

Her breath went out. "Oh, no. By whom?"

"I don't know. That's what I have to find out. And before whoever it is finds me." Burke rose from the floor and stretched out beside her on the bedcovers. "You never had any hint you were being watched?"

"No. Never. But what is it? Why are you in such trouble?"

"It's very complicated."

She was silent.

He felt for her face, fingers touching eyes, nose, lips, chin—a blind man seeking sight. Her cheeks, at last, were dry. "I'm really not sure why they want me," he said. "I thought at first it was because they were afraid I knew something potentially damaging, but now I think it has to be more. I've been given too high a priority. Too many are involved. Too many have died. There has to be something else."

"Couldn't you simply go away somewhere?" she asked. "I mean, just disappear and to hell with them?"

"Not unless I was willing to spend the rest of my life running, hiding, and waiting for a bullet in the head. Besides," he added wearily, "I've gotten others into it now. I couldn't just run out on them."

Turning slightly, she drew him closer and held him. They lay this way; he above the covers, she beneath.

Suddenly, there were things he had to know. "But if it were possible," he said, "if I somehow could get away somewhere, would you go with me?"

"Yes."

"Even knowing what you do?"

"I never look gift miracles in the mouth."

"You'd leave your job, your work?"

"My work is hardly a calling."

"And what about the tall, dark-haired guy with the moustache?"

"Who?"

But he had felt her body tighten, and waited.

"You sneaky bastard," she said.

"Once a spy . . ."

"That's unfair."

"I couldn't help it. Even dead. I had to look through your bedroom window once. Just to see you."

"How . . ." she stopped. "How much did you see?"

He could not answer that.

"Oh, God," she whispered and turned away from him. "I feel a little sick."

"It doesn't really matter," he lied, remembering the extinction he had felt.

"I'll never be able to look at you again."

"Yes you will," he said, and switched on the bedlamp.

"Richard, that's cruel."

Gently he turned her so that she faced him again. "Who is he?"

"Didn't you check him out?" she said flatly.

"I didn't want to know. I was dead."

"And now?"

"I'm no longer dead."

The lamplight soft on her face, she frowned as though adding up an expensive bill. "I work for him," she said tonelessly. "He's married, but we had a kind of arrangement. It fitted both our needs. He was never you. No one could ever be you for me again. But I could at least laugh with him, share, talk, feel like a woman. After Tony said you were dead, I punished myself for a long time. I wanted to bury myself. I almost did. Paul helped lift me out of it." Her mouth fell open and she sighed. "And that's pretty much the whole story."

Burke was silent. So his name was Paul, he thought, and felt something dark go out of him. An exorcism? But there were no devils here, just the usual clay.

"I love you," she said. "I've never stopped."

He touched her lips with his fingers, still blind even with the light.

"What's going to happen to us?"

"I don't know," he said honestly.

"And you're sure we can't run?"

"I'm sure."

"Oh, Lord . . . Lord," she whispered and gave him a kiss as dizzying as the one they had shared earlier, except that the strangeness was out of it this time, some of the new uncertainty.

Burke breathed a sweetness that had floated on the air one hot summer night long ago. "Let's go back," he said. "Let's go back at least three of these last goddamned years."

They did. And somewhere in the middle, as if born out of the regret and hurt of every mistake he had ever made, like an offering he did not deserve and had never expected, some small hope stirred in him again and he thought, maybe, just maybe it can still be all right.

He was ready to leave at first light, about an hour before the watcher was due.

"Please don't die on me again," she said.

"Not even as a joke."

She was holding him hard. "When will I see you?"

"I don't know, but you can count on it."

"I will," she said.

13

Burke called the answering service and asked if there were any messages for Arthur Radin. "Yes, Mr. Radin," said the operator. "Edgar Burns called and said he would like to speak with you as soon as possible."

"What time did the call come in?"

"At 9:08 this morning."

"Thank you," Burke said.

At exactly 12:08, he called David Tomschin's assigned number, a service station booth on Second Avenue and Sixtieth Street. He heard the receiver picked up on the first ring. "David?" he said.

"Yeah." The tone was flat, thick.

"Is anything wrong? I haven't heard from you in a while. You okay?"

There was no answer and Burke thought the line had gone dead.

"David, are you there?"

"Yeah, I'm here."

"What's wrong?"

"I've been locked up," said David hoarsely.

"What?"

"I've been jailed. I've been stuck in a goddamned dungeon for almost two weeks. My girl, too. No phone calls, no lawyers, no nothing. What happened to the Bill of Rights?"

He stopped and Burke could hear him breathing heavily. "Who did it? Who picked you up?"

"That bald, pink-faced guy I told you I kept seeing. Always smokes a pipe. He said his name was Ellman. Sam Ellman. You know him?"

"I once met him, but it was years ago." Burke took a moment. "I'm sorry, David. Did he put much pressure on you? Are you all right?"

"Don't worry. I didn't tell him anything. I just said I hadn't seen or spoken with you since the hospital and stuck with it."

"When did you get out?"

"Yesterday."

"Your girl, too?"

"Yeah."

"Why did they let you go?"

"Dolores, my girl, was finally able to get someone to call a lawyer she knew. He went to the District Attorney's office and threatened to make a stink. Ellman was sore as hell but had to let us out."

"Did he say why they were looking for me?"

"Yeah. He invented some crap about you turning into a double-agent or something. He made you sound like the latest model Benedict Arnold. The bastard's Jewish, and he even appealed to our mutual Jewishness to get me to tell him what he wanted. You wouldn't believe some of the things that came out of his mouth. He gave me this whole bit about how great America has been to him and his family after the pogroms of Europe, and how there's nothing he wouldn't do for the country. And he said that I, as a Jew, should feel the same way, that Russia was persecuting the Jews even today, and that you'd sold out to the Russians. Which meant that in protecting you, I was hurting my own people." David laughed harshly. "I mean, the guy was really reaching."

David fell silent and Burke waited.

"The funny thing is," David went on, "that after awhile he was actually starting to remind me a little of this uncle I've got—Uncle Louie—same bald head and pink face, same phoney, salesman's personality, same flag-waving about what the country's done for the Jews. I swear he even gave my Dolores a TV set while she was in the hole so she wouldn't have to miss any of her soap operas. Now is that a sweet little ole' *landsman,* or isn't it?''

David made a small sound deep in his throat that may have started out as a laugh, but reached Burke as something quite different.

"You're sure you're okay?"

David did not answer.

"David?"

"No, I'm not okay," David blurted hoarsely, his voice twisted with a sudden fear and trembling. "I'm scared. I'm scared shitless. I can't eat or sleep and my insides are jelly. All I keep doing is looking over my shoulder. I'm afraid that bald son of a bitch isn't through with me." He took some breathing time. "What do you think. You know about these things. It's your goddamned business. Do you think he'll pick me up again?"

Burke did not answer at once. He was beginning to feel like the original man in the glass booth. Something came over the wire like the whispering in a forest, and he could almost see David's fear. "I'm not going to lie to you. He probably will."

"Oh, God," David whispered.

"I'm sorry I had to get you into this."

"I'm not blaming you. It's not your fault. I just don't know how to handle this. I'm scared of what I might say if they ever really went to work on me. Just being in that lousy hole almost put me out of my skull. I guess I'm claustrophobic or something." He stopped, breathing heavily against the mouthpiece. "I know I can't really hurt you any," he rushed on. "We already burned your picture negative and I don't know anything to give them but a lousy answering service number. But I keep thinking of those two guys we buried up in the Catskills. What if I really busted and told them about that? I mean I'm the one who shot them, for Jesus's sake! I could spend the rest of my goddamned life in the slammer."

"Take it easy, David. They haven't got you, and you haven't told anybody anything yet."

"Yeah, but they might, and I might."

Burke was silent.

"I can't just sit and wait to be picked up again," David moaned. "I can't take that chance. I know me and I know the kind of shape I'm in. I'm not proud of it. I wish I could be tougher. But why kid myself? I'm not tough. Not in that way. So I've got to do something."

"What do you mean?"

"I've got to get out of it. I've got to lose them. I've got to go away somewhere until it all blows over, or you settle it one way or another. I've got enough money. I can just hole-up somewhere under another name and write."

"It's not that simple, David."

"Why not? What's to stop me from packing a bag, pulling some cash out of the bank, and taking off for California some night?"

Burke sighed. "You're not going to lose them that easily. They probably have you under surveillance this minute."

"I haven't seen anyone following me. I don't see anyone now."

"I told you once. The only time you'll see them is when they want you to. Take a look out the booth. Is there anyone sitting in a car, walking a dog, reading a paper, standing in front of a store, or just strolling past?"

After a moment, David said, "Yeah."

"Yeah, what?"

"They're all here. I guess it could be any one of them."

"Or none," said Burke. "They're not that obvious. I just wanted you to have an idea of your chances."

"So what am I supposed to do? They'll bury me if I'm picked up again."

The silence on the line was heavy as a scent. To Burke, it stretched and hung almost palpably.

"I didn't say it was impossible," he said at last. "It can be done. But I'd have to help you."

"You kidding me?"

"I haven't seen a surveillance yet that a good pro couldn't break out of."

"Shit. That's probably just what Ellman wants. It's a real sucker move. I haven't gone through all this crap just so the bastards can pick you up trying to help me."

"Listen, David . . ."

"Forget it."

"Will you shut up a minute and listen to me. I'm not making any noble gestures. I happen to think you're right. If you're picked up again, they will bury you. And that's not going to do either of us any good."

"But what if Ellman set the whole thing up? I mean, couldn't he have fixed it so Dolores could get a message out, have us released, and then pull you into just this kind of trap?"

"Of course. In fact that's exactly what I figure he did do. Don't you think I know that? I know you're the cheese in this thing. But I happen to be a very tricky little mouse."

"I still don't like it."

"You don't have to," said Burke and his mind was far ahead, working.

"Please," David begged. "I feel like such a cry-baby, such a weak sister."

"Now cut that out. You've been fine. They've put the big squeeze on and you've given them nothing, not a damn thing. I just want to get you out of this while we're both still ahead."

"What about the others? What about Lilly, Pam, and Hank? What's happening to them?"

"Nothing. At least nothing like the kind of thing you've been through. They're under surveillance, of course, but you seem to be the one they're concentrating on."

"But why me?"

112

"I don't know. You're just lucky, I guess."

"Ha . . ."

"Just give me a little time to work things out, and I'll get you out of this clean. Where's your girl? Where's Dolores staying? Has she moved in with you yet?"

"Yeah. This morning."

"Good. Concentrate on her for awhile. My guess is that they're not going to be bothering you for a while. By then, I should have you clear of them."

"I . . . I appreciate it."

"I got you into this. The least I can do is get you out."

14

The professor was absolutely, Burke decided, the worst driver he had ever seen. Suicidal was probably the only word that came close to describing his performance at the wheel of a car. It was a miracle he had survived to become an old man. Driving not too far behind, Burke had seen him sail serenely through stop signs and red lights, make turns from wrong lanes, cut off cars to the screeching of brakes, and, in general, leave a growing trail of near disasters across a small, undeserving section of the southwestern part of the state of Maryland. And he'll be fine, thought Burke. I'm the one who'll finally end up getting totalled.

Of course the old man had no idea that he was being followed, although this was the fourth day that Burke had him under surveillance. Only when the professor turned in for the night, which he rarely did before 2:00 A.M., did Burke allow himself to bed down in the Volkswagon van he had rented for that purpose. Among other things, the simple fact of the old man's energy astounded him. On no more than three or four hours of sleep a night, he put in a workday that could have exhausted an Olympic athlete. Burke himself was bleary-eyed from trying to match his pace for just the past ninety-six hours.

There was another squeal of brakes ahead as Professor Kreuger, perhaps lost in a fresh analysis of some dimly remembered, eighteenth century political theory, ran his seventh stop sign. Burke winced and shook his head, but could not help smiling. That was some professor. One of the last of a special but

114

sadly vanishing breed, with heart, intellect, and integrity, and enough human warmth to match the rest. Who was there to replace teachers like that when they were finally gone?

Burke saw him turn onto Route 95, going south towards Washington, and a moment later did the same himself. Watching the cars ahead, as well as those in his rearview mirror, he saw nothing suspicious. Just as he had also seen nothing suspicious for all of the past four days. Which, in itself, had begun to bother him. They should have had someone watching the old man by now. It was ten days since he had dangled that supposedly irresistible piece of bait in front of Millang, and something should have happened. Yet nothing had. Even if Millang was not involved with the Service in some way, he should have been able to contact someone who was . . . or else gotten back to the professor himself. But since Burke had received no messages at all from the old man during this period, he could only assume that neither of these events had taken place. And this was what he had found most disturbing.

"I don't understand it," he told Angela during one of his nocturnal visits. "I just can't believe I could have figured this so wrong."

They were sitting over a 4:00 A.M. pot of coffee in her kitchen, a tiny, windowless room that Burke enjoyed because it provided a warm (if false) illusion of continuing domesticity. This was his third visit, but the flood of feeling that had swamped him the first time had not diminished. They could have been two adolescents. It was that kind of springtime wonder.

"Maybe you'll still hear from him," she said.

"No. If I haven't heard by now, I won't hear. That's how these things work. There's a pattern you recognize after a while." "Somehow, they aren't sold on the professor," he said. "I can't think of any other reason why they wouldn't have reacted. Unless they just don't believe Tony could have been careless enough to leave anything important lying around.

Which happens to be true. This guy was a machine. He ate detail for breakfast. But even a machine can make a mistake. And why would they doubt his father?"

Angela's finger traced a vein on the back of his hand, a loving explorer in the promised land. "Could they be afraid the professor was suspicious?"

"About what?"

"That Tony might not have really been a suicide?"

"It's possible. But even so, they wouldn't simply ignore it. They'd want to find out why he was suspicious and what he actually knew. One way or another, they'd have to contact him."

"What are you going to do?"

"I don't know. But it's got to be something. I can't just sit and wait anymore."

She lay her head against his hand. "Sometimes I feel so terribly guilty."

"Why?"

"Because you're in trouble and I'm happy."

She raised her head to look at him and they stared at one another like two prospectors, partners, who have just come upon an extraordinary find. "I promise not to be indiscriminately happy," she said. "Just at special moments. And in between, I'll give equal time to worrying about all the trouble you're in."

"Please leave the worrying to me. I'm very good at it. I'd rather you were just happy."

"Indiscriminately?"

He leaned over and kissed her, holding it long and hard, as if trying to learn everything about her with his lips. "Absolutely indiscriminately."

"And you promise it won't bother you?"

He nodded. "What about what's-his-name? The guy with the moustache. Paul."

"I told him it was over."

"Didn't you give him any reason?"

"I just said I'd met someone else I cared about." She smiled. "Someone who wasn't married. So it wasn't even a lie."

"Any regrets?"

"Not really. I'm a basically monogamous type, darling. I always was. One love quite fills me up. There's no room in me for any more than that."

"He might fire you now that you've stopped putting out."

"Don't be vulgar. That's not why I was hired. I happen to be very good at my job."

"Sure, but I'll bet you're better in bed."

She made a face. "Sexist pig. That part of you sure hasn't changed."

"I can still try."

"Don't you dare. Not when I have three dry years to catch up on," she said, and happily led him out of the tiny kitchen and back into the bedroom.

Burke smiled as he drove, keeping the professor's weaving, green Chevrolet in clear sight, but remembering the woman who had once been his wife. The totally absorbing business of his survival had made a miser out of him, had made him save most of his thoughts for just trying to stay alive. But with nothing to do now but drive, he indulged himself, and thought of Angela and those last moments in bed. It had been a peak, passionate experience, a sensual flood that had swept away all the lonely years, all thought and memory of dying, all fear of what still lay ahead. It had all disappeared there in that warm, scented bed, in that dark room with the barred windows. He had not realized how much he had missed simply the joy of her flesh, the feel of a body he had once known as intimately as his own. They clung fiercely to one another, kissing with such force that their lips became bruised and puffy. She was wild, unable to get enough of him, surprising even herself.

"My God, I'm liable to really kill you this time," she gasped.

"Please. Kill . . . kill."

"What's wrong with me?"

He was too busy to answer.

"I'm turning into a crazy nympho."

"Terrific. Keep turning."

"It's embarrassing. I feel so wanton. When will I finally have enough of you?"

"The minute we get married again."

She laughed. "That's nasty."

"No. More good love affairs are ruined by marriage than by anything else."

"And that's cynical."

"But true."

"Not for us," she said. "It was never that way for us."

He did not comment.

"Was it?"

"Was what, what?"

"Was it ever that way for us?"

"Hey, come on," he said. "You interested in talk or some real action?"

"Both."

"A man can't do both."

"You can."

And, incredibly, he could.

Afterward, she smiled. "See? I told you."

Drowsily submerged in love, he licked her throat like a happy cat.

"There's definitely something to be said," she whispered, "for all resurrections."

But the real trick, he thought now in his rented van, was being able to stay resurrected. It would be too bad if it didn't last, for Angela as well as himself. Losing him twice would be doubly hard for her. He knew about such loss. He had been introduced early to the concept of resurrection, to both its hopes and disappointments. His father had gone down on the *Arizona* at Pearl Harbor, and although his body still lay trapped somewhere underwater, for years Burke had waited for the miracle of its rising. It had been a secret wait. He had shared it with no one, not even his mother. The whole idea had been too crazy, too blasphemous, even for a kid. To believe his father could actually pull off something that only Jesus

118

Himself had so far managed to do was surely too much. Still, the man had been his father, and from the day his mother had first taken him to visit the memorial at Pearl Harbor when he was seven, and he had stood staring at that great, rusted hulk, jutting from the waters of the harbor, he had carried the private fantasy inside him. In it, his father had always appeared in his beautiful white, summer dress uniform, his face solemn, his eyes weighted with the responsibility of his brand new lieutenant's stripes, just as it was in the photograph that had stood for years on the piano at home. Otherwise, the rising was pretty much like the paintings Burke had seen of Christ's own, with his father's body rising mistily from the water like a great kite, one hand raised in greeting as he drifted toward him. As Burke grew older, and his mother converted both of them to Christian Science, he adapted to a less realistic version of his father's resurrection, with the spirit as more the source and constituent of his father's life substance. But when his mother, not too long after, tried and failed to talk herself out of a terminal cancer, even this vision faded and his father was finally twice dead. And because he was older, the second dying hurt more than the first.

I must be very careful not to do this to Angela, he thought. As though any such result would be solely his to control.

The professor's Chevrolet turned off Route 95 at Silver Spring, and Burke followed. There was less traffic here and he allowed the distance between them to lengthen another hundred yards. Checking the rearview mirror, he saw a tan station wagon coming up behind him and slowed until it had passed and turned off to the right. Professor Kreuger was driving more slowly now, as though uncertain of where he was going. Reaching a busy intersection, he stopped half way across as horns blared from three sides. Then he turned off to the left and drove into a large shopping plaza.

119

It was late afternoon, a busy shopping time, but the parking area was huge and had many empty spaces. The old man stopped in a section with few cars in it and Burke parked about seventy-five yards behind him. Another wasted day, he thought, wishing he could at least close his eyes for a while and grab a little sleep. Surveillance had always been the least favorite part of his work. It was tiresome, dull, and usually futile. Most of those who had something to hide, or who were professionals, could somehow manage to break the best of surveillances. The others rarely had anything going on that was worth discovering. In this instance, he was following the professor not because he expected to come upon any big discovery, but because he simply had no other alternatives.

Waiting for him to leave his car for whatever shopping he had come to do, Burke was struck again (as he had been outside his kitchen window weeks before) by the terrible solitariness of the old man's daily existence—the reading, eating, and sleeping alone, the absence of anyone close, anyone to share with, to touch, to confide in. Of course he had his work, his students, but when he closed his door at night who was there to make him feel loved, to soothe his human fears, to tell him he was not alone and closer to death than he wanted to believe? Who was there to remember him as he had been when he was young? Because Burke himself felt more fortunate, because he suddenly had Angela again, he ached all the more for the old man. Ah, hey, professor, he wanted to say, I know how it is. Up until a few days ago, I was even more alone than you. And though I'm thirty years younger, I may be even closer to death. Besides, none of us are really that different. We're all in this place together, and the final going always has to be done alone.

Burke stared across seventy-five yards of concrete at the back of the green Chevrolet, but the old man still did not come out. When a few more minutes had passed, he began to worry. Had something happened to him? Maybe a sudden fainting spell or even a heart attack? He seemed healthy enough, but at that age anything could happen, and usually without warning. Then he realized Kreuger could also just be sitting there and thinking, or going over some notes, or jotting down an idea, or simply reading one of the many books he was always carrying about with him. During his four days of watching the old man, Burke had become an expert on his more visible eccentricities. So there might very well be nothing wrong with his sitting alone in a parking lot for a while.

A moment later Burke saw a man walking towards the green Chevrolet. He had not noticed where he came from, whether from another car or from the shopping mall itself, and only spotted him when he was about thirty feet from the Chevrolet. He was of average height and wore a dark hat and a light coat with the collar turned up against the wind. For an instant, watching from his van, Burke sensed something familiar about him. He had no idea what it was. Perhaps it was his slender build, or the slight forward tilt of his head, or his walk, a quick purposeful stride that vaguely reminded Burke of other times, other places, and maybe even of people long gone. He had sensed the same thing many times before. It was part of his tradecraft automatically to collect bits and pieces like that and store them away for possible future use. Most of them were worthless. But every once in a while, at some utterly unpredictable moment, one of them could save your life.

When the man was within ten feet of the professor's Chevrolet, and clearly headed for it, Burke picked up a pair of high-powered binoculars from the seat beside him. But before he could sight and focus, the man had opened the car door and disappeared inside.

It seemed he had something.

But what? Whoever the man was, he had taken pains to meet the professor alone and on neutral ground. Which meant he was almost certain to be someone Millang had contacted. Parking lot meetings in cars were hardly a normal part of the old man's daily routine. But if Millang had arranged the meeting, if this finally was the contact they had been waiting for all this time, why hadn't the professor notified him as planned? During the past four days of his surveillance, Burke had regularly checked with the answering service number he had given the professor, but had received no messages. Of course, he had not called in for the last few hours. Also, this meeting might have come about too quickly for the old man to set their elaborate call-back arrangements in motion. Which was all beside the point, anyway. The only thing that mattered was that someone was here.

Burke focused his binoculars on the rear window of the Chevrolet, but the angle was bad and he could see nothing. Carefully backing out of his parking space, he circled the mall and chose what he hoped would be a better viewing position at a safe distance. But the visibility was equally bad from here, with the slope of the rear window reflecting the light in such a way as to make the glass opaque. Burke considered moving again, then decided against it. He had been foolish to move the van even the first time. It was not unlikely that they would have someone watching the contact's back in a situation like this, and a van cruising from one place to another in the same parking lot would arouse suspicion. He was getting careless. Any rookie would have known better. You could be careful, careful, careful, then blow it all in a moment of thoughtless enthusiasm.

He put down the binoculars in disgust. That, too, was stupidity. Did he think he was off in the woods, somewhere? Imagine being seen using high-powered glasses in a suburban shopping mall. Feeling coldly on edge, he checked every car within his field of vision but saw nothing to be disturbed about. The only occupied car was a black Cadillac Seville in which a couple sat talking, and he had spotted them earlier. Occasionally, they kissed and hung onto one another. They were not young. Probably married, thought Burke, only not to one another; he felt a tinge of sympathy. But whether the feeling was for them, for two aging lovers having to steal a few crumbs of affection in a parking lot, or for their imagined spouses, he was not certain.

So once more he found himself waiting, although this time in reasonable comfort, and with the excitement of positive results immediately ahead. This could be an important breakthrough. He had not, after all, been wrong about Millang. The simple fact of a contact was no real proof, of course. Millang might have merely passed on the baited information to someone he knew in the Service, and still be no part of it himself. But Burke did not really believe that and, confirmed or not, felt the satisfaction of having his judgment vindicated. That this might prove a significant step towards his survival was not even part of his satisfaction at the moment. He was too hooked into the glow of a professional pride he had just about forgotten. He was still pretty damned good at this stuff, he thought, and could almost envision Tony as he would have once looked at a beautiful debriefing like this, with that great, secret face seeming to say nothing, but the pleasure still busting out of both eyes. Terrific, terrific, his eyes would have said, but just remember who taught you, baby.

Okay, Burke thought. The debt is hereby acknowledged and proper credit given. Retroactively.

He looked at his watch. They had been together in that car for fifteen minutes. Which was much too long. According to the instructions he had given the professor, this first meeting was to have established just two things: some proof of the Service contact's authenticity, and arrangements for a second meeting at which the alleged top-coded document would be handed over. Five minutes, or less, should have been all the time required. Conditioned to having such things go off on a tight schedule, Burke began to fret. When an estimate was this far off, something had to be wrong. He had great confidence in the professor, but age was always a factor and he could have lapses. Simply driving behind him was an ordeal. Then he felt guilty over so harsh a judgment, and thought . . . You should be as sharp as that old man. So just relax.

But he decided to allow only five more minutes. If nothing happened then, if the contact did not leave the car, he would drive past and find out what was going on.

Restlessly, he glanced over at the middle-aged lovers in the Seville, saw them embracing and wished he had Angela with him. At least the waiting would be more palatable. Not a bad idea for the Service. They should introduce the use of sexually mixed pairs for the long, dull surveillances. Efficiency through sexual titillation. He saw the woman's head suddenly drop out of sight so that her companion seemed to be sitting alone behind the wheel. Oh, lovely, Burke thought, and felt himself wanting Angela more than ever. Beautiful. And under any and all conditions. God bless the human animal, he thought in silent benediction, and its sublimely opportunistic sexuality. Or was it just one of the unadvertised options that came with fourteen-thousand-dollar Cadillacs?

Then the professor's car door opened, the man got out, and Burke instinctively reached for his binoculars. He decided he would take a chance on using them.

They did him no good. The man was walking away from him and it was impossible to see his face. Burke put down the glasses and started the van's motor. When he saw the professor's Chevrolet move towards the parking lot exit, he drove slowly after the man who, instead of getting into a car of his own, headed directly for the line of stores in the mall. Hurriedly, Burke parked in another spot and got out to follow.

The mall was one of the new, enclosed types and Burke saw his man go through the nearest entrance and disappear in a swirl of shoppers. Running to catch up, he found him again about fifty yards ahead. At this point he was not even bothering to check his own rear. If the man had any back-up operating, they would have had him spotted by now anyway and he would deal with that if and when it occurred. The only thing he was interested in right now was not losing the man. Which was all wrong, of course, but here he was.

Once more, he felt his earlier sensation of familiarity. It wriggled in his gut like a nest of worms. It worked on him as he bucked through the crowds. The man's coat was loose and shapeless, his collar turned up, his hat pulled low over his eyes, and he might have been anyone.

Then the man turned to go into a department store and Burke caught his first glimpse of his face in profile, saw, from perhaps a distance of thirty yards, fragments of nose, cheek, and chin, saw just a single deep-set eye. Only the worst remained. He should have known it before. He should have recognized that walk instantly from seventy-five yards away in the parking lot. Because there had surely never been anyone else on the planet who walked precisely the same way, no one with as quick, impatient, and purposeful a stride as Tony Kreuger.

By the time Burke reached the store itself, the man was gone.

Tony, you sonofabitch, he thought.

He sought the soothing darkness of a nearby bar and put down most of a double bourbon in a single gulp. This one was a beauty, he thought, and ordered himself another drink to fuel further speculation. Paradox. The more liquor-soaked his brain, the more decisively it seemed to function today. But he would happily have given up a lot of bourbon to have sat, unseen, in the back seat of the professor's Chevrolet for those fifteen or twenty minutes this afternoon. What a discussion that must have been. How had Tony gone about explaining things to the professor? How had he tried to justify the unique cruelty of making a father attend a beloved son's funeral? And what reason had he given for wanting a lifelong friend dead? Surely some sort of explanation must have been offered. Or maybe not. Maybe no answers or explanations were handed out that afternoon in the green Chevrolet. Maybe it was enough for Tony to just fall back on that great, catch-all Kreuger Commandment, which merely declared in letters of stone: It had to be done.

But would that really be enough for the professor? Surely a man like the professor would require a lot more reason than that to betray him. And if he did want more reason, what would Tony tell him? What new fiction would he create? Unless no lies were needed. Unless Tony had knowledge of certain lethal truths that he, Burke knew nothing about. Which brought him full circle to the big question: Why now? What had happened recently that he did not know about, that suddenly made it so vital for him to be eliminated?

Then having finally had enough of questions he could not answer, he paid his check and left the bar.

It had grown dark outside and it took him a moment to orient himself. Crossing the parking lot, he walked a trifle unsteadily as the air hit him. It was a clear night with a great many stars and Burke paused in the middle of the lot to stare up through the darkness. Once, a long time ago, he and Tony had walked together on a similar winter night. Burke remembered it. They had just come off an assignment that had turned out better than either of them had expected and they were both feeling good, and life was full of promise, and food and drink were waiting for them in a warm sweet-smelling restaurant. "Lord, we're lucky," Tony had said softly . . .

126

only that, nothing more, although for him that was a great deal. And Burke, for an instant, almost thought the words had come from his own mouth because he had had the exact same feeling.

Where had that feeling gone now? And what had happened to the life so full of promise?

Finding the rented van, he started what he knew was going to be a long, lonely drive back to New York.

15

Burke sat in his car, hands in his coat pockets, fingering clusters of dimes and quarters—dimes in one pocket, quarters in another. He was parked under the defunct West Side Highway at Fifty-third Street, about fifty yards from the long line of Hudson River piers. The latest of the Queens was in, her lights glowing through the dark, each bulb throwing its own halo. A sea-going Christmas tree, he thought, crammed full of good things. How nice if he and Angela could be aboard when she sailed in the morning. For a moment he enjoyed a happy vision of the two of them walking up the gangplank together, saw them finding their cabin, watched them closing and locking the door as the engines took hold. Maybe, just maybe, they would consider coming out for occasional meals. Ships had always intrigued him. Any kind. From fishing trawlers and tugs, to luxury liners and battle wagons. He sometimes wondered whether it was because his father lay buried in Pearl Harbor. A fact that had just the opposite effect on his mother, who absolutely refused to set foot on anything afloat. When he was nine, he told his mother he wanted to be a sailor when he grew up. The fury of her reaction kept him from ever mentioning the subject again.

He glanced at his watch. It was 10:49, exactly eleven minutes from calling time. The phone booth he planned to use stood across the street under a corner light. The gas station behind it was dark, closed for the night at 10:30. Earlier Burke had checked out the phone itself to be certain it was in working order.

128

Lately half the street phones in New York seemed to be broken. There was apparently something about the telephone company that inspired more than the normal public inclination to vandalism, thievery, and scatological attack. Many booths had taken on the look and stink of toilets. And what moral judgment, what significant philosophical statement did that offer upon the blessings of urban communication?

Silly, random thoughts. Burke was trying hard to distract himself from what lay ahead. He was not looking forward to this call. None of the calls he had to make these days were good, but this was sure to be one of the worst. He had wondered how long it was going to take before the professor left the message requiring him to call back. He had thought about it, dreaded it and finally talked to Angela about it. "The worst of it is," he said, during one of his nighttime visits, "that I really care about that old man. Damn it, who needed this? Wasn't I rolling around in enough crap without having to fall into this too?"

She said nothing. What he needed mostly, was the chance to talk out his anger and frustration, and she was the only one he could talk to. Just two nights before he had told her about discovering Tony alive. Though shocked herself, she had helped him absorb the hurt, commiserating, holding him, finally trying to soak and rub the worst of it away in a hot tub. In the steaming water she had worked gently on his arms, legs, body, as if each belonged to the child they'd never had. And whatever the water failed to bless, she took care of later with love.

Burke laughed harshly. "Talk about irony. I mean the professor was desperate to help, was actually grateful for the chance. It was a personal vendetta for him. He'd not only be saving me, but be taking vengeance on the villians who'd murdered his son. Now his son turns out to be alive, and I end up the bloody villian."

"You don't know that, Richard."

"Don't know what?"

"That he regards you as the villian."

"How else can he regard me? Tony is his son! And if Tony wants me dead—whatever his reasons—then he'll want me dead too." He stared broodingly at the slight cleft in her chin, then leaned across the narrow kitchen table and kissed it. Her hand slipped to the back of his head, held him for a moment, released him. "Aah," he sighed. "What the hell. At least he has his Tony back."

Her eyes offered love. "You know something? You're a very nice man."

"I'm not a very nice man. I'm a very angry, confused, and frightened man. But occasionally I have you. Which is something I never expected to have again. And once in a while, thinking about that, or looking at that special place on your chin, it helps me be a bit nicer than I am."

"My strange-faced love," she smiled.

"I'm that, all right." But then he was lost in it again. "I don't even know where I am now. I thought if I could trace this to its source, I'd at least have a chance to do something positive. Now I come up with Tony, of all people, and haven't any idea at all what that means. Other than that my once good friend believes the country would somehow best be served by my removal from it."

"What are you going to do?"

He thought about it. "Take off my clothes."

"And then?"

"Make love to you."

"And after that?"

"After that, I'll probably lie in bed beside you, wondering when the professor is going to leave his message. Then I'll try to figure out how that sweet, gentle old man plans to set me up so his resurrected son can blow my brains out."

"Aren't you going to sleep at all?"

"I can't afford to waste the time."

But he did sleep. And so soundly that she had to waken him when it was time to go. Startled, he jumped, naked from the bed. "What time is it?"

"Five o'clock. I almost didn't wake you. I was tempted to just let you sleep."

Shivering, he struggled into his clothes. "Great. Then I'd have had to stay all day and into tomorrow night."

"So? Would that be the end of the world? You could rest. You need it. Look how you look."

"Okay, Ma."

"Never mind. How long do you think you can keep running around like this?"

Working into his pants, he did not answer.

"Don't you think you could take twenty-four hours in a row of me?"

"What twenty-four hours? You'll be leaving for work soon."

"I'll take the day off."

He stopped dressing. "Could you do that?"

"I'll be sick."

"You're never sick. You haven't been sick in twenty years."

"I'll be sick tomorrow."

He looked at her and things were going on inside him. Then he slowly began dressing again.

"You've got a whole new face, but nothing else is new, is it?"

"I guess not," he said.

Afterwards, away from her and alone, he felt the residue of disgust. He was hopeless. He'd never learn. On the edge of eternity itself, he'd still deny himself longed-for pleasures. And for what? It certainly was not the old puritan work ethic. He had no work. He had only the business of staying alive. Which was getting to be a full time job, but would still not have suffered appreciably if he had indulged himself for twenty-four hours.

In his car under the elevated highway, he glanced at his watch once more. Six minutes to go. He

131

measured everything in minutes these days—they crawled, hardly moved at all. Only the years seemed to fly. Looking back, he was unable to separate one from the other. He had been so young. When had he gotten middle-aged? What had happened in between, and why didn't he feel any different? If you were middle-aged, shouldn't you feel middle-aged? Still, when he looked in the mirror, his face was young, falsely so, but young. The miracle of modern surgery. Every man a Peter Pan. At the age of ninety, body and brain a shambles, he'd be able to die an apparent juvenile. Except that he was far more likely to die at forty-five. He thought about that for a moment. So? And what if they did keep him from reaching his next birthday? What was the big loss? Had he ever really savored the process of living that much? Sometimes he suspected he moved from one day to the next more out of a sense of habit than of genuine desire. Or if not habit, then perhaps out of a stubborn sense of duty. Oh, he was stubborn, all right. If everyone was supposed to live as long as humanly possible, then by God, that was what he would do. And how foolish, really. He had no firm contracts. If the struggle simply to keep moving from one minute, one hour, one day to the next finally became more trouble than it was worth, where did it say that he had to keep pushing it.

Burke smiled bleakly out at the phone booth and let himself toy with the idea. All he'd really have to do would be to speak to the professor, allow himself to be conned into another meeting, and then let Tony pump a bullet into the back of his head. Tony was competent. He had never been a bungler. If he did this, he would do it right. And wasn't it always classier, more fitting, to be kissed off by a friend?

Very funny. He really ought to arrange a reunion of his whole hospital gang so he could share his jokes with them. They could do with a few laughs these days.

But just the thought of his four fellow plastics smothered all trace of his poor gallows humor. There was nothing funny about what he had gotten them into. And every day that passed seemed to make it worse. During the past thirty-six hours he had either seen or spoken to all of them, and nothing promising had come from any of it. Having arranged a trial run for David, he had watched him walk up Fifth Avenue at high noon and picked out at least four people tailing him. So breaking him loose, as he had promised, was obviously not going to be easy. Lilly, more involved with Frank Harkevy by the hour, still thought she was going to be a big help, but had to be heading straight for disaster. Yet what could he do to stop her? As for Pamela and Hank, the latest news from them was that Pam had been fired from her fifteen-year career job with a major corporation solely because of Service pressure, and had no chance of being hired anywhere else. The only plus factor for these two was that they at least had each other and were less alone than before. Could he perhaps take a small piece of credit for that?

Sitting there, guilt rode him like a horned beast. They deserved better. Yet what could he have done differently? Surely he hadn't wished any part of this on them. If blame was to be placed, it had to start with the simple bad luck that had thrown them into the hospital with him.

At 10:58 he left his car, walked across to the telephone booth, and dialed the public phone in Maryland where he knew Professor Kreuger would be waiting. He heard the old man answer. Then the operator asked for the long distance toll charges and Burke deposited some of his hand-warmed dimes and quarters. When the gongs finally stopped sounding, the old man said, "This is Henry Condon," which was the code name Burke had assigned him.

"Arthur Radin calling."

There was a fairly long pause and Burke could hear the old man's breathing, rushed and labored, over the miles of wire. Yet he was not unsympathetic. Son or no son, Burke knew how the old man felt about him. This was not going to be easy for either of them.

"Richard, how are you?" The voice was strained, raspy, as if suddenly compelled to demonstrate its age.

"Hanging in there, professor. How about yourself?"

"Truthfully, I've had a troublesome few days. Very troublesome." There was silence. "Richard, I have something shocking to tell you."

"Yes?"

"Tony . . . my son . . . he's not dead."

Burke's mouth opened. Nothing came out.

"He's alive, Richard. The reports of his suicide, of his death were all carefully manufactured lies. His funeral was all a performance. The whole thing was a fraud. It was done only for your benefit. He's the one who is actually heading the search for you. I still find it hard to believe, but it's the truth. Tony is alive."

Surprise! Burke stared blankly out of the phone booth. Life was crammed full of all sorts of cute little twists, but what was this one all about? Why was the old man blowing the whole thing by telling him? Where was the expected con job? Where was the trap? Caught totally unprepared, Burke said nothing.

"Richard? Are you there? Are you all right?"

"I'm all right."

"I know how you must feel. I know how it hit me when I found out. I didn't know whether to laugh, cry, or be angry. Finally, I managed to do all three. But of course it's different with you. He's not your son."

"No, he's not. But he's my friend. Or, rather, he was."

"Curiously enough, he still thinks he is."

"And what do you think?"

The old man took his time on that one. "I think Tony does feel he's still your friend. He's quite miserable about this. But I also think he's an utterly single-purposed fanatic who is quite ready to kill you because he believes this to be in the best national interest."

The operator asked for more money and Burke clanged in the required number of coins. Then he said, "I knew Tony was alive, professor. When I didn't hear from you after our last meeting, I spent a few days following you. I saw Tony when he met you in that shopping mall. I got over my shock back then." He paused. "The rest of what I felt I'll probably never get over."

"Good Lord! Isn't it possible to surprise you people with anything?"

"You just did."

"You didn't expect me to tell you?"

Burke smiled faintly. "Come on, professor."

"Surely you should have had a better opinion of me."

"Well, he is your son. What am I?"

"Someone I've known, regarded highly, and cared about for a great many years. A friend who trusted me. A man I'm sure would never have hurt and tried to use his own father as my son did me."

"He wanted you to call and set me up for him?"

"Yes."

Burke was silent.

"I'll tell you this, Richard. I may seem to talk about this easily, but that's not how I feel. Things have taken place inside me these past days. You don't know . . ." He broke off. "Couldn't we meet somewhere if we're very careful?"

Burke did not reply.

"No, I suppose not," said the old man. "You have

every right to doubt me. You can't know what I intend. And I'm certain I'm being watched, in any case. Although not now, not at this moment. I was very clever at getting out unseen to make this call. I went back to my office for some night work and left the building through an old tunnel dug by abolitionists to help escaped slaves. Then I borrowed a friend's car to drive to the phone booth." He laughed softly. "Which gives you a fair idea of what necessity can do to a basically simple, forthright man."

"Just try to relax. There's no one waiting for the phone, is there?"

"No. Not at this time of night. There's not a soul anywhere."

"Then take your time. I've stacks of dimes and quarters. We're under no pressure. Just take it easy and tell me what you can."

"Yes, yes, of course. I'm ashamed of myself. I don't know what on earth is the matter with me. I've never felt quite this way before. But then I've never been in this position before, have I? I suppose the worst part of all—at least for me—was that Tony would actually allow me to believe him dead, would actually put me through the funeral services and what came after. I'm his father; he knows me. He knew what his alleged death—by suicide, no less—would do to me. Yet he did it. It takes a very special type of man to be able to do something like that to his father. Imagine," the old man intoned distantly. "Imagine him actually letting me think he had blown his brains out."

Burke waited, watching an occasional car go by, gazing past the *QE 2* at the lights on the far shore. There were questions to be asked, things he had to know, but he did not have the heart to break in on the old man's mourning.

"Remember," he went on, "when you first came to my house to tell me he was not a suicide, that he had been murdered? Remember how I called him my son, the patriot? How I spoke of his dedication, of his loy-

136

alty to our country? Do you remember all the things I said that night, Richard?"

"Yes."

"My son was dead to me that night, but I was very proud of him. Tonight he's alive and no different than he's ever been, yet I'm not proud of him at all. Do you know why? Because I have come to the unhappy conclusion that somewhere along the way, he managed to stop being human. I have no idea when it happened, but it happened. I've raised a dedicated patriot with no heart. God help us all, he's solid red, white, and blue clear through."

The old man sighed softly along the wire. "And don't think I'm unaware of the relationship you two shared all these years. I know what you meant to him. He could not have cared more for a brother. And insane as it sounds, he still feels that way. We've spoken of it very intensely these past few days. We've discussed you in great depth, Richard. We had to. Since Tony was trying so hard to get me to lead you into an ambush, it was necessary. But somehow he failed to convince me your death was absolutely vital to the well-being of the nation."

"How did he try convincing you?" asked Burke, grateful for the chance to get down to it at last. "What arguments did he use?"

The old man laughed. "Believe it or not, he actually started off by very solemnly reminding me that we were father and son, and that the mutual love and trust we'd enjoyed over a lifetime should surely be enough to make me do as he asked without question. I told him that as far as I was concerned, he had displayed appallingly little love and trust by letting me believe him a suicide. I also told him that for me, love and trust stopped quite a bit short of murder. This was not murder, he said. Morally, it had to be regarded as the unfortunate but necessary death of a soldier in a continuing war. He claimed that regardless of what the politicians in Washington said, the United States was engaged in a death struggle with the forces of world Communism, and that every step we took towards détente, was a step closer to our own destruction. He insisted that he and others had a job to do as soldiers in this war, and it was a job that sometimes had to be done by any means possible."

"Yes, yes," said Burke carefully. "I know all about that. I've lived with that sort of morality for twenty years. But exactly when and why did I, Richard Burke, suddenly get to be such a threat to our battle against world Communism? Why now? What have I supposedly done?"

"Well, Tony did tell me pretty much the same things you told me about that abortive assassination in Lebanon. And then . . . ."

"Lies," Burke cut in. "I'd figured out it wasn't Lebanon long before Tony turned up alive. There was too much pressure, too much going on for just that. And now with Tony not having been killed to eliminate all ties to that blunder, it makes no sense at all for them to need me dead because of it."

Automatically, Burke dumped more coins into the black box.

"Please," he said. "Think about it. In all your discussions with Tony, did he ever say anything about me, personally, about anything I might have said or done, anything that may have happened recently that concerned me?"

"Curiously," said the professor, "when we did talk about you, it was complimentary. Tony spoke of his feeling for you, of your tremendous integrity and sense of ethics." The old man paused. "But as a matter of fact," he went on more slowly, "Tony almost seemed to make the compliments sound like accusations. It was as if such traits might be admirable enough in someone engaged in any of life's more normal pursuits, but could be a decided handicap in the Service. In fact he said it was this,

138

more than anything, that finally caused you to fail in Lebanon."

Burke nodded encouragingly at the night air. "Okay. Good. But was there anything else? Did he mention any specific examples?"

"Of what?"

"Of how my integrity and sense of ethics proved to be a handicap in my work."

"Well, yes. He said he actually gave up any real hope for your future in the Service many years ago because of it. He indicated that something happened at that time, apparently on one of your assignments, to which you overreacted so strongly, about which you were so violently judgmental, that he should have gotten rid of you at once. He said that only his personal feeling for you stopped him. And he has come to regard that as one of the worst mistakes he ever made."

Burke stood gripping the receiver. "And that was all?"

"I believe so. Except for a bit of swearing at you and your damned narrow views, and at himself for his foolish sentiment." The old man laughed dryly. "Imagine. My son the machine, berating himself for the sin of sentiment."

Burke said nothing. The headlights of an approaching car came at him and he turned until they had passed.

"Do you have any idea what he was referring to?" the professor asked.

"Yes."

"Is it of any help?"

"I doubt it. It was so long ago and so much has happened since. I don't see how it could be pertinent to what's going on now."

"Richard." The old man's voice was hesitant. "Are you sure you couldn't simply go away somewhere and disappear? Wouldn't that be the best way to handle this?"

"I'm afraid there is no best way. Besides, I've gotten others involved. If I disappeared now, they'd never be left alone, never have a moment's peace."

The line was silent.

Burke said tiredly, "I guess that's it, professor. Thanks for your help. And I appreciate your not trying to set me up."

"Apparently there was no way I could have done it in any case."

"It's the lack of intent I appreciate."

"Be careful, Richard."

Burke smiled at nothing. "You know me, professor."

"I obviously don't know anybody," said the old man.

Burke heard him hang up. He was aware of a faint trembling in the booth, the vibration from some invisible engine. It made him feel he was about to be launched on a voyage. Collecting his remaining change, he left the booth.

The wind off the river tore at him as he walked towards his car and he bent his head. The unseen ship's engine chugged more loudly and the smell of diesel fuel haunted the air. Shivering, he got into his car, started the motor and heater, and sat staring out at the running lights of the *Queen Elizabeth,* as though he had the insane notion that if he looked at them long and hard enough they might work some magic and lift him free. Suddenly the best of his thoughts depressed him for there seemed to be a quiet madness attached. Demons hid along the piers and swam in the dark waters below, waiting for him. Let them wait, he thought. He had the worst of the crop inside, dozing quietly in his chest. They had been there for almost eighteen years, and it was apparently time to call them awake.

Yet he wondered what good it would do. What could he find among them now, that he had not found in all these years? Wake them and they would just start chewing at him all over again. How could they have anything to do with what was happening to him? Still, it had involved some effort for the old man to scrape up even this faint hope of a clue. The least he could do would be to give it some thought.

So with the motor running and the heater starting to melt the worst of the chill from his bones, he lit a cigarette and allowed himself to dig through old burial grounds.

16

In Burke's mind it always began the same way, with all of them moving steadily and well, in a long, loose column, through the thinning trees. He could see the dark banks of the stream below, and beyond it, the green slope of the hillside. On the other side of the slope, out of sight and about a mile distant, was the border. In a bit more than an hour they would be over it. Not counting Tom Ludlow and himself, there were twenty-three of them: eleven men, nine women, and three children. The youngsters were in their early teens, two boys and a girl, with wide, dark eyes, smooth faces, and incredibly white teeth. It all seemed like an exciting excursion to them. There were not supposed to have been any children in this group, but a mistake had been made somewhere along the line and by the time it was discovered, nothing could be done.

Ludlow had been angry, but as far as Burke was concerned, the kids' presence would not affect the group adversely. He actually enjoyed having them along and did not expect any trouble. This was the seventh group they were taking through, and nothing had gone wrong with any of them. Ludlow had a submachine gun slung over his shoulder and Burke himself carried a pistol and carbine, but so far there had been no need for weapons. Ludlow knew every foot of the border area and the posting and pattern of the patrols well enough to avoid all critical points.

None of the others in the group were armed. Ludlow would not permit it. A man with a gun in someone else's contingent had once panicked, fired on a passing patrol, and almost caused a disaster. Now in Ludlow's groups no weapons were allowed. Burke disagreed with the ban, feeling that in an emergency they might need the extra firepower, but he did not argue the point. Ludlow was officially in command, knew the country and people far better than he, and did not take kindly to having his judgment questioned. During the weeks that Burke had worked under him, he had found his superior to be a decisive, confident man who knew what he wanted done and went about doing it with a minimum of fuss and discussion. Which was perfect for this type of operation. Still, Burke did occasionally find himself irritated with Ludlow's obvious arrogance towards those he was there to help.

Tony Kreuger had briefed Burke on his new commander before sending him on the assignment. "You probably won't like Tom Ludlow," he said. "He's not your kind of man. But he'll be good for you. He's exactly what you need right now. He's cold, clinical, and conceptually sophisticated enough never to lose sight of the broad picture. He's not one of us, not a Service man. He's an oil specialist, working undercover for the State Department. I'm sure he's also C.I.A. But he knows everything there is to know about this business. So watch and learn from him."

Six weeks later, following Ludlow through the shadowed coolness under the trees, the butt of his carbine rapping against his lower back, Burke was still watching him. There was an arrogance in even the way he walked with these people, he thought, like a shepherd moving his flock to another pasture. When they spoke to him or asked questions, he rarely bothered to answer. The fact that they were frightened and uncertain, were leaving their homes for a doubtful future in a foreign place, meant nothing to him. Since it was currently part of America's policy to help these people escape a cruel and repressive regime, he was helping them escape. He was interested in nothing more. Tall, slender, aloof,

143

his back rigidly straight under the weight of his Tommy gun, he was surely something less than a Moses, Burke thought, leading his people to the Promised Land.

As they headed down towards the stream, Burke hoped he hadn't learned too much from him. Never mind what Tony had said. There was very little that this man could teach him that he really wanted to know.

The stream was fairly shallow where they crossed it, but some of the women and older men still had to be helped. Burke stood up to his knees in the fast-moving water, lending a hand to those who stumbled over hidden rocks or showed signs of fright. Ludlow watched the crossing from partway up the steep slope ahead. He said nothing, but Burke could feel his impatience from just the tilt of his head.

Burke watched the small band trudging slowly up the hill. It moved like a wounded beast, dragging itself along. Only the three youngsters seemed to have any energy left, and they were using that to help carry some of the heavier articles for the older people. Burke had been involved in this sort of operation for less than two months, but at this moment it seemed as though he had been doing it all his life. He felt part of a permanent, never-ending stream of refugees. Escape seemed to have become the absolute condition of existence. Over the border and back, over the border and back, always with another frightened, exhausted group, always with the sad souvenirs of forsaken lives, always with the border patrols out there, threatening. But this was the last, at least as far as he and Ludlow were concerned. Ludlow had told him the night before. They would be coming back in for undercover work in the cities. "We've done our share of escort duty," Ludlow said. "And without losing a single one."

True, thought Burke. Other teams had lost as much as twenty per cent of their people to the security police, while they themselves continued to show a perfect score. And this was all Ludlow. Burke was happy to give the State Department man full credit. Whatever else he thought of him, the guy knew what he was doing. He was good. Everything he touched went off with the precision of a fine piece of machinery. Regardless of his motivation, he had gotten almost three hundred people safely out of the country.

There were trees at the top of the hill and this was where they rested. From here Burke could see the long ridge of rock, with the stand of pine just beyond, marking the border in this area. The trees were about a mile away, but the air was so clear that they looked closer. It was almost all downhill from here, and merely the sight of the easy slope ahead was cheering. People talked and joked, and their voices were bright. These were the moments, thought Burke, that made the rest of it worth doing. His mood was expansive enough to embrace even Ludlow, who stood benignly a short distance from the clustered group, smoking, and at that moment looking almost human to him.

"Richard!" Ludlow called and Burke walked over to join him.

"Why don't you start now," Ludlow said. "We'll follow when you wave an all-clear from that stand of pine at the border."

Burke turned and looked at his people. They had settled into an easy quiet. Some lay stretched out on the grass, others dozed, sitting against trees. All seemed stamped in attitudes of immortal grace. Classic Renoir, he thought. Then he slung his carbine and started down the slope towards the border.

He was at the bottom of the hill, just starting the gentle rise near the border, when the first shots went off.

Instinctively he dove flat out into the high grass. Sonofabitch! And on the last trip out, he thought. Then he unslung his carbine, flicked off the safety, and peered cautiously up at the trees, three hundred yards ahead. But as the firing went on, he realized it was coming from somewhere behind him. It came in short staccato bursts, in the spat-spatting of a machine gun. He swung around in the grass, but could see nothing but the dark cluster of trees on the hill he had just left. A patrol must have come on them from the rear, he decided, and started back up the hill. He ran hard and straight, not bothering to zig-zag or look for cover.

Gasping for breath, leg tendons straining, Burke reached the first of the trees. It was totally quiet. They had drilled all their groups in taking cover and keeping still if they ever came under attack, but this was extraordinary. When it came to discipline, there were none better than Ludlow. Crouching, his carbine ready at the hip, Burke pushed farther into the grove.

There was an explosion in the back of his head. Everything turned black. Then there was nothing.

He came out of it slowly. The colors started seconds before his brain. He was into the reds, yellows and blues again. At least he was not dead, something told him. But when he tried to move, he couldn't, and changed his mind. I'm dead, he thought, and everyone was wrong about what being dead is like. It was not nothingness. It was just very quiet, with only a soft, whirring, clicking sound coming from somewhere. Also, there were all these colors, and when you tried to move your arms and legs, something held them.

Then Burke opened his eyes and found he was not dead after all. He was not even lying down. He was sitting up. And the reason he was unable to move was that his legs were tied together at the ankles, and his arms were lashed behind him around a small tree. As for the soft whirring, clicking sound—that, he saw, came from Ludlow's camera. Apparently Ludlow was taking pictures one after the other, (focus, whir, click, focus, whir, click) in the same swift, efficient way he did everything. Then Burke

146

saw what he was taking pictures of, and quickly shut his eyes once more.

Oh, Christ! he thought. Oh, dear, sweet Jesus Christ!

It was a charnel house under the trees, a bucolic butcher shop, a sun-dappled grove of the dead. All of them. None had escaped. Burke did the counting from where he sat. Twenty-three. He counted them again. The total was still twenty-three. They lay as they had been hit. The surprise was still on some faces. Others had no faces at all. Still others lay face down, arms extended as though in flight. He saw that a young girl and her grandmother were together, side by side. The old woman's arms lay across the child's body in an apparent last minute attempt to shield her.

And the soft whir and click of the camera went on . . . and went on . . .

Finally, it stopped and everything was very still, with only the breeze moving through the tall grass. But then there came a low moaning from somewhere off to the right, and Burke watched as Ludlow lifted his Tommy gun from a branch, flicked the action from automatic to semi-automatic, and ended the sound with a single, carefully placed round. The guy was never one to waste ammunition, thought Burke.

Ludlow hung up his machine gun once more, turned, and saw that Burke's eyes were open. He studied Burke from where he stood, as if trying to make vital judgments merely from the way he looked. Then he came over. "I'm sorry I had to put you out, Richard, but I had no choice. I simply couldn't take a chance on how you'd react."

Burke said nothing. I must be very careful, he thought. One wrong word or look and I'm as dead as the others. He hasn't decided yet, but it's very close.

"I'm also sorry about the youngsters," said Ludlow. "As you know, they were't supposed to be in this group."

Burke's glance drifted past where the girl lay and

147

focused on the two boys. One had taken several rounds in the chest and his shattered ribs stuck out through his bloodied shirt like white splinters. The other, a small, skinny kid with a perpetual buck-toothed grin, had caught one in the forehead. Nothing remained above his eyes.

"I know it's difficult, if not impossible, for you to take the long view right now," Ludlow went on, a professional lecturer in a butcher shop. "But in the end, this little episode may well save a hundred, even a thousand lives for each one it cost."

Burke decided it was time that he spoke, that he at least said something. "I don't understand. I don't understand anything at all."

"Of course you don't. But believe me, Richard—I conceived and executed this entire operation very carefully. Every feature was weighed with the utmost precision. In spite of what you may think, I'm not a cold-blooded monster. I don't regard human life lightly. If I took twenty-three lives here today, you can be sure it was only because I felt the results would justify the sacrifice."

"What results?"

"The same ones we've been after in this place for more than ten years: a reasonably democratic government and an important source of oil for our future."

Burke stared at him. The man was incredible. This was no act. He actually believed every word he was saying. He had just slaughtered twenty-three men, women, and children and there was still no sweat on his face, no pain or doubt in his eyes, and not a hair out of place on his head.

"I'll explain," said Ludlow, and took three rolls of film from his pocket and showed them to Burke. "I have pictures here of twenty-three innocent people, murdered at the border by the soldiers of a repressive regime, a government bought and paid for by the Russians and already despised by most of the population because of its brutality and corruption. These

148

photographs will be blown up into posters and spread throughout the country. They'll give us the martyrs we need to create the final groundswell of riots and strikes that will immobilize the economy, bring down the Russian-backed puppet regime, and allow us to put in a democratic government favorable to the United States."

"Just like that?"

Ludlow's smile was almost beatific. "No, Richard. Not just like that. A great deal of time, effort, personnel, and money have gone into this, and still more will have to go into it before we actually see these results. But we are almost there. The big thing we lacked were the martyrs to set off the final spark of emotionalism. And that's what I've provided here today."

Oh, God! thought Burke. The martyr-maker. Martyrs provided on demand for all occasions. Another wonder of the twentieth century. What an exquisite improvement over the limited goals of the autos-dafé and inquisitions of the Middle Ages. Oh, God, he thought and shut his eyes. He did not want to have to look at Ludlow's face. He was afraid he might not be able to keep from spitting in it. And if he did that, if he displayed even the smallest fraction of the horror and loathing he felt, this intellectual animal would have no choice but to kill him.

"Are you all right?" Ludlow asked.

Burke forced open his eyes. "These damn ropes are tearing my arms apart."

"I'm sorry," said Ludlow, but made no move to do anything about the ropes. "They were for your own protection as much as mine. I needed time to explain, to let you understand reasons. I didn't tell you before, because I knew you could never have gone along with it. It's not in your nature. Which is why, unless you change drastically with age and experience, your potential for this work has to be limited." Ludlow looked at him, closely. "Do you understand, Richard?"

149

Afraid to trust his voice, Burke nodded. But he saw that Ludlow was not convinced. Do it right, he told himself. He glanced up and met the tall man's eyes. "You were right. I don't know what I might have done if you hadn't knocked me out." He paused, trying to pace his performance with as much skill as he could muster. A not especially talented actor, auditioning for his life. "Apart from everything else, I feel simple and stupid. You had a tough enough job without having to worry about me complicating it even more."

Ludlow was still studying Burke's face. He had never looked more like a predatory animal. A flush of danger, of unmistakable threat, came off him and Burke felt he could spring either way. He could sense the beat of his pulse almost as clearly as he felt his own. In the silence they could have been sitting in smoke. I can be dead in the next ten seconds, thought Burke. Insanely, he felt more curious than afraid at that instant.

Ludlow drew a knife, bent, and cut him loose. "Come on," he said quietly. "We have a lot to do."

It was almost six months before he was able to return to Washington and speak to Tony about it.

"What about you?" he asked Kreuger. "Did you know what he planned to do?" Burke spoke softly, but there was something very close to murder in his eyes.

Kreuger shook his head. "No."

"You're a fucking liar."

"Well, if I've got to be a liar, I suppose that's about the best kind to be."

"I'm not joking, Tony."

"I know you're not joking. But if you think I'm going the Hamlet route with you, you're crazy. When you get that accusatory, soul-searing look of tragedy out of your eyes, and want to talk about this thing rationally, then maybe I can help make some sense out of it for you."

"I've got this crazy hang-up," Burke said. "I find it tough as hell to talk rationally about murder. And I just hope to Christ I never get sick enough to make sense out of the deliberate slaughter of twenty-three innocent people."

From behind a cluttered desk, Kreuger stared evenly at Burke. He seemed capable of remaining that way forever.

It was Burke who was unable to hold the silence. "Well?"

"Well, what?"

"Did you know in advance?"

"I've already told you I didn't, and you called me a liar."

Burke chewed his lip. "I'm sorry about that. I suppose I'm still upset."

"I never would have guessed. I mean, you cover your emotions so terrifically."

Burke permitted himself a grudging smile.

"Listen, schmuck," said Kreuger. "If I had known what Ludlow planned, do you really think I'd have sent you, of all people, on that job? My God, you're the last one I'd have chosen. With your kind of conscience and moral strictures, you should have been a goddamned monk. What the hell are you doing in this stinking business, anyway?"

Burke started to answer, but changed his mind.

"As it happens," Kreuger went on, "all I knew about Ludlow's mission was its overall purpose, which was to create enough dissension to get the Russians out of there and us in. He never shared the details of how he intended going about it with me or anyone else. I'm not even sure he knew himself until very close to operation time. The guy is inventive as hell. He did a really amazing job over three. Approve of his methods or not, you've got to admire his results."

"Admire?" Burke stood up. There was a sudden heat in him that could not be contained sitting down. "All I want to do when I think of that sonofabitch is kill him. I want to cut him in half with one really beautiful burst and see his guts in his hat."

He broke off and dropped back into his chair. "Ah," he said softly. "Have you ever seen what a .30 caliber burst can do to a twelve-year-old body?"

"Richard . . ."

Burke's eyes cut him off. "Please. Don't be reasonable with me. I love you like a brother, but I swear I'll strangle you if you start being reasonable with me. I couldn't take it right now."

Kreuger looked as though he had swallowed something bad. The skin seemed to be stretched too tightly across his cheeks and jaw, and his mouth was a gash.

"Richard, I don't approve of what he did. I admit his methods were ghastly. But neither can we ignore their ultimate results."

"I piss on their ultimate results. That's exactly the kind of thinking which led to the Holocaust. That's exactly what decent, intelligent Germans said about Hitler and his Nazis at the beginning. Well, they and the world soon found out differently. In the end results and methods turn out to be the same."

Kreuger's expression was neutral. "It's over, Richard. The best you can do now—the best for all of us—is just to move on and forget it."

"I'll move on, but I won't forget it. I'll never forget it."

"You're talking like a maniac."

Burke stared straight through Kreuger. "That sonofabitch is mine, I tell you. I was the one up there with him. I was the sole surviving witness to what he's capable of doing. And I was the one who let him walk away from it and turn himself into a hero, an American Lawrence of Arabia. So he's got me to contend with from now on. Do I make myself clear?"

"Very clear."

"And do you believe I mean every word I say?"

"I believe it."

Burke sagged wearily in his chair, as if only now,

by having fully exorcised every last demon through confession, would he be able to take his first unconstricted breath of air in six months and relax. "So what do you think?" he asked.

"What I think," said Kreuger quietly, "is that you're going to need an even longer vacation than I expected you to need when you walked in here an hour ago and I had my first good look at your face."

The vacation turned out to be for almost three months, and came close to being a permanent one, as Kreuger was quick to tell Burke when he finally called him back to Washington.

"I want you to know you're here against my better judgment," Tony said. "Twice I had pretty much decided to wash you out. And if it had been anyone else, I'd have done it. But I finally decided to put it up to you. Do you want to stay in?"

The question was not new to Burke. He had been asking it of himself for the past three months. He nodded, "Yes."

"Why?"

"For the same reasons I first came in. Because I believe the work is important, that it has to be done, and that I can do it well."

"Without blinding emotionalism?"

"Yes."

Tony looked at him until something stirred between them. They both felt it—first hot, then cool, then hot again.

"Okay," Tony said. "You're in. Though I know I may be making a bad mistake. If I am, we'll both pay for it later. But I figure you're young and smart enough to toughen up the soft places. At least I hope you are. If you're not . . ." he shrugged.

Burke said nothing. What would be the point? He had already made his decision. He was remaining in the Service. And anything further he might have said on the subject would have made that patently impossible. He knew Tony was not fooled by his apparent acquiescence. His friend was no dummy. He was only too well aware that his feelings about Ludlow and the twenty-three dead had not changed during the past few months and probably never would. But he was evidently willing to accept an unspoken truce on it. Burke was also willing. And that was how it was left.

Now, more than eighteen years later, Burke sat in a rented car with the motor and heater going, and thought about it. According to the professor, Tony regretted not having dumped him way back then. Okay. Having flunked out on that hill in Lebanon, (another hill in his life) Burke had finally justified such a judgment. But what did Ludlow and an eighteen-year-old incident have to do with the fire under him now?

Could it really have something to do with that murderous sonofabitch again?

Burke gazed up at the prow of the majestic *Queen.* Murderous sonofabitch. Eighteen years, and in his mind the two words were still synonymous with Tom Ludlow. For him the man still populated his own spectral landscape, etched with trees, a hill and the pale light of a recurrent nightmare. A far cry from the reality of the present, with its shimmering capitals and halls of power. Ludlow had built a sparkling career, Burke often thought, on the bloody remains of twenty-three bodies. Yet who knew the truth about them other than Tony, Ludlow, and himself? As far as Washington and the world of national and international politics was concerned, Ludlow had somehow pulled off the coup of the decade by bringing four million barrels of oil a day into the internal combustion engines, factories, and homes of the American people.

Unfair, thought Burke. Even the devil deserved credit for his talents, and Ludlow's gifts were considerable. The slaughter of innocents had been only one of the many cards he had played. With or without

that long-ago killing ground the man would undoubtedly have gone far. It was just that each time
Burke saw his picture in a newspaper or magazine,
or heard him speak on television, he felt the same old
bitter dread stir in his gut. Look at him. See that
handsome face. Watch those sharply penetrating
eyes. Listen to that deep, mellifluous voice. Pay close
attention. Don't ever forget.

But time and the human condition being what
they were, he did push the memory into the background. Remembering those past deaths was not his
principal occupation. He was neither mad nor ob-
sessed. He did not spend his time baying at moons.
His life was complicated, busy, worrisome, and dangerous enough in the present, for him not to hug the
memory of earlier disasters. He usually had enough
calamities running along more current tracks. It
was just that from time to time over the years, some
event or meeting would jar his memory and it would
all come flooding back. At times he had actually
been in the same room, hall, lobby, or building with
Ludlow, and the result was instantly electric, at
least for him. So far as Ludlow was concerned, neither his face nor his eyes showed a thing. It was as
though they had never met. Which may simply have
been his always exceptional control. Since their
work together during those months had been about
as deeply undercover as you could get, there was no
reason for them to recognize one another publicly. It
was wiser that they did not. Still, considering the
way Burke himself felt at their being close enough to
touch, he always half-expected some slight reciproca-
tory sign—perhaps a change of expression, the flut-
ter of an eyelid, something. Although it may have
been a foolish expectation for another reason. Seven,
ten, thirteen, fifteen years later, (the four times
when they had actually been within sight of one another) Ludlow had probably not even recognized him
out of context. Faces did change with time and
Burke's had aged exceptionally.

Another thing. The entire hilltop incident had undoubtedly had a far deeper, more lasting effect on Burke than it had on Ludlow himself. As far as Burke knew, it may actually have been one of many for him, a routine job of unofficial, patriotic murder. If so, Ludlow was not likely to be bowled over by the sight of someone he may just possibly have remembered from some dim time zone out of the past. And in a way, when Burke thought of it at all, he considered this last possibility the most obscene. Twenty-three insignificant lives. A minor event, not worth remembering. This, if true, would be the worst.

But who knew what was true these days about Thomas Worthington Ludlow? Though their lives had once briefly touched, they had since been moving at different levels of widely separated worlds. While Burke listened to the words of popular songs, Ludlow marched to the drumbeat of history. He dined with prime ministers and presidents, danced with their wives, and appeared with depressing frequency on the cover of Time Magazine. Once inadvertently picking up one such copy on a plane, Burke had stared at the increasingly charismatic face and thought, I'll be damned if the sonofabitch isn't turning into one of our national treasures. And indeed, his list of credits had grown steadily more impressive. He had during the past few years led senior diplomatic missions to four important foreign capitals, negotiated settlements for two potentially crippling national strikes, arranged emergency economic assistance for several crumbling democratic bastions in South America, and served as Special Security Advisor to the President during a period of critical Far Eastern confrontation. Currently it was rumored the President would appoint him Secretary of State, as soon as his present Secretary could be gracefully gotten out of the way. If so, Burke thought, Ludlow would probably have a contract out on the Secretary in a matter of weeks.

Or was he still being unfair? The man did, after

all, have a long career of nationally recognized achievement behind him. How long did he deserve to be vilified for an eighteen-year-old transgression?

For as long as he lived, thought Burke.

Then having thought this, something in the deep of that faraway hilltop wood, something once sweet and as filled with hope as a young girl's smile, was finally able to travel out of the memory of those longtime dead and straight into him. And sitting here in this car, eighteen years and a continent away from where they lay buried, his heart welcomed it.

17

The rain was unnecessary. On this of all nights, Burke thought, he could very easily have done without the rain. Wind-driven, it came down in sheets, so that even with the high-speed wipers going, the windshield was never really clear. Peering through the torrent at the road ahead, Burke experienced the sensation of being in a curious underwater world. Occasional lights shimmered and there was the swift movement of other cars, but it was all very silent and strange.

Although he had taken this same drive two nights before as a trial run, it had not been raining then. This made a difference. Another difference, of course, was the tension. Tonight was no rehearsal. It was for real. And regardless of careful planning and favorable odds, no operation of this sort was ever entirely free of threat. He had not mentioned any of this to David on the phone. He had simply said, "I have it all worked out. I'm getting you clear of them the night after next."

"Yes?" David's voice started off tentative, frightened, but quickly improved. "Hey, that's great."

"I guess you want to take your girl with you."

"What?"

"Your girl," Burke said. "From what you've told me, she's important to you."

There was a pause on the line. "Can't . . ." David's voice was hesitant again. "Can't she meet me later?"

"No. They'll be watching her. You either take her now, or not at all."

"You mean you can actually get both of us away?"

"Yes."

"Then I guess Dolores comes along."

"All right," said Burke. "Pack a couple of bags and take enough cash out of the bank to keep you going for at least six months. Do you know where you want to go?"

"I was thinking of the San Francisco area."

"Do you or Dolores know anyone there?"

"No."

"Good. Now listen carefully. You'll be driving. Not your car. You'll start out in your car, but then dump it and use one that I'll be giving you. I'll also give you a new driver's license and ownership papers to go with it. You're going to have a whole new identity. No one is to know about this. Not even your parents. No one. Understand?"

"Yes."

"You can tell your parents you're off traveling. But only when you're well on your way. And don't call them after that because their phone will be tapped. And don't write them because the postmark will give you away."

"Okay."

"Will they worry about you?"

"Hell, no. They'll just be relieved at not having to look at my face."

Burke was silent for a moment. "It's not a bad face, David. When I tailed you on Fifth Avenue the other day, I saw you with your new beard. I thought you looked fine. Very macho."

"It's good camouflage."

The wire hummed against the traffic noises.

Burke said, "You're sure this is what you want? You're absolutely certain you want to get out of here and away?"

"Yes."

"You don't sound very happy about it."

"I'm scared, for Christ's sake!"

"There's no need to be."

"How the devil are you going to get two of us away in a car with them watching?"

"Don't worry about it," said Burke. "All you have to do is what I tell you. Now listen."

David listened and Burke gave him directions for getting to what Burke described as a country road that ran through an upper-Westchester woodland. David was to allow about an hour and fifteen minutes for the drive and arrive at the rendezvous point at exactly 9:00 P.M.

"That's all?" David asked when Burke had finished.

"That's about it. I'll be there when you arrive. It'll be black—no lights or houses or anything around, but I'll wave a small flashlight. When you see it, stop your car and cut off your headlights. Then flick the lights on for a second, only a second, and turn them off again. You got that?"

"Got it."

"One more thing. Keep these instructions to yourself. Not even Dolores is to know them. Just take her along with you. I know she's terrific and you've already trusted her with your life, but my life is involved in this too and I like to make my own judgments about that. No offense to Dolores."

"Sure."

"See you at nine o'clock."

"I sure appreciate this."

Burke smiled into the mouthpiece. "It's my pleasure."

Some pleasure, thought Burke, driving through the rain forty-eight hours later. Still, if everything went well, it would all be over in an hour. God, he hoped there was no foul-up. The kid had been through enough. He deserved a break. They all did. In his mind his four fellow plastics always ran together like quadruplets. He seemed incapable of thinking of one without the others. Even now. At last accounting there was nothing new with Pamela and Hank. She was still out of a job and blacklisted; he was still agonizing over the killing. With that hanging over them, they didn't need any new catastrophes. But evidently Lilly did. "Hey, wait till you hear this!" she had almost shouted into the phone less than twenty-four hours before, and Burke braced himself.

"I think I'm afraid," he said weakly.

"Don't be a wise guy. When you hear this, you'll be crazy for me."

"I'm crazy for you now."

"Are you ready?"

"Ready," he sighed.

"Frank wants to help. He thinks he knows who's after you and why. He's disgusted with what's happening and wants me to make arrangements for him to meet you and . . ."

"Lilly!" It cut her off in midsentence.

"What?"

"Are you saying he knows you've been in touch with me?"

"Hey, come on. The guy's nuts about me. He's been living at my place ever since those two apes went to work on me. There's nothing he wouldn't do for me. For some reason you refuse to understand that. You're so screwed up and suspicious from being a goddamned spy so long, you've forgotten how people can feel about each other. Of course I told him I can reach you. I told him weeks ago. We're in love!"

Burke took a moment to calm himself. I must remember her motives, he thought. She's doing this for me. I must be careful not to hurt her. "Did you also tell him how you get in touch with me?"

"I just said we had this complicated system of phone calls set up."

"Did he ask about numbers or where you called or anything like that?"

"No."

"He's not with you now, is he?"

"No! Christ, you infuriate me. I don't know why I even want to help you. What an ungrateful bastard."

"Not ungrateful, Lilly . . . just skeptical."

"What dirty people you must have known."

"I'm afraid so," he said and clanged some coins into the box.

She passed a moment in hurt silence. "Well, do you want to hear the rest, or don't you?"

"Of course I want to hear. But you're going to have to allow me my little doubts without taking them personally and sulking."

"Up yours."

"I love you, too," he said gently. "Now get on with it and tell me what suddenly made your Frank so disgusted with the Service that he's ready to betray it, his oath, and his country to help me."

"It's not sudden. He's been disgusted with some of the things he's had to do for a long time. He has these awful nightmares. Sometimes he wakes up in a cold sweat, screaming. If you saw and heard him as I have, you wouldn't be so skeptical."

Burke fingered the receiver and said nothing.

"But what happened Saturday night really set him off," she went on. "We were driving out to Amagansett after the show, when Waldo and Kevin—those same two apes—stopped Frank's car at gunpoint and tried to kidnap me. Frank refused to let them. Then they had this godawful fight and Frank shot them both. I mean he killed them." She paused. "Or maybe you think that was a performance, too."

"Well . . ." he said. "You've really had a time of it."

"I've had better nights. But does that convince you of how Frank feels about me?"

"I've never doubted that. Just as I'm sure you care for him. But that still didn't stop you from doing everything possible to use him to help me."

"My God, he killed two of his own people to keep

162

them from hurting me. Does that sound as if he was trying to use me?"

He needed a little time on that one. "Well, Lilly, do you really know for sure that he killed them?"

"Of course I know," she shouted across the wire. "I was there. I saw."

"Okay, let's go into that," Burke said carefully. "Exactly what did you see?"

"I saw him shoot them."

"You saw the actual shooting?"

"I told you I did."

"Where did it happen?"

"On a small road a few miles from Montauk Highway. They made us turn off there."

"Then it was dark where it happened?"

"Yes, but there was a moon and I could see them lying there, all bloody."

"Where were they hit, Lilly?" Burke's voice was very soft on the wire. "Where were they all bloody? What parts of them?"

"Their faces. They were lying on their backs and I saw their faces. It was awful."

"It was dark. How much could you see?"

"Enough. Too much."

"Did you see any specific physical damage, any holes in their faces, any features shot away?"

She did not answer.

"I'm sorry to have to do this, Lilly. I know how it must be for you. But it's important."

"Their faces were just all dark and bloody," she managed. "I couldn't see anything else."

"Did you perhaps accidentally touch the blood? Did you get any of it on your hands or clothing?"

"No."

"Okay, what happened then?"

"What do you mean?"

"What did Frank do next? Did he bury the bodies?"

"No."

"You mean he left them lying there?"

"He dragged them behind some bushes."

"What about their car? They did have a car, didn't they?"

"Frank drove that into the woods and left it behind some trees."

"And that was it?" said Burke. "You and Frank just drove away?"

"Yes."

"Have you seen anything in the papers about bodies being discovered on Long Island?"

"No. But Frank said the police have orders to keep these things quiet when they happen. But I guess you know that."

"Yes. That's true."

"He also said you'd probably be blamed for the killing anyway."

"That's also true," Burke said flatly. "God knows how many killings have been hung on me so far."

Neither of them spoke for a moment. Then Burke said. "What did you say those two agents' names were?"

"Waldo and Kevin. Waldo was black. Does that mean anything?"

"Sure. It means the Service is an Equal Opportunity Employer. Do you know their last names?"

"No." She was silent. "You don't believe Frank really killed them, do you?"

"Would you hate me if I said I didn't?"

"No. I'd just pity you for being so wrong and of so little faith."

"I've been wrong before. But please, just give me a little time to check this out."

"I'll give you a little time to kiss my ass."

"Promises, promises," he said.

The rain eased as Burke turned off the Taconic Parkway onto Route 100, and the visibility was better. He slowed, watching for his first landmark. Five minutes later he saw it, a burned-out diner on the left side of the road. Everything was black. He was in a heavily wooded area without a house in sight. Checking the rearview mirror, he saw a single pair of headlights far behind him. The lights kept pace for about a mile, then disappeared onto a cross road. Burke spotted his second landmark off to the right, the foundation of a house someone had once started, then abandoned. He lowered his window for a clearer view and took a gust of rain in the face. Braking carefully, he suddenly saw the opening in the trees on the left side of the road and steered into it. The trail was unpaved and just wide enough for a single car to get through. A wall of trees crowded close on both sides. If a car came from the opposite direction, there would be no way to pass. Burke bumped along the trail for several miles, drove around a sudden, sharp bend, and parked just off the road in a small opening between two trees.

Moving quickly, he took a bag of demolition equipment out of the trunk and carried it back along the trail for about twenty-five yards. Then he packed his charge at the base of a tall swamp maple he had chosen for this purpose the night before, attached the wires to an exploder, and returned to the car. Glancing at his watch, he saw that it was 8:42. If David was on time, he had eighteen minutes to wait.

At exactly 9:01, Burke saw headlights flickering through the trees and went out to meet them. He turned on his flashlight, waved it, and saw the headlights stop. Then the headlights disappeared, came on briefly, and went off once more.

Burke walked towards the car through the rain. "Everything okay?"

"Yeah," David said. "There were some lights behind us on Route 100, but they disappeared when we turned off." His voice was high with tension. "This . . . this is Dolores."

"Hello, Dolores." In the flashlight's beam, Burke saw wide, dark eyes in a soft, incredibly young face.

"All right, let's move quickly," he told David. "Take the keys out of the ignition, bring your bags, and follow me."

"You mean I just leave the car right here, in the road?"

"That's what I mean."

Burke led them the short distance to his car. "Wait inside," he said. "I'll be with you in a minute."

This time Burke ran as he went back. He had already seen the following headlights through the trees. They were closer than he had expected. Reaching the exploder, he swiftly checked his connections. Then he lay flat behind a rock and pushed the plunger. There was a cracking roar and Burke felt the blast from the explosion roll over him. His face pressed against wet leaves and dirt; he breathed the smell of the explosive as it rained pieces of wood. When he looked up, the big maple lay across the road. He was pleased. He had not tried something like that in ten years. That's right, he thought. Just lie here congratulating yourself and in two minutes you'll be plucking bullets out of your ass. But the headlights were still a quarter of a mile away.

Burke trotted back to the car. He slid into the driver's seat, started the motor, turned on the lights, and swung forward onto the road.

"Do you think those lights back there are them?" David said.

In the glow of the dashboard Burke's face was dripping but relaxed. "I know it's them. But that maple should hold them for awhile."

"You're a very smart man," said Dolores.

Burke glanced at her as he drove. "And you're a very pretty girl. David's lucky to have you with him. But you look twelve years old."

"Sure. And I also remind you of your kid sister."

Burke laughed. "Is that what men always tell you?"

"Yeah."

"I have no kid sister. But if I did, I'd be happy to have her look like you."

"Thanks."

"I'm sorry you got locked up because of me. Was it rough?"

"Nah. I'm used to it. I used to get picked up for hustling all the time. It don't bother me none."

Amazing, thought Burke. And with that face. "Where are you from?"

"Paraguay. But I came here when I was five, so I guess that don't count much anymore."

"Your family still there?"

"She has no family," David answered for her. "Just an old grandfather she sends money to. He's too weak to cut cane anymore and he'd starve, except for her. He sends her all these letters that a priest writes for him because he never learned to write. You should see them. They're beautiful. She keeps them in a cigar box and reads them to me. An illiterate old Paraguayan cane-cutter, and I swear they sing."

Burke braked as the car bounced and splashed through some ruts. He loves this girl, he thought with vague surprise. He's proud as hell of her and he absolutely adores her. Somehow, this cheered Burke inordinately.

"How long do we have to stay on this lousy road?" David asked.

"Only a few more miles," Burke said. "It feeds right into Route 103. From there, we'll go west to Route 9, then north to Dobbs Ferry, where I'll leave you. Then you two can take off on your own. Are you tired?"

"No."

"Then I think you'd be better off driving straight through the night. Let Dolores spell you at the wheel

167

if you get sleepy, but put as many miles behind you as you can before morning. You have a full tank, so you won't need to stop for gas before you're well into Pennsylvania. Just don't get picked up for speeding or anything else. Once you're out of the state, there's no need to rush anyway. Take your time. Stay off toll roads and turnpikes wherever you can. It's a big, beautiful country. Enjoy yourselves." Burke smiled a bit ruefully. "I envy you both."

Steering with one hand, Burke took out an envelope with the other and handed it across the girl to David. "Here's your driver's license and car ownership. Your new name is Jimmy Cooper. I hope you won't have to keep it too long."

"Thanks. How much do I owe you?"

"Nothing."

"What do you mean nothing? The car alone must have cost almost five thousand bucks."

"It's a going-away present for you and Dolores."

"No!" David exploded. "No presents. There's no reason for any goddamned presents. I . . ." He stopped himself as Burke glanced at him. "I appreciate it, but I've got plenty of money and I . . ."

"Please, David. Money happens to be the least of my problems right now. So it's only a small thing, really. I'm just trying to say thanks for all you've done. Consider it my need, not yours. Okay?"

David turned to Dolores for support, but found none. Looking ahead through the headlights' beam, she might have been trying to count the trees along the trail. Her lips were pursed in concentration, and her face carried a delicate expression of cool reserve. At that moment she did not look nearly so young. "Okay," he said. "Thanks. But what about you? What are you going to be doing?"

"More of the same—trying to find out why they want my head." Then the thought of Tom Ludlow suddenly intruded and Burke fell silent. More frustration. Now he had to sweat out Ludlow's return from a much publicized conference in Paris. And until the man did get back, there was nothing he could do but alternately brood and hope. "Anyway," he went on, "watch the personal notices in the *San Francisco Chronicle.* If I want to get in touch with you, my message will be addressed to Jimmy Cooper. And if you have to reach me for any reason, address your notice to Arthur Radin in the *New York Times.* You got that straight?"

"Yeah."

"There's just one other thing," Burke said. "If they do pick me up—or if anything happens to me—it's important that you know. Once they're finished with me, you'll be all right. I don't want you having to hide indefinitely. So I've worked something out. I'm going to leave a prepaid notice at the *Chronicle* with special instructions. They'll get a call from me every two weeks telling them not to run the notice. If ever I don't call for four weeks in a row, they're to automatically run the notice on the fifth week. It will say, 'Jimmy, come home. All is forgiven.' If you see that, you'll know it's over for me and you're in the clear."

"Did David tell you I was a hooker?" Dolores broke in hurriedly.

"Yes."

"But not anymore, not since I went to live with him. Now all I do is cook and clean and screw just for fun. I even read books. David gave me *A Farewell to Arms.* It's by Ernest Hemingway. Did you ever read it?"

"A long time ago."

"You remember how it ends?"

"Don't tell her," David cut in. "I'm trying to teach her to read the right way—front to back."

Dolores giggled.

"That was sneaky," David told her. "And you promised."

169

"I only promised not to look at the back of the book."

David started to say something more, but Burke did not hear him. He was leaning forward in his seat, staring through the windshield. "I don't believe it . . ." he said softly.

Coming around a sharp curve, the headlights had suddenly picked out four men standing behind a car that was parked sideways across the road. The men had guns pointing straight at them. They were no more than twenty yards away. Without warning they opened fire.

Burke swore and gunned the motor as the car lurched forward, wheels spinning wildly in the mud. "Hold on and get down. We're going through."

"Wait!" David yelled. He made a grab for Dolores, but was jolted back against the door. Shots were exploding in bursts of automatic fire. Then they crashed into the front end of the other car and David's head went into the windshield. Burke swung the wheel, cut it back, and swung it again. He felt the car shudder, hesitate, then leap forward once more as it tore clear. Shots were going off all over the place now and he heard glass shattering. A moment later they were on Route 103 and speeding west. Burke glanced at his passengers. David was leaning against the door. His arms were around Dolores, clutching her tightly. They both seemed to be unconscious. Burke kept driving.

Parked in a small clearing, surrounded by darkness and trees, Burke pulled at David's arms.

"David, let go."

David opened his eyes. "What?" he mumbled.

"Let go of her."

"Who?"

"Dolores."

David glanced down and looked at the girl in his arms. Dolores's head was resting against his chest and he looked at it long and carefully. Then he turned and looked at the holes in the windshield. No lights were on and it was hard for him to see. He blinked, then wiped his eyes with the back of his hand.

"I think I'm bleeding."

Burke had stopped pulling at his arms. "You went into the windshield. It's not bad. Just a few cuts."

"Where are we?"

"Off Route 9, somewhere near Dobbs Ferry."

David nodded consideringly. As if just discovering his hands, he moved them across Dolores's back. "You got away from them, huh?"

"At least for now."

"Good. I'm glad."

Burke was silent.

"It was me who set you up. I told Ellman where we were meeting: the time, the exact spot, everything."

Burke still said nothing.

David began rocking gently with Dolores. "It was the only way he'd let us out. He said he'd bury us if I didn't cooperate. And when I found how you'd lied to me, I guess I went a little crazy."

"I never lied to you, David."

"It's okay. It doesn't matter now."

"It matters to me."

"Ellman said you'd sold out, that you were a double agent, working for the Russians. He said that was why they were after you."

"That's not true."

David closed his eyes. Still rocking, he pressed his cheek to Dolores's hair. "He showed me pictures," he said tiredly. "He had it all on film. You and a Colonel Igronsky. You were getting paid off. He showed me how you changed attaché cases at Heathrow Airport in London."

"Ah, David." Burke shook his head. "I'm afraid he just turned that one around for you. It was Igronsky

171

who was the double agent for us. It was I who was paying him."

David rocked in the darkness. "Well . . ." Delicately, one hand patted Dolores's shoulder. "Well, what do you know. I mean, that's really funny, isn't it?"

"David . . ."

"Ellman promised you'd get a fair trial. He said there'd be no shooting. The bastard. They started shooting the minute they saw the car. They never gave you a chance."

Burke watched him. The rain made a hollow, metallic sound against the roof of the car. Overhead, a plane's engines struggled through the weather.

"They never planned on any trial, did they?"

"No."

"Oh, shit."

"There was no way for you to know."

David rocked with Dolores, an old Orthodox Jew lost in his evening devotions. After awhile, he started to cry. He wept without sound and the tears ran down his cheeks and mixed with the blood.

Burke studied him with great care. He might have been researching a monograph on grief. He refused to look anywhere else.

"In the head . . ." David said softly. "She weighs a hundred and three pounds and they had to go and shoot her in the goddamned head. They're inconceivable. They knew she was in the car." He began to rock harder. "In the goddamned head. I mean, did you see what they went and did to her?"

"Yes."

"Okay . . . okay. So where's the sense to it?"

"There is no sense to it," Burke said gently, accepting his assigned dialogue without question.

"What kind of enemy was she of the fucking Republic? I mean, where was the threat?"

Burke said nothing.

172

"A hundred-and-three-pound, nineteen-year-old ex-hooker and the sons-of-bitches had to go and . . ."

He broke off. Burke sat stiffly behind the wheel and waited. From a long way off, he had suddenly remembered an even younger girl.

"I beg your pardon," David said with quiet dignity. "I'm sorry. I know this is real heavy. It must be very embarrassing for you to have to sit and listen to this kind of shit."

"No, no . . ."

David absently stroked the girl's hair. His hand was dark and slippery with blood. When he spoke again, he had stopped weeping and his voice was more controlled. "Okay. So who's neck do I hang it on?"

"That won't help her."

"No. But it'll sure help me."

"David, listen . . ."

"I don't want to listen. I've already listened my girl right into a hole in her head."

Burke saw how it was going to be.

"It's got to be Ellman, of course," David rushed on. "My own fucking *yiddishe landsman.* My good old Uncle Louie. He's the one who lied to me about you. He's the one who baited me into setting you up. He's the one who promised there'd be no shooting. So even if he didn't actually pull the trigger himself, he's the one who really killed her. Right?"

But Burke chose to reject this particular part of his assigned dialogue.

"So what am I going to do about him?"

"Please. Haven't you had trouble enough? Forget about him, will you."

"You forget about him. I'll forget about him when I'm dead."

"If you start pushing this," Burke said wearily, "I'm sure he can arrange that for you too."

"You mean you won't help me?" David's voice had

gone all fuzzy around the edges again. "Is that what you're saying?"

Burke measured the younger man's mood and condition. "I'm saying don't act like a suicidal idiot. We both need time on this. You won't do anyone any good by screaming for instant vengeance. In time maybe you'll get your payment—if that's what you still want. But you're crazy to personalize something like this. A lot more than just Ellman is involved. He didn't kill Dolores. He's just following orders. Which might not make you feel any better, but happens to be the way it is."

But David seemed to have lost interest in anything Burke had to say on the subject. Rocking the dead girl once more, he stared off into the night.

Burke touched his arm. "David, did you hear me?"

"I heard you."

"Are you okay?"

"Yeah. Sure. I'm great."

"There are a couple of things I'm going to have to tell you to do."

"Go ahead. Tell me. That's what I'm best at, doing what other people tell me to do. That's how I ended up getting a bullet into my girl's head."

Burke waited.

"All right," David said. "I'm listening."

"I left a car near the train station in Dobbs Ferry this morning. We'll drive there together now, then separate. You'll have to drive this wreck back to New York alone. I don't think they'll have any roadblocks set up. There are too many directions to cover and their personnel are limited. In any case, it doesn't really matter if you're picked up. It'll just save you the trouble of having to get in touch with Ellman. You did everything he told you to do, so you're in the clear. And since you can no longer be of any use to him with me, I'm sure he's finally finished with you."

"Yeah? Well I'm not finished with him."

Burke ignored the threat. "Now about Dolores . . ."

David stopped his rocking.

"I think it would be best if you didn't travel with her," Burke said gently. "I think it would be best if you left her here and let Ellman make the necessary arrangements later tonight or in the morning."

David was staring at him. "You want me to leave her here alone? In the rain?"

Burke said nothing.

"No. I'm not leaving her."

"She's dead, David."

David's eyes were as black as his beard. "Didn't you hear what I said? I said I'm not leaving her."

"All right," Burke sighed. "Then let me help you put her on the back seat."

"I'm keeping her right here with me."

"David, you can't drive with . . ."

"You just shut up, damn it! Don't you tell me what I can't do."

"Then get her to Ellman as fast as you can. If someone happens to spot you with her, it could get complicated."

But David had already tuned him out.

Burke headed out of the grove and ten minutes later pulled up alongside his own car. With Dolores leaning against David's shoulder between them, neither man had spoken during the short drive. Now, Burke said, "You know how to get back from here?"

"I'll take the Saw Mill River Parkway right down to the Henry Hudson."

Burke looked at him, once again measuring. He seemed more resigned to than satisfied with what he saw. "I'm sorry about Dolores, about everything."

David studied a hole in the windshield with its halo of shatter. It appeared to be the absolute focus of his concentration.

"Please. Don't go and try anything stupid about Ellman. Just be patient. Use your head."

David nodded distantly.

"You're sure you can manage?"

"Yeah."

"Stay in touch," said Burke, and got out of the car, into his own, and quickly drove away, as if to have hesitated or to have even glanced back would have made it impossible for him to leave at all.

18

The message from Sally Warden (Pamela's code name) had been clocked in at 8:42 P.M. and Burke returned it precisely three hours later from a booth on Ninth Avenue and Fifty-third Street. It was the first time that Pamela herself had called. Until now it had always been Hank. Burke had a feeling there was trouble even before he heard her voice.

"What is it?" he said. "What's wrong?"

"Don't ask." But it was only a last ditch effort at the old bravado. "Everything's wrong. They know Hank killed that agent . . . Bishop."

"What do you mean they know? Who's they?"

"A man named George Reese. He's the one who's been working on us from the beginning—the one who cost me my job—and the one who got me out of bed at four in the morning to look at Bishop's body in the morgue. He's who they are." She paused. "And the damnedest part is, he always comes across as such a decent type. Do you know him?"

"Yes. At least, I did. And he is a decent type."

"Well right now I wish he were dead," Pamela said and started to weep.

Burke listened to the small unhappy sounds coming across the wire and waited. Everybody finally cried. But this woman was the last he had expected it from.

"Okay, tell me about it."

"Just give me a second." Burke heard her blow her nose. "God, I'm a mess."

"Just take it easy. You've been under a lot of pressure."

"I'm okay now. Hank doesn't even know I called you. He'd be furious if he found out. He thinks you've got enough problems without our adding this to them. And he's probably right. I'm sorry."

"Will you cut that out. You're only in this because of me. Now tell me what they have on Hank."

"That's the real reason I called. I wanted to find out if you thought they were only bluffing. They said they found hair and blood samples on Bishop's body that matched Hank's. They said there was also some flesh under Bishop's fingernails that came from the back of Hank's hand when Bishop scratched him during the fight. They said they had enough on Hank to put him in jail for the rest of his life, and that they could put me away also as an accessory. Is that . . ."

The operator signaled for more money and Burke went through his usual coin and gong ritual.

"Do you think they're bluffing?" Pamela asked.

"Not if the forensic people really have what Reese says they have."

"Oh, God."

"Have they arrested Hank yet?"

"No."

"Why not?"

"Reese is trying to squeeze him into making a deal. He says he's no cop and doesn't want to be vindictive. He claims to understand how Hank got sucked into this whole thing, and that it's more vital to the national security to get you than to punish him. He's sure we know where you are and how to get in touch with you. He says he'll let Hank off if he cooperates."

Burke stared out at the traffic moving downtown on Ninth Avenue. "What did Hank say to that?"

"You know Hank. What do you think he said? He told him to go fuck himself."

"That's my boy."

"Sure," she said flatly. "Your boy's ready for just

about anything in your cause, including self-immolation."

Burke heard the bitterness in her voice. He did not blame her for it. She had every right to be bitter. He just wondered at its having taken so long in coming. "And you?" he said quietly. "I take it you're less inclined to such sacrifice."

She left that one alone and the wire hummed over her silence.

"What would you like me to do?" Burke asked.

"I don't know," she said miserably. "But something!"

"Well, I suppose I could give myself up."

"You said it, not me."

She started to cry again and Burke put some more coins into the box even though the operator had not requested any money. She wept for what seemed a long time, and Burke thought it best to simply let her get it out.

"I'm sorry," she said at last. "I guess you must think I'm some bitch. I swear Hank would knock my head off if he ever heard me. And he'd be right. Christ, I don't know what's wrong with me. No, I mean, yes I do. I'm just scared for him. I'm so scared for him I can't sleep nights." She fought for control. "But you don't really know how I feel about that punchy bum, do you?"

"I've guessed."

"No. You couldn't possibly have guessed. I couldn't have guessed myself. It's something I never expected to be able to feel anymore. It's absolutely crazy. But let me tell you something . . ."

And she told him, leaving out, it seemed, nothing. Burke listened without interruption, putting in more coins when necessary, but pleased to let her share a range of emotions that surprised him. She had always seemed so cynical and tough. Still—when you felt, you felt, and none of them were that different. But what was he going to do about Hank? This was the real problem and this was what he was thinking about when he saw the car slow as it approached the curb. Four men in a sedan would have worried him at anytime, so he was out of the booth and running before it even came to a full stop. And this time it was just as well that he worried.

My God, she's been setting me up, he thought with cold surprise. She's been holding me on the phone while they traced the call. Then he had other things to think about.

Knowing he had to get off the street, he ran low, crouched over, keeping the line of parked cars between himself and the following car as a continuing shield. He was running west towards Tenth Avenue, the street a tunnel between two walls of tenements. The street was empty at this hour and he cursed himself for not having used a booth in a more crowded area, closer to Broadway. A lot of people around would have at least kept them from firing. This way he was a duck in a shooting gallery. As soon as one of them developed sense enough to get out of the car and onto the sidewalk behind him, he'd be finished. Then glancing back as he ran, he saw that one of them had—a big, bulky man with a submachine gun. Wonderful, he thought, and dashed up the stoop of a tenement just as the man opened fire.

He felt the strangely painless shock of metal tearing into his left arm and knocking him into the vestibule. The second door was locked, but it was all glass and Burke kicked his foot through, opened it and ran up the hall stairway in front of him. Gasping, the nerves in his legs wriggling, he pushed himself up five flights to the roof. Reaching it, he found wide areaways between the buildings on either side. There was no place for him to go but down. He felt an old misery settling on him. Then he took out his revolver and attached the silencer he kept in an inside breastpocket of his jacket. Reluctantly, he stepped to one side of the stairhousing and waited.

The man with the machine gun came through the door without even slowing, an eager, unwary hunter. Burke fired once and there was only the soft whoosh of the silencer and the thump as the man fell. Pocketing his revolver, Burke dragged the man away from in front of the door and out of sight. It was not easy. His left arm was numb and of little use and the man was heavy. Then he took the submachine gun and went back into the shadows to wait once more. He had avoided looking at the man's face. He might have known him. If he had, he had no wish to find out. Whoever he was, Burke thought, he had not been very smart to come barging through the door that way. A small enough error in another line of work, but big enough to kill you in this one. Maybe it was the machine gun's fault. The damn things were so powerful, made you feel so impregnable, you tended to get careless. He hefted the weapon in his good arm, not feeling the least bit impregnable. But he was grateful not to have to face three armed men with just a revolver.

Where were they? He wanted to get this over with as quickly as possible. He was a good clotter, but was still losing a fair amount of blood. If he passed out now, he'd be through. There was little doubt about that. He started to think about Pamela and what she had done, but quickly stopped himself. This was not the time. He had to focus on staying alive, nothing else.

Then, worried about whether he would be able to aim and fire the machine gun with only one good arm, he sat down with his back to a ventilator, drew up his legs and leaned the gun-barrel across his knees. It held steady. Good. But he would have to get them all with the first burst, he thought, because that was the only chance he was going to get. He had been concerned about the shots down in the street being reported to the police, but apparently no one had heard them. Or if they had heard, they'd chosen not to notice. What a town. You could fight a small war on the sidestreets, and the good citizens would go right on minding their own business. It was a city of almost religious noninvolvement. Don't bother us, it said. We got our own troubles. And they had them, all right. But God help you if you ever needed someone.

When they came at last, it was with far greater caution than their dead colleague. Burke saw the big fire door slowly swing open, its scratched metal glistening in the moonlight. A man eased his head out like a cautious turtle, looked around, then stepped onto the roof. "Walter?" he called softly.

From the shadow of the ventilator where he sat, Burke saw him clearly, saw the tough, broken face over the barrel of the submachine gun resting across his knees. Well, he thought. It's Reeves. It's George Reeves himself.

Like the first man, Reeves was also carrying a Thompson gun. He was crouched slightly, holding the automatic weapon in front of him. The gun's muzzle pointed straight at the place where Burke sat.

"Walter?" Reeves called again.

Burke could feel his heart banging against his chest. He looked at the wedge of the front sight in the slot of the rear sight, the top of the wedge cutting the center of Reeve's chest. A second man came through the door and quickly knelt to the right of Reeves. Then the third came out and dove flat out, off to the left.

"Where the hell's Walter?" hissed the last man.

No one answered.

Burke sat waiting for a clean, sure shot. He had to be able to get them all with a single burst. If just one made it back downstairs or behind the stairhousing, he was in trouble. George Reeves. Imagine that. Last seen ten years ago on a mountain in Peru, and now waiting to cut him in half with a Tommy gun on a New York roof. The always surprising exigencies of the Service. Dimly, he remembered something about a mentally retarded daughter whom Reeves was always worried about, and wondered how she was.

How could she be? Well, George, he thought. It was never easy, but was a little less hard when they were faceless. He supposed George felt the same way about him. Unless he believed all the lies about his selling out, which he probably did. Why shouldn't he? Still, they had worked together, gone through things. Sentimental crap. George would believe what they told him to believe.

Out of caution, Burke kept his finger pressed forward against the trigger guard to keep it away from the trigger itself. This thing could go off much too easily. If he was going to get just one chance, he wanted it to be the best one possible. He had an urge to touch his bad arm to see if the bleeding had stopped, but was afraid to let go of the gun. Feeling himself getting bleary-eyed, he blinked to clear his sight. Come on, he thought. You can't wait there all night. Let's get on with the damn thing.

"Okay, let's spread out and cover the roof," said Reeves. "He's got to be up here someplace."

"But where the hell's Walter?" asked the second man, obviously not too anxious to go probing the dark places.

"Probably dead," said Reeves and moved forward and to the right. "Let's go."

The other two rose and moved also, and for a moment they were almost in a straight line. Gently, Burke squeezed the trigger, shifting the barrel slightly to the right as he felt the quick lurching of the gun against his shoulder. It was just a single short burst that sounded little different from the backfiring of a motorcycle. The three men fell. They had not gotten off a shot. Reeves went down on his back, the other two forward on their faces.

Burke slowly pushed himself up. He walked over and looked at the three men where they lay. None of them moved. He forced himself to look at Reeves' face. Somehow, he felt it to be necessary. In the moonlight the tough face appeared as tough as ever. Burke felt no special sensation at his survival. The odds had been four to one against it, but it just meant four more dead. My brother, my enemy, he thought, and wondered how many lives his own was finally worth. Given some kind of mortal scale, how was he supposed to make that particular judgment?

Instinctively, he wiped all fingerprints from the stock and barrel of the submachine gun and placed it beside the man who had carried it. Then he took a final look around and left the roof. He went down the stairs quietly, holding to the bannister with his good hand and still grateful and amazed that no door had opened, no cry been raised. Stepping over the broken glass in the vestibule, he glanced cautiously out into the street. The agents' sedan was double-parked a short distance away. A patrol car was parked right behind it, with a cop at the wheel, and Burke started to duck back. Then he saw the cop's partner, standing and writing what was evidently a parking ticket. When the cop finished, he tied the summons onto the sedan's windshield wiper, got into the patrol car and rode off.

Beautiful, thought Burke. Four bodies up on the roof, and New York's finest were diligently keeping the streets of the world's greatest city safe from double-parkers.

He found a cab on Ninth Avenue, got out half a block from Angela's apartment, and was in her bedroom at 1:35 A.M. He woke her gently. "It's only me," he whispered.

In the dark her arms went around him. "What do you mean, only you. What's this sudden humility?" She kissed him. "Mmmm," she purred. "This is even better than what I was dreaming."

On his knees beside the bed he clung to her for a moment. The bent position had made him dizzy.

"What are you waiting for?" she said. "Why have you still got your clothes on?"

He stood up and switched on a lamp. "Don't be frightened. I'm fine. But you're going to have to help me a little."

She stared at him. Then she saw his left coat sleeve and her face went white. "Oh, my God."

"Easy," he said. "I told you I'm all right."

She sat up in bed, closed her eyes, and breathed deeply several times. When she opened her eyes, she had better control. "Okay . . . okay. What do you want me to do?"

"First, you'd better help me get my clothes off. I want to see what this thing looks like."

His coat and jacket came off with little trouble, but his shirtsleeve was stuck to the wound. They went into the bathroom and he sat on the edge of the tub. "I'm really a great little clotter. I clot quick as all hell. Doctors are always crazy about my clotting." He saw that her face was still white and strained. "You're not going to faint on me, are you?"

She shook her head.

"You're sure?" he said anxiously.

"I'm sure, damn it. Just tell me what I'm supposed to do."

Following his instructions, she cut away his shirtsleeve, then soaked the remaining piece of fabric with warm water until it came unstuck. But when the wound was exposed, she had to turn away. "I'm sorry," she whispered. "I guess I'm not much good at this."

"You're good at more important things. And how often do I get shot, anyway?" He was busy studying the damage to the upper part of his arm. "It missed the bone. It went right through. Right in and out. I'm lucky."

"Boy, are you lucky."

He smiled. "It's all comparative. Do you have any kind of antiseptic and bandages?"

She found some peroxide, gauze, and surgical tape. Then steeling herself, she was able to do what had to be done. Afterward she helped him out of the rest of his clothes and put him to bed with a large brandy. He lay there, sipping his drink, luxuriating. "You

185

know something? I think I could learn to like getting shot."

"Does it hurt very much?"

"Only when I laugh."

"You're not funny." She had put on a robe and sat stiffly on the bed beside him. The color was back in her cheeks, but her eyes were moist and she kept chewing her lip. "Another few inches and you'd be doing your laughing all the way to the morgue."

"Yes, but I'm not."

"What happened? Who shot you?"

"What's the difference? It's over and done."

She glared at him. "Don't you dare start shutting me out again. If you don't tell me what happened this minute, you can take your fucking bullet hole out of my goddamned bed and get straight to hell out of here."

"You talk pretty dirty. You're not that young."

"Richard!"

"Okay. If you come lie next to me and promise not to cry, I'll tell you."

"No promises," she said and lay down beside him on his good side. "If I want to cry, I'll damn well cry."

He told her, his voice low and even and losing itself quickly in the hidden bedroom, among the mingled odors of peroxide, brandy, and Arpége. It was for his own needs as much as hers. He had stopped being a solitary animal. He did not intend to be one ever again.

"Oh, God," she murmured when he had gotten it all out. "Four of them."

"I couldn't help it. I didn't want it that way. There wasn't anything else I could do about them."

"To hell with them," she said fiercely. "Do you think I give a damn about them? I'm glad they're dead. They deserve to be dead. All I meant was that there were four of them trying to assassinate you with their miserable machine guns, and somehow you're alive here in my bed, while they're dead up on that roof. I just thank God for the miracle."

Under the covers he touched what he considered to be the equal miracle of her flesh. "You think God is on our side?"

"Who else's? We've got right, haven't we?"

He loved the "we." He had come to adore that particular pronoun. "I hope so. At least, I like to think so."

"And right is might, isn't it?"

"Absolutely."

"Then thou art twice armed," she intoned.

"Damn right."

"And thou shalt surely smite them good with the jawbone of an ass."

"If it's all the same to you," he said, "if it doesn't damage your lovely Biblical allusions, I'd be much happier smiting them with a standard .38 caliber service revolver."

But she was already off into her next resentment. "And that bitch," she swore softly. "How could she have thrown you to the lions like that? How could she have done anything so rotten?"

"I guess she was just frightened. I don't know. Pam's a good woman. People react to fear in different ways."

"That wasn't just different. It was murderous, inexcusable."

He sipped his brandy and said nothing.

His silence bothered her. "For God's sake, Richard. The woman as good as pointed a gun at your head and pulled the trigger. If it was up to her, you'd be dead this minute. And look at you. You're so calm and tolerant about the whole thing, I could spit!"

"Would it make you feel any better if I jumped up and down and swore?"

"Damned right."

"I'm too tired right now."

"I don't understand you. When did you suddenly turn into a Mary Poppins?"

He smiled faintly, "Fantastic. I've just shot four men to death and the lady calls me a Mary Poppins."

"You know what I mean."

Burke stared deep into his glass, as if searching for something important at the bottom. "That woman hardly knew me, Angela. All we'd ever shared were a few days together at the hospital, and the hope of a new and better shot at things. Yet because of me—because she tried to help me these past weeks—she's had her career ruined, become partly responsible for the death of a government agent, and found herself and a man she cares about facing a murder indictment. Would you say that's a fair list of sacrifices to have made for someone you barely knew?"

Angela did not answer.

"I'd say so. I'd say that's way above and beyond. So if the whole thing finally got too much for her, if she finally had to bend and give them what they wanted —me—I'm afraid I can't really hate her for it."

She moved closer to him under the covers. "I've been thinking. I've been thinking you're actually a lot nicer than I am."

"Not really."

"Yes, really." She leaned over and sipped some of his brandy. "I'm very glad they didn't kill you tonight. You know that?"

"Yes. Me too."

He waited for the question which, through repetition, had become *the* question for them and part of a necessary ritual.

It came. "What's going to happen to us, darling?"

"We'll be okay," he answered on cue, deciding he enjoyed the pronoun "us" equally as much as "we."

"You promise?"

"I promise."

"When?"

"I don't know."

"How?"

"I'm not exactly sure," he said. Which may not have been very reassuring, but was still a lot better than the "I don't know" it had been just a week or so earlier. The change depended, for a possibly greater certainty, on Tom Ludlow's anticipated return from Paris. But because the whole thing might also prove to be a total dud, Burke had told Angela nothing about it. Still, in the absence of any other hope, it had begun to look brighter each day.

"Hey!" She suddenly sat up, the ritual over.

"Hey, what?"

"I'm going to call in sick tomorrow and stay home and take care of you." She saw him about to protest. "And if you dare say one word about getting out of this bed and going home tonight, I swear I'll shoot you in the other arm myself."

Lying back, Burke grinned at her, feeling like a happy idiot, knowing he was going to remember the way her face looked then—anxious, warm, and loving as she sat on the bed beside him—remember for as long as he was able.

19

Lilly had dreamed up the entire plan herself. She had not even told Burke about it. What would have been the point? she thought. He only would have thrown cold water on the whole idea. When it was over, and she had been proven right and he wrong, she would make him eat every one of his dumb, cynical judgments without salt.

The advance arrangements were simple enough and involved just Frank and herself. She simply told the agent that Burke had agreed to see him. "He'll meet us in the parking lot of the Fountainhead Diner in Syosset on Wednesday night," she said. "Do you know where that is?"

"Sure, I've stopped there on the way to the beach. What time?"

"1:00 A.M."

He kissed her. "You're sensational."

Forty-eight hours later, Frank picked her up at the theatre after her performance and they drove over the Fifty-ninth Street Bridge and onto the Long Island Expressway. She sat close to him and they listened to soft radio music and did little talking. With some surprise, she found her palms wet. "My God, I'm nervous."

He touched her arm. "There's nothing to be nervous about."

"What if your people are following us?"

"Do you think you're dealing with an amateur?" He grinned, showing strong, even teeth in a wide mouth. "I made sure we had no tail even before we crossed the bridge."

"What would they do if they caught you?" she said, somehow finding it easier while she was talking.

"No one's going to catch me."

"You once said this would be treason. What do they do to you for treason?"

"First or second degree?"

"There are different degrees?"

"Always."

"Which would this be?"

"First," he said. "Aiding and abetting a known enemy of the republic."

"What would they do to you for that?"

"Cut off my right testicle."

She made a face. "I don't think that's very funny."

"My God, neither do I."

A fog had begun to roll in as they drove farther out on Long Island, and their lights shone wetly through it. Here and there the flickering neon tubes of junk-food restaurants, drive-ins, and real estate offices broke through the thickening mists and their effect was oddly foreboding in the quiet night.

"We're just about there," Frank said, and moments later Lilly saw the big, red neon sign spelling Fountainhead Diner.

They drove around to the parking lot at the rear and pulled into one of the marked-off spaces. The area was large and unlighted, with perhaps a dozen cars scattered about. Jukebox music came faintly from inside the diner, but otherwise there was no sound. Behind and along one side of the lot, there were pine woods.

"Do you see his car?" Frank said.

"I don't know what he's driving."

He looked at her.

"I asked, but he wouldn't tell me. He said it would be better for me not to know." She pretended to study the other cars in the lot. They were all empty. "I guess he's not here yet."

191

Frank glanced at his watch. "We're five minutes early."

They sat without speaking and Lilly was abruptly aware of a sharp pain in her stomach. It felt as though someone had stuck a knife in her and all the love, all the good feeling she'd ever known was draining out. Why? Touching the place, she was almost surprised at the smooth, unbroken feel of the flesh under her clothing.

A white Thunderbird drove into the lot and she saw Frank's hands tense on the wheel. But a couple, a man and woman, were in the car. They parked and got out, laughing a trifle too loudly and holding onto one another as they walked towards the front of the diner. What a luxury, Lilly thought, to have nothing more on your mind than the guy you're with and something to eat. It seemed impossible to remember a time when things had been that simple for her, and equally impossible to imagine them ever being that way again. And it had all started because she had once gone into a hospital to have her nose and breasts done. Yet how could you look for reasons with something like this? If you tried, you could end up in a rubber room.

A man walked around from the diner entrance and started towards his car. Frank leaned forward, studying him through the windshield, then relaxed once more in his seat.

"How did you know that wasn't Burke?" Lilly asked.

"Wrong build. Burke is taller, wider across the shoulders. He can change his face, but not his body."

The things you had to keep in mind, thought Lilly. These were details that had never even occurred to her, yet might easily have ruined everything. And what else of significance had she overlooked?

A big, silver-grey Mercedes rolled into the lot, paused as the driver searched out a parking space worthy of his considerable investment, then glided into a spot about thirty feet away. Lilly considered the car and the single man inside. This one seemed to meet the necessary requirements. "There he is," she said. "That's Burke."

"In the Mercedes?"

"Yes."

He was out of the car before her mouth had closed on the final 's.' Sprinting past a grey Plymouth, his fist pounded the hood and three men burst out and followed him. Lilly stared. The men had evidently been lying flat, out of sight, waiting for his signal. All four men, she saw, had pistols with attached silencers in their hands. Then there were all those soft, whooshing sounds and the Mercedes's windshield exploded into fragments. Lilly opened her mouth to scream, but found a small part of a great horror jammed in her throat like a rock. "Oh, Lord," she whispered.

She watched the rest of it as if paralyzed. Although there was not really that much more to see. Two of the men simply got into the Mercedes and drove it away, the third man took off after them in the Plymouth, and Frank walked slowly back to where she sat, waiting. The entire incident had taken no more than a minute, and no one but Lilly had seen or heard a thing.

Frank got in beside her but she was barely aware of him. She had her eyes closed and was breathing very slowly and carefully.

"I'm sorry," he said.

She went on with her breathing.

"It had nothing to do with us, with you, with how I feel about you. You've got to understand that."

She nodded slowly. There he was, right on cue with his dialogue. It was like a play that Burke himself had written for her, a bad play. It didn't deserve the single performance it was getting. Next comes the part about not knowing he was going to fall in love with me, she thought.

"It's my job, Lilly. I make no apologies for that. I just never expected . . ."

193

"To fall in love with me," she finished.

She opened her eyes then and looked at him, wondering why he didn't look different in some way. "And your friends, Waldo and Kevin," she said. "You didn't really kill them the other night, did you?"

"No." He turned away, moving cautiously on the seat, as if fearful that any sudden movement might frighten her into leaving. "Whatever you think about Burke personally, he had this coming. He was a gun at our heads. He sold us out—you, me, the country—all of us. And for a few lousy bucks. I don't understand a man like that. I don't understand what goes on in his mind. Even so, there was no satisfaction in this for me tonight, Lilly. I don't take human life lightly. Not anyone's. And to have had to make you part of it was probably the single toughest thing I've ever had to do."

My poor darling, she thought wryly. If there was no satisfaction in it for him now, how was he going to feel when she really zonked him? But God Almighty! A man was dead for no better reason than that he had decided to stop for a bite to eat. And she had fingered him. Talk about insanities. Still in a state of semishock, she felt the first icy intimations of what lay ahead.

"Frank?"

He turned quickly, anxiously. She saw the hope in his eyes and hated knowing she was going to enjoy punishing him. "That man you and your playmates just shot up wasn't Burke. He wasn't anybody I even knew. He was just some poor slob who happened to run out of luck and drive in here at the wrong time."

Frank stared at her, "But you said . . ."

"Never mind what I said. You also said." Her eyes had gone cold and she was finally angry. "All I'm trying to tell you is that you shot the wrong guy full of holes."

"I don't understand."

"You will, you bastard!" She was well into it now,

194

riding it coldly. "Oh, you had me fooled, all right. You had no trouble there. I was stupid enough to believe everything you told me. Burke was where you ran into trouble. He was the one who didn't believe you. He told me that Waldo and Kevin probably weren't dead, that the whole thing was just a set-up to con me. But I couldn't buy that. So I worked out this bright idea to show him how wrong he was about you, that you meant what you said about wanting to help him, that it wasn't just going to be a trap." She shook her head. "Well, I showed him all right."

Frank said nothing. Things were happening to his face that he did not seem to know about.

"Damn you!" she swore. "You're unspeakable—all of you—a pack of wolves. It was bad enough I was wrong. But who expected a goddamned massacre? Who expected you to shoot some poor bastard full of holes before I could even get my mouth open?"

He made a vague, helpless gesture. "I . . . we thought he was Burke."

"So?"

"So you don't just casually walk over and talk to a man in Burke's position. If you try, you're dead, and he's gone."

In the car they sat together but were apart. Several more cars entered the lot and others left. Above the diner the neon sign added its baleful red glow to the shifting fog. Once Frank started to raise a hand to touch her, but changed his mind and let it fall.

When he finally spoke, his voice was low, weighted with anguish. "It's what I do, Lilly."

"I know."

"Please don't hate me."

She felt sick, almost feverish, and moved closer to him, trying to keep her nerves from fluttering.

"We'll be okay," he promised.

She groaned. "I don't know. That poor man. What am I going to do about that poor man?"

He misunderstood. "We'll take care of that. Christ! Wait till they find out he's not Burke."

"But I killed him. And for no reason."

"You didn't know what would happen."

"Sure. I'll tell him that."

"It's too bad, but these things happen. I could tell you stories . . ."

"I don't want to hear any of your dirty stories. Mine are bad enough." She clung to him. "Hold me," she whispered, shivering. "Please. Just hold me. I think I'm going out of my mind. All I can think of is that poor man. All I can think is that if it weren't for my goddamned nose and tits, he'd still be alive."

20

Burke woke early, prodded by a confusing mixture of pain and expectation. The pain came from having slept with too much weight on his bad arm, in spite of almost two weeks of recuperation. The sense of expectation was more elusive, and his sleep-fogged brain groped for reasons. Then he opened his eyes and saw the four oversized reels of recording tape stacked on the floor beside his bed. "Aah . . .", he sighed, and rolled over onto his back.

One cigarette, he promised himself, just one, and then I'll get up and get to it. He lay there, savoring the rare luxury of these few extra moments in bed. The spartan. Usually, on normal mornings, to be awake was to be instantly out of bed, as if even the slightest delay would start him on a swift slide into decadence. But this was no normal morning. On this morning, he thought, he was entitled to his small reward. Then he wondered whether he was really rewarding himself by staying in bed or just stalling. Maybe he was simply afraid of what he might find when he got up and started to listen. Finally, he had the tapes. And he expected so much of them. What if they produced nothing? An unpleasant thought, but a definite possibility. More than a possibility. The odds actually favored his finding nothing.

Still, he was hopeful. A long time ago he had decided that hope was his natural state. Or, if not natural, then at least his chosen state. Certainly it was more pleasant to live with than despair, which might offer a ready enough cushion against disappointment but not much else. Better to soar and perhaps fall, than to crawl through tunnels of depression. He had felt exactly this way, soaring, while driving back from Washington only a few hours ago. With the tapes safely on the back seat of his car, he had the sensation of flying home. And he had no idea what he would find on the tapes. It was enough that he had managed to get them.

Even in concept, he had found the idea exciting. Electronic surveillance had always held a special fascination for him. Its potential was awesome. And in this case, because his future might hang on its results, he could almost feel himself sliding into the metaphysical. Ten days before, he had tried explaining some of this feeling to Angela.

"The newer techniques are fantastic," he told her, "straight out of science fiction. No one is safe from them. It's like an attack by psychic particles. There's no reasonable defense. With the right expertise and equipment, you can crawl into anyone's life."

"It sounds frightening."

"It is." He smiled. "Unless you happen to be using it in a good and proper cause."

"Which you are," she said.

"Which I am," he agreed.

It was the second day of his rest and rehabilitation treatment in her apartment and he had already told her the whole thing, told her all about Tom Ludlow and the hilltop and the twenty-three dead. He had told her as part of his new anti-solitary-animal-philosophy, despite its being stupidly unprofessional to share with anyone what you weren't required to share. He had started out telling her coldly and dispassionately, but it got away from him somewhere near the end. She listened without comment and was sensitive enough to leave it alone for a few hours. When she judged the time right, she said, "You think Ludlow is involved?"

He picked at the gauze, covering his wound. The action had become a nervous tic, a continuing need to touch, to affirm.

"Leave that bandage alone," she told him. "Do you want to give yourself blood poisoning?"

"Nag, nag, nag. I might as well be married to you again."

"Don't you wish."

He looked at her. "Of course I wish."

"You didn't answer my question," she said, avoiding his eyes. "What about Ludlow? What do you know about him?"

"Only what I've told you. Plus what I've read in the papers over the years. Anything else I might feel about him is exactly that—what I feel." His hand started towards the bandage again, but he stopped it. "From what the professor told me, Ludlow and that whole incident on the hill were evidently very much on Tony's mind. And if an eighteen-year-old itch suddenly needs scratching, I figure there has to be a better reason for it than just nostalgia. Especially for someone like Tony."

"But if it does have something to do with Ludlow, why now? Why after all these years?"

"That's what I have to find out. I've just been waiting for him to come back from his Paris conference. And according to the news reports, that should be in a few days."

"What are you going to do then?"

He picked at his bandage. "Crawl into his life."

Of course, it was not that simple. To begin with, his wound had taken more out of him than he had realized or was willing to admit. Hard, sustained physical action made things shake inside him. But refusing to take any more recuperative time, he brushed aside his weakness along with Angela's concern. "The sonofabitch is back," he told her the following week. "I have to get moving." So he moved. Perhaps not as fast nor as vigorously as he would have liked, but at least he was taking action. Which, in this case, had to originate in Washington.

Thomas Worthington Ludlow, he discovered, lived in a century-old, Federalist mansion in Georgetown with his second wife (his first wife had died of cancer several years before) and a middle-aged housecouple. Consulting a recent renovation and building plan he had photocopied at the County Hall of Records, he was able to learn whatever he needed to know about the physical layout of the house. He also copied the floor plans of the houses on either side of Ludlow's. Then he holed up in a motel room, studied what he had, and decided on the equipment he would need.

Acquiring the equipment was no problem. Since he knew of every major electronics supplier in the capital area, he was able to pick up scattered pieces in a variety of places without arousing curiosity or suspicion. Even before Watergate, the town had a flourishing reputation as the bugging capital of the world. It was said that if you listened hard and carefully enough in the small hours of the night, you could literally hear the air over the city crackle with electronic devices. But the hard part was getting the equipment safely placed. To be caught or even observed in that particular act would wash out everything.

So he watched Ludlow's house, along with the houses on either side, almost around the clock. He saw their occupants come and go, noted their hourly and daily patterns, and weighed the possibilities open to him. It was unrelievedly hard, exhausting, and (as always) tedious work. The only time he was not bored, the only time he felt himself come alive and the adrenalin start pumping, was when he saw Ludlow leave or arrive at the house.

At such moments, wherever Burke happened to be—whether standing up the block, sitting in his parked car, or walking or driving slowly past—he felt so bright a pain in his arm and chest that it seemed to be threatening to tear a nerve. Sometimes, then, he would close his eyes and almost be able to imagine himself dead and in his private Hell. Since boyhood, he'd had his own personal vision of Hell, with mobs of naked people running through the snow, just running; no hellfire and brimstone, as in Dante, but only this frozen white landscape with all these poor slobs running and never stopping and never getting anywhere either. But not anymore. In his current vision of Hell, Burke was tied to a tree on a sun-dappled hilltop, while Ludlow kept snapping pictures of his ungrateful dead.

When the time was right, when Ludlow and his wife were off dancing at an embassy ball, and the housecouple were safely at their weekly church bingo festival, Burke went into the house with his equipment. Five generations of Ludlow wealth had gone into the house and its furnishings but to Burke, getting his initial breath of the close, overheated air, it was like being the first to enter a dead Pharoah's tomb. A fragrance had been left behind, faint as the whispers in a bank vault, and he felt a stir of pity for the woman who had worn the perfume. He had seen the second Mrs. Ludlow leaving and entering the house, a beautiful woman of perhaps half Ludlow's age, who probably needed no one's pity, least of all his. Nevertheless, he felt sorry for her. He had no idea why. Unless he sensed that no ultimate good could possibly come to anyone through close association with this man.

He worked quickly and well, pleased again at finding he had lost none of his skill. Like swimming and bike-riding, he thought. You just don't forget. He bugged two rooms: the upstairs master bedroom and the downstairs study, including the telephones in each. He carefully counted his tools as he put them back into their bag. Seven out, seven in. Forget a screwdriver in this business and you had an earthquake. Then he ran fine, barely visible wires into an unused basement storeroom of the adjoining house on the right, where he had set up his recording equipment two nights before. He made the necessary connections, flicked on the master switch, and left the dusty storeroom through the same rear, basement window he had entered fifteen minutes before.

It was a full week before he returned to the basement. Anxiously, he checked his equipment. The four specially made, oversized, voice-activated reels he had used were almost completely full. Together, they would carry more than forty hours of recorded sound. Burke removed them from the machine, replaced them with four fresh reels as possible insurance, and drove back to New York with them that same night. He was tempted to stop off at Angela's before going to his own apartment, but it was almost 4:00 A.M., her watchers would be coming on duty in another few hours, and he decided that for once in his life he needed sleep more than love.

He parked his car and carried his four precious reels of tape upstairs. A weak, sick perspiration seemed to leak from his body as he undressed. He felt drained. But there was also a soft, pleasant singing in his head. An angels' choir? More likely the devil's own glee club tuning up. Yet sliding into sleep, there was one beautiful, euphoric moment when he was sure things were going to turn out all right. But he did not remember this afterwards. When he awoke, there was only that confusing mixture of pain and expectation—and, of course, the four reels of tape beside his bed.

"If you really want to learn about people," Tony Kreuger had once told Burke during the early years, "just listen to them speak. And I don't mean only what they say. I mean the way they say it."

Burke recalled this as he listened to the first of the tapes. If he knew nothing at all about Tom Ludlow, if he had never met or even heard of him, he wondered what sort of image he would get from simply hearing him speak. For a while he tried listening coldly, dispassionately, pretending he was hearing the words of a stranger. But he soon gave up the attempt; both futile and stupid. This was no stranger he was hearing. It was Tom Ludlow. There was no way he could make himself forget that. And why would he want to try?

Still, there were surprises. There always were, Burke had found. They were all walking icebergs . . . two-thirds under water. Some hid even more. But rarely in the bedroom. And it was here that Ludlow turned out to be curiously abandoned, with a whimsically playful approach to sex that Burke would never have expected from him.

"Whose big, hot pistol are you?" purred the second Mrs. Ludlow.

To which came the heavily sugared reply, "I'm lil' pink pussy's big hot pistol."

Burke picked at his shoulder as he listened to a long run of heavy breathing and sweet mouthings.

"Big . . . hot . . . pistol's . . . all primed to go off," came the rhythmically passionate grunts.

"Go . . . go . . . go . . . !"

"Ride . . . ride, lil' pink pussy!"

"I'm ridin' . . . I'm ridin' . . ."

"Oh . . . oh . . . oh . . . !"

End of that segment.

Okay, big hot pistol, let's get on with it. Burke poured himself some fresh coffee. History books should be written with greater focus on the bedroom, he decided. It would help humanize the world's leaders. It was very hard to strike awesome poses while approaching climax.

A phone call from his daughter must have wakened Ludlow later that night.

"Did I wake you, Daddy?"

"No . . . no. It's all right. What is it, honey? What's wrong?" Ludlow's voice was instantly anxious and alert.

"I was dreaming about Mom again."

"The same things?"

"Pretty much. Only this time it was about that week we all went to Virginia Beach together. It was when we had the sailboat. Remember?"

"Of course. It was a lovely time."

"Yes, but why didn't I know it then?"

"You knew it," said Ludlow.

"No I didn't. Not really. I kept fighting with Mom all the time. And over such stupid little things."

"We all do that."

"Sometimes it seems all I ever did was scratch at her."

"She knew how you felt."

"I don't know whether she did, Daddy. And that's what bothers me more than anything."

"She knew. I've told you that before, darling."

"I wish I could believe it."

"It's the truth."

"I still miss her very much."

There was a pause. "So do I," said Ludlow.

Burke speeded up the tape. There was obviously going to be nothing in this portion that would be of any help to him. If anything, the reverse was true. This sort of thing only blurred his focus. He already knew that everything in life was not clearly black or white, that the human psyche had many varying sides. He needed no further lessons in that. All he needed now was some sign that this cutesy-pie stud and sensitive caring father was somehow involved with a great many people wanting him dead.

It was a long process. Because the tapes had been voice-activated, because when no sound was being picked up by the microphones, the recording machinery did not roll, the reels carried no blank places. The almost forty hours of tape carried almost forty hours of voices. The only thing that Burke could do to hurry the listening procedure along was to speed up the tape during those sections that carried the housecouple's voices or Ludlow's wife, gossiping with friends or speaking to local tradespeople. There appeared to be very little of that. But even this area proved to be not entirely without interest.

Rushing the tape through one of Ludlow's wife's calls, Burke abruptly slowed it to normal speed.

"I'm afraid I'm going to have to cancel out Tuesday," Jeanne Ludlow was saying. "Tom is flying to New York with the President for that United Nations thing and he wants me with him."

The unidentified male voice said, "Suddenly?"

"The President is taking his wife, and Tom wants me along to hold her hand."

"Oh, shit," said the man.

"Exactly. You know I'd much rather hold yours, darling."

"My what?"

She laughed coquettishly. "Whatever—it will have to wait for Friday."

"Unless Tom decides he needs you somewhere else."

"Don't be bitter, love. A husband does have some rights."

"Do you know it's been almost ten days? If this keeps up, you'll have me playing with myself."

"Don't you dare. That's criminal waste."

"This is the third time in two weeks you've had to cancel out because of Tom. What's this sudden need for your presence?"

"I don't know. But he does seem to be under especially heavy pressure lately. Even his moods have been strange."

"Do you think he suspects anything?"

"About you?"

"No. About those three other guys."

She giggled. "He doesn't think of me enough to suspect anything. Between his work and his daughter's calls, he's lucky if he gets a chance to breathe." Her voice took on a whining note of complaint. "You'd think the kid would have him climbing walls by now. But when it comes to her, he has nothing but patience. Her and her poor, dead mommy. I don't blame her for feeling guilty. She ate her mother's heart out while she was alive. Now that the woman is dead, she whines day and night."

"You're a tough lady."

"Am I? I don't mean to be. But I suppose I am kind

of resentful of Susan." She paused. "How could you love such a tough lady?"

"You have a tender ass."

"Well, that's telling it like it is."

"It was supposed to be a joke."

"Freud says nothing is said in a joke."

"Oh, fuck Freud."

"For that," she sighed, "I think I'd rather have you."·

Burke moved through the remainder of the segment quickly. In one form or another betrayal was apparently the order of the day. But of course it always had been. Many years before, he had been assigned to a full month of electronic surveillance and it had left him slightly paranoic on the subject. Whom could you trust? Were people really like nests of hibernating snakes? Or was the potential for betrayal an endemic part of the human condition and therefore acceptable on that basis? As he grew older, he stopped wrestling with such troubling philosophical concepts. He found it bad for his work as well as his psyche. He finally settled on a manageable peace. For sanity's sake alone, he decided, you had to stop trying to judge and understand the species, and just do your best to survive it. Some joke. But the segment of tape had at least contributed three additional features to his gradually rounding image of Tom Ludlow—namely, that he did seem to be under especially heavy pressure lately, his moods had become strange, and that his wife had apparently given him a large, pointed pair of cuckold's horns.

The hours ground on and the tape ran, stopped, speeded up, slowed, and ran again. It was like taking a long trip through someone's life, Burke thought. And he was so deeply immersed in it, that when the sound of police sirens or other traffic noises occasionally intruded from the streets below, it took him a moment to realize he was in his own apartment. Food was not important to him at any time, and he bothered even less with it now. When he thought

206

about eating at all, when the gnawing in his stomach became a distraction, he chewed on some bread and cheese. He became, in turn, impatient, bored, and worried. What if he followed the tape to its end and came up with nothing? What if this whole concept of Ludlow's involvement was actually no more than that—a concept? What if he found himself right back on square one? What if, what if, what if? Easy, he told himself. You've done this kind of thing before. You've grown middle-aged and half-senile doing it. You know the nature of the work. You know you have to dig through tons of crap to come up with even a gram of the shiny stuff. So just stop nagging at yourself and listen.

Then he came upon a fairly good stretch. Perhaps not gold, but with enough glitter to make him listen more closely. It was a telephone conversation with a man whom Ludlow addressed as Chris, with whom he was on familiar terms, and who evidently had something to do with running his financial affairs.

"What about the stocks?" Ludlow asked at one point. "Have you started unloading them yet?"

"A few small blocks. It's a shaky market. We have to be careful not to unsettle it even more."

"I don't care about the market. I just want it done. And as quickly as possible."

"We're going to get hurt on the price that way."

"So we'll get hurt."

"I don't understand why you insist on . . ."

"Chris . . ." Ludlow cut in quietly. "It's not necessary that you understand."

"Unless that appointment of yours is closer than rumors have it, you're not going to have to worry about possible conflict of interest problems for some time yet."

"I'm giving you a month. No more. At the end of that time I don't want to have a single share of common stock listed in my name. Is that understood?"

"You're crazy. It's going to cost you a fortune."

"Is that understood?" Ludlow's voice had taken on a cutting edge.

"If you'd only put some of that stock in trust . . ."

"Chris!"

"Okay, okay."

They clicked off.

Burke thought about it as he speeded the tape through some bedroom conversation followed by the usual sex. Interesting. It looked as though the rumors were true. Apparently Ludlow was going to be the next Secretary of State. And what plans had been made, what secret sessions held in Oval Office cabals to get rid of the current Secretary? He would probably hand in his resignation at the proper moment, Burke thought, for the customary personal reasons. Which meant what, as far as he, Richard Burke, was concerned? Probably nothing. Unless, and this was really reaching, since the Senate's approval of the appointment would be required, there might be some fear of his suddenly bursting forth with embarrassing accusations about the hilltop massacre.

Unlikely.

To begin with, who would believe so wild an accusation? Especially when brought by an unfrocked, faceless agent against so illustrious a national figure as Ludlow. And it would hardly be important enough for so much activity on the part of the Service. They wouldn't want him dead just for that. Or would they? What was it that Machiavelli, in his infinite political wisdom, had once said? "He who establishes a dictatorship and does not kill Brutus . . . or he who founds a republic and does not kill the sons of Brutus, will only reign a short time."

A bitter and cynically wise quote. But he was not even near to being Brutus, no Secretary of State had yet to be a dictator, and the republic had been well founded more than two hundred years ago. So much for Machiavelli, as applied to Richard Burke.

Nevertheless, there was enough built-in abrasion

in the segment to hold his attention a while longer. Or maybe, he thought, it was just having the rumor of the possible appointment confirmed that really hit him in the gut. So the wages of sin were finally high and honorable office. You murdered twenty-three men, women, and children, and eighteen years later they made you Secretary of State. Like a delayed-action fuse, a sudden sickness broke loose in him, as if something dead and rotten from the past was spreading through his system. Leaving the tape running, he went into the bathroom, knelt, and retched into the bowl. Eighteen years came up out of him along with the suddenly soured cheese and bread, came out with all the stink and crud of its long festering. Finally, there it went. Then kneeling on the hard, tile floor, he was afraid the poison had infected his brain as well as his stomach because he seemed to be hearing the voice of Tony Kreuger. Easy, he told himself for the second time in as many hours, or you're going to turn yourself into one very sick boy. This was no time to be imagining voices. This was a time for coolness and control and quiet, passionless thinking. This was a time for cold facts.

But the cold fact was: he was hearing Tony's voice. Grabbing a towel, he mopped his mouth dry as he went back to where the recording machine was going. He reversed the tape, then started it forward again at the point where he heard the dialing of the telephone in Ludlow's study and Tony's voice saying, "Hello?"

"Anything new?" Ludlow asked without amenity.

"Nothing good."

"What's happened?"

"We've lost a few more people and we're worse off than ever. We don't even have any promising lines out anymore."

"Congratulations."

"Well, we knew it wasn't going to be easy," said Kreuger.

"Marvelous. That makes me feel immeasurably better."

"I have an idea I'm going to try."

"Yes?"

"We've been using his wife, his ex-wife, much too subtly. We can't be that cautious anymore. It's been a waste. I don't believe he knows she's even in the city."

"So?"

"So I want to make sure he knows. And I want him worried enough to get a little careless."

"And how are you going to manage that?" Ludlow's voice was cold. "Right now I'm the one who's worried enough to get a little careless. We're going to run out of time if this drags on much longer."

"We're all doing our best, Tom," Tony said quietly. "And we've lost some good people doing it."

"I know, I know. This whole business is making me impatient and edgy. There's so much at stake I'm starting to have nightmares about it. Imagine. One man."

"I suppose there is almost classic irony to it."

"If I was less directly involved, I might be able to appreciate it more. As it is, I sometimes wonder whether we're not getting a bit paranoid about him. We could be exaggerating the threat, you know. There is that possibility."

"We've gone over that a hundred times. Are you willing to take that chance?"

Ludlow did not answer.

"I'm not," said Tony. "I know Richard. And I don't think we're exaggerating the threat in the slightest. He's a walking timebomb. If I wasn't wholly convinced of that, I'd never have gone this far to begin with. You know how I feel about him. So you also know no part of this has been easy for me."

"Yes. Of course." A long, deep breath fluttered over the tape. "All right. What's this idea of yours about his wife?"

"I don't especially like it. But as you said, time is

running out. I'm going to make her a burglary and assault victim that will hurt her enough to put her in the hospital. Then I'll arrange heavy news coverage to insure Richard's knowing about it. He cares about that woman. I don't think he'll be able to resist seeing her under those conditions."

"I hope you're right."

"It'll take a few days to set up. I'll be in touch if I have any news."

There were several more moments of conversation before the phone connection was broken, but Burke only half-listened. When he heard them hang up, he turned off the tape and sat very still, staring at it. His stomach, still unsettled, sent new messages of dread. He had been right about Ludlow, but this knowledge only added to the infection. Tony had called him a threat, a walking timebomb, yet there had been no mention of why. And Ludlow's appointment as Secretary of State was still not reason enough.

Then his mind went to Tony's plans for Angela and he swore at himself for not thinking of her first. How self-absorbed could he get? Tony had said the thing would take a few days to set up, but it was hard to pinpoint the exact date on which the conversation had been recorded. Fortunately, it was near the beginning of the last reel. Which meant it had probably been taped within the past day or two. He checked the time. He would have to wait at least another two hours before Angela's watcher left at midnight and it would be safe to go over there. His good friend, Tony. He had thought himself past reacting to these things, but suddenly felt threatened with a fine madness.

Raging, frustrated, unable to bear the best of his thoughts, feeling the panic of a trapped animal with hounds near to ripping his flesh, he turned on the tape once more. He speeded through the houseman's argument with a cheating plumber, listened to another segment of the big hot pistol communing with

211

his lil' pink pussy, heard a long stretch of Susan Ludlow's guilt-inspired efforts to exorcise her dead mother's ghost, and accepted the small satisfactions of several more adulterous conversations conducted by Ludlow's wife.

Then near the end of the reel the tape was again activated by a ringing telephone. "Yes?" said Ludlow.

"Hello, Tom." It was a husky, male voice that sounded tired and, to Burke, vaguely familiar. "Sorry I couldn't get back to you sooner, but it's been one hell of a day."

"I can imagine. I was just wondering whether the doctor had anything more to say."

"He's putting me into Walter Reed on Friday for some additional tests. It'll just be overnight. The press release will call it a routine physical."

Burke slowly straightened in his chair. He had just realized why the caller's voice sounded familiar. It belonged to the president of the United States.

"You still feeling lousy?" said Ludlow.

"It's really more tiredness than anything else. There's no pain. It's just that halfway through the day, my ass starts dragging."

"Then leave the office earlier."

"Know any more good jokes?"

"If you really want to, you can do it."

"Bullshit. Wait till you're in here. You'll soon see what I mean. You sure you're ready to stick your balls in the big ringer?"

"I'm not sure of anything right now," said Ludlow.

"You suddenly sound like I feel. What's the matter?"

"Nothing. It's just that every once in a while I guess this Burke thing starts getting to me."

"It'll be taken care of. Forget it."

"I wish I had your confidence."

"When you've been in this office as long as I have, when you've seen what can be accomplished from this particular room, you'll have my confidence."

"We're running out of time."

"I told you to forget it. When did you become such a damned worrier?"

Ludlow grunted softly. "I suppose when you first told me I was going to be president."

Burke reached out with his good arm and switched off the tape. He did not want to hear any more for now, not for at least another few minutes. He did not feel capable of accepting another word. It was enough to have learned that the president of the United States, with the full might of his office behind him, evidently headed the growing list of those who wanted him dead. Talk about overkill. This was in the same category as exterminating a roach with a nuclear warhead. But even more incredible at that moment was the fact that Tom Ludlow, in some as yet unexplained way, was apparently slated to become the next president of the United States.

Moving slowly, a sudden invalid, Burke pushed himself up and walked to the window. The Hudson flowed darkly, looking cold and dangerous far below. Downriver on the New Jersey shore among the piers and warehouses a huge electric sign etched its statement to the world in letters of fire: KELLY'S KATFOOD. Burke stared out at it. Search the night for help, dig for clues to your future in the surrounding blackness, and what did you come up with? KELLY'S KATFOOD. Perfect. It was absolutely fitting. The electric oracle spoke with unforked tongue. Put your faith in KELLY'S KATFOOD, it declared, and your illusions would remain intact, would never be subject to betrayal. There were lessons to be learned here, but it was too late for him to learn them. He had already spent most of his life committed to loyalties and beliefs that could not stand up under hard examination. And he couldn't blame Tony for that. Very early, his friend put him on warning. "Believe in nothing and no one. Believe only in the state. That's the only thing we're working for—the perpetuation of our form of government. Nothing else matters.

Nothing else can stand up under investigation."
Well, he hadn't taken the warning and Tony had
been proven right. Nothing else could stand up under investigation. He had shown himself to be naive
and sentimental and it had turned out to be fatal to a
lot of people. Still even now he did not consider himself capable of acting otherwise.

Burke turned away from the window, went back to
the tape, and switched on the machine once more.

"Not having second thoughts, are you?" he heard
the president say.

"You know me better than that. Sometimes I
think I've been preparing for this all my life. Maybe
I have, if you believe in fate, or destiny, or whatever."

The president laughed softly. "What I believe
about fate, Tom, is pretty much what you believe:
that every now and then it has to be helped along
with a shove in the right direction. My getting sick
may have been pure fate. But all the rest . . . my deciding not to run for a second term, my keeping it
quiet while I set you up in my place, my twisting the
necessary arms to make certain there's no slip-up at
the convention this summer . . . well . . ." He chuck-
led again. "I'd say that all comes under the heading
of pure shove."

"And I appreciate it."

"You don't have to appreciate a damned thing.
You should know by now there's nothing personal in
this for me." The husky voice had turned dry, sar-
donic. "At times, I'm not even sure I like you. The
only thing I really care about is that you're the one
man I know with enough strength, brains, background, and prominence to get elected to this office,
and then run it the way it has to run if we're going to
survive the chaos that threatens the world today.
And perhaps most vital of all, you're without either
sentiment or conscience. Whatever has to be done for
our survival, I know you'll do—whether it be the
wasting of a dozen enemy cities in a pre-emptive

strike, or sacrificing a dozen of our own to save the rest. The nature of our world is such, that for a leader to indulge himself in sentiment or conscience is to abandon his people. History has proven itself to be totally amoral. It doesn't know what a conscience is. Try running a country according to Sunday School principles, and you'll soon be presiding over a catastrophe."

For the first time, Ludlow himself laughed. "Do you think the people would elect me on that platform?"

"The people are fools. Left to their own devices, they'd invariably elect all the wrong leaders for all the wrong reasons. Which happens to be one of the built-in hazards of our democratic process. Fortunately, they're rarely left to their own devices. They're usually conned, bullied, or mesmerized into performing at least an approximation of the proper action."

The president coughed harshly, hackingly and it took him a moment to regain his breath. "Take yourself as an example," he went on more quietly. "If you and Kreuger are correct in your estimate of the situation and our friend, Burke, did start screaming about your being a mass murderer the minute he learned you were about to run for the presidency, the good people of Ameica would sooner lynch than elect you. Never realizing, of course, that the very qualities that made it possible for you to shoot those people for the good of the country are the same qualities that would make you a superb chief executive."

"You make me want to stand up and cheer," said Ludlow.

The president was coughing again. "Christ," he gasped bitterly. "And there was a time I could talk for ten hours straight without even a goddamned sip of water."

"You'll feel better."

"Sure."

"I hear they're doing remarkable things with chemotherapy."

"I'll still be dead in three years."

"You never know about these things."

"You don't know. I know."

"Listen," said Ludlow. "You're only president, not God."

"You mean there's a difference?"

They both laughed.

"I'll speak with you tomorrow," said the president. "And for God's sake, stop worrying about Burke. I'm sure we'll have him before we have to announce you."

"And if we don't?"

"Then we'll stop him the minute he comes out of his hole to do his screaming. And finally he'll have to come out to be heard."

"Tony Kreuger has a theory about that," said Ludlow. "He doesn't believe Burke will do any screaming at all if he finds out I'll be running for president."

"What do you mean?"

"Kreuger remembers Burke's reaction to the episode in question eighteen years ago. He thinks he'd sooner kill me than see me president. He thinks he'd feel that strongly about it."

"Your friend Burke sounds like an utter fanatic."

"He's a good, essentially moral man."

"That's exactly the stuff utter fanatics are made of," said the president. "Do you want protection?"

"Hell, no! Not now, anyway. If we have to announce my candidacy before we get him, we'll talk about it then."

They hung up a moment later and Burke switched off the tape. He felt battered as a shipwrecked sailor, yet somehow relaxed. Finally, it all made sense, and there was an odd sort of relief in simply that. Just knowing a reason was a special kind of luxury for him. They were right to want me dead, he thought

216

with a feeling very akin to elation. Perfectly right. They had absolutely no choice in this.

He squinted at the silent reel of tape, seeing it as though it were far away, half-hidden in mist. Righteousness, he thought heavily. Everyone was always so damned sure of their righteousness—Tony, Ludlow, the president himself. And anyone who disagreed, anyone who dared think differently, was branded fool, traitor, or infidel. The murderers of the Crusades, the animals of the Inquisition, the slaughterers of how many legally sanctified tribunals were also sure of their righteousness . . . breaking bodies, pouring blood, untouched by anguish, always certain that theirs was the one true way, their solution the one bearing God's holy image.

All right, he thought, and his brief elation was gone. At least I know it all.

Shortly after midnight he picked up a cab on Broadway and had the driver let him off two blocks from Angela's apartment. The watcher was gone, but it was not until Burke was in the apartment and actually saw her that some part of the tension went out of him.

He kissed and held her. "Miss me?"

"Mmm. Don't ever leave me for that long again." She pulled back to examine him. "You look awful."

"Thanks."

"Didn't you get any sleep at all?"

"Enough."

She laughed. "That's funny. I mean my saying you look awful. With that new face of yours, how can I really know how you look? Good or bad."

"Does my face still bother you?"

"Yes. I can't stand your looking so much younger than I."

"Okay, we'll have a job done on you too," he said and heard a faint whisper of something unpleasant.

She put both hands to her face, fingers pulling the skin taut. "I could do with a little tightening."

"Angela . . ."

The single word and the way he said it was enough to set sirens screaming. It changed her entire mood. "What is it? God, I'm stupid. Here I've been prattling like an idiot and haven't even asked you what happened." She looked at him. "You've found out something, haven't you?"

"Yes. Pretty much the whole thing. I'll tell you about it later. Right now I have to get you out of here, fast. Tony's tired of waiting for me to discover you by myself. He's going to put you in the hospital and give it to the media so I can't miss it."

"What do you mean put me in the hospital?"

"Burglary . . . assault . . . probably a little nice, friendly rape thrown in for flavor."

"Are you serious?" She shook her head impatiently. "What's wrong with me? Of course you're serious. When is all this supposed to happen?"

"I'm not sure. It could be anytime—tonight, tomorrow night, the night after that. But it'll happen."

She was already in motion. "What should I take?"

"Pack one bag."

He followed her into the bedroom, pulled down a valise from a closet shelf for her, then watched as she filled it. She worked in silence, frowning a little in concentration, doing what had to be done quickly and efficiently. How beautifully she moves, he thought, and how well she has learned to accept things. No fuss, no wasted anger, no whining, no self-pity. Christ, I'm lucky. Then realizing how few would have considered him lucky at that moment, he laughed.

"What's so funny?" Bent over the valise, she did not turn or miss a beat.

"I was just thinking what a cute ass you have."

"A woman's ass isn't supposed to be funny. It's supposed to be erotic."

"Later it'll be erotic."

She took an armful of sweaters from a drawer,

chose two for the valise and returned the rest. "Will I ever be coming back here?"

"I don't know."

"Should I pack for hot or cold?"

"For a while it's not going to matter. You won't be doing any moving around. Whatever else you'll need later we'll buy."

"Are we rich?"

He smiled. "Money's not going to be our problem."

She threw some jeans in the bag. "Where are we going?"

"To my place. At least for now."

"Will I be able to call my office?"

"You mean the guy with the moustache?"

"He deserves some word."

"One short call."

"What should I tell him?"

"Whatever you like."

"Please, Richard, I suddenly can't think."

"Just say you have to leave town for personal reasons. A family crisis of some sort. Illness. Whatever. Tell him you're sorry to have to cut out without notice, and you have no idea whether you'll even be back." He was watching her eyes but could not tell what she was thinking. "How is he going to take that?"

"Miserably."

"And what about you?"

"I've reached the point where the only thing that can make me miserable is not being with you."

"Well, we've sure come to this the hard way." He kissed her. "Come on, let's get out of here. This place is suddenly making me very nervous."

He had her leave the house first and watched her walk west until she reached Park Avenue. Then he followed with her bag. He did not want to get into a taxi with her in this area in case they checked back later. But they did pick up a cab together on Broadway, left it on West End Avenue about four blocks from where he lived, and walked the rest of the way.

She gazed up at the faded elegance of the building on the corner of Riverside Drive and Eighty-fourth Street. "I've wondered where you lived. I like it. It has great dignity. And practically nothing has that anymore. Does it also have a view of the river?"

"Absolutely."

"Then I love it."

He went in alone to check the lobby and elevator, found them clear, then quickly brought her upstairs and into the apartment. With the door finally locked behind him, he closed his eyes and leaned back against it.

She looked at him anxiously. "You okay? Your arm bothering you?"

"You're bothering me. It's different than being alone. I was never this nervous about myself."

She came close and her body pressed his. "Is that because you're so crazy for me?"

"Damned right."

"Isn't that lovely," she said and went to explore the apartment, hurrying from room to room like a child in search of hidden presents. He followed, watching her face with its changing expressions, feeling the joy of her presence.

"It's insane," she said, "but I'm almost glad Tony forced us into this."

"Yes, wasn't that nice of him? It pays to have friends in high places."

In his studio now she stopped before her unfinished portrait still on the easel. Looking at it, she was obviously moved.

"I'm afraid it's not very good," he apologized, always a bit self-conscious about his painting where she was concerned. She was too perceptive about such things, understood too much. It made him feel stripped down in front of her. "I started it right after I saw you at the museum that second time. You weren't happy that day and you sat for awhile in front of Rembrandt's *Old Woman.* Do you remember?"

"I remember. Where were you?"

"In the next gallery, quietly dying."

"Is that why you painted the tear on my cheek?"

"I'm not sure. I guess I just needed to see you crying for me a little."

"I cried for you. A lot."

"Yes, but I never saw."

She turned then and he saw. "It's beautiful," she said. "I only wish I looked that good."

"You look better."

"Maybe ten or fifteen years ago."

"You just looked younger then, not better."

She smiled. "My God, you really do love me, don't you?"

"Did you ever doubt it?"

"No. Not really. Just as I didn't doubt my loving you. But that was never my problem. I told you. My only problem then was not being able to live with you."

"And now?"

"Oh, I can manage to live with you very beautifully now. It's just that the bastards won't let me."

"Well, you're at least with me."

"Isn't it wonderful? I swear I feel like a bride." She hugged him, but came back to reality fast. "Now tell me everything you've found out."

He told her over whisky and coffee, watching her face all the while, finding there an almost exact reflection of his own feeling. Did love finally create its own emotional clones? At times it did seem so. She had become a virtual mirror image of the way he felt, seemed attached to him through an invisible network of fibers. And at the end, out of this same incredible union of feelings, her first words actually duplicated his own initial reaction . . . "At least we know it all."

But what practical value this fact would have for their future remained to be seen. In the meantime, thought Burke, it was enough that they were alive, whole, and together. He thought very much the same thing while they were making love later and, after that, as she lay sleeping beside him for the first time in his bed, in his apartment. He thought it as he listened to her soft breathing in the warm, friendly dark. "Sonofabitch," he whispered with the total lucidity that seems to come only in those few final seconds before sleep, "what else is there?"

21

David Tomschin stood beside the open grave, squinting into the sun and not really listening to the words of the priest. Some of the words were in Latin and he would not have understood them anyway, but this had little to do with his lack of attention. What he was concentrating on mostly, was the feel of the revolver in his right-hand coat pocket. The gun and its intended purpose were the only things that made the small ceremony bearable. Without them David was sure he would either be screaming by now or else dashing for the horizon. Which would have upset the priest no end, he thought. As it was, the poor man was disturbed enough by certain of his attitudes, as well as by the depressing lack of mourners.

To David funerals were nothing more than a performance in any case, and he would not have bothered with this one at all if he had not felt Dolores would have wanted it. So he had gone to a nearby Catholic church and talked to a priest. The priest was warm, kind, very sincere, and asked a lot of questions.

"What was your relationship to the deceased?"

"I loved her."

"I see," said the priest, although he did not really see at all. "Then you were not married?"

"No."

"How did she . . ." The priest glanced at his notes. "How did Dolores die?"

"She was shot."

The priest looked like a middle-aged choir boy—blonde, blue-eyed, scrubbed, and shining. Still, his eyes could show pain. "Aah." He hesitated. "She . . . she didn't shoot herself, did she?"

"No, Father."

He appeared relieved. "Does she have any family?"

"No. Not here anyway. She had a grandfather in Paraguay."

The priest's glance held steady, not sliding off his face as most people's did, and David was impressed. What a way to have to judge people, he thought . . . by how well they can put up with my face.

"I take it Dolores belonged to no church, had no priest, no confessor of her own?"

"No, but she believed in God and was very religious. She had all these small, plaster saints. I don't know what I'm going to do with them now. Would you like to have them, Father?"

"If you want to give them to the church, I'll be happy to accept them. Are you Catholic?"

"No. I'm Jewish. But I've done a lot of reading about your God, as well as about six or seven others."

"They're all really one."

"With all due respect, Father . . . I have this theory about God actually being a Committee. I mean, I can't believe anybody could have messed things up for us this badly all by Himself."

The priest looked unhappy. "You're too young to be so bitter."

"Take a good look at my face, Father. This kind of thing ages you fast."

"What happened?"

"An accident. Or one of the Committee's little jokes. You can take your choice."

The priest's choice was to change the subject. "You don't want a church or chapel service?"

"No. There'll just be me there. And maybe one other person." Then almost compulsively, David heard himself add, "She was a prostitute. Not at the end. But before that."

224

The priest looked at him.

"I just thought I should let you know."

"Did you expect it to make a difference?"

"I don't know, Father." David felt stupid. "There might have been special kinds of prayers."

"God doesn't split hairs. We're all His children."

David nodded. Sensational. The only catch was in getting yourself to buy it.

The priest arranged for a gravesite on Long Island, and two days later they drove out in David's car, a very short, single-unit cortege behind the hearse. The cemetery itself was new and flat, with acres of unused open space. Five years before the entire area had been potato fields and the land still stretched, treeless and unbroken, to the horizon. A bell rang as they entered the gates, and the priest told David to park for ten minutes while the hearse went on alone. "They have to prepare things. The bereaved are often sensitive to the sight of raw earth."

They sat together, facing sky and brown grass. The sun was bright and seemed to hold the promise of spring. David stared straight ahead. There had been little conversation during the drive out. The priest had tried several times, but David barely responded. Now the priest said, "It won't help her, you know."

David looked at him.

"The gun," said the priest. "It's not going to do your Dolores any good at all. Not one bit."

"I don't know what you're talking about. What gun?"

"The one in your right-hand coat pocket."

David said nothing.

"I had a waterfront parish for thirteen years," said the priest. "It got so I could spot a pistol under four layers of clothing at fifty yards. And I've yet to see anything good come out of one of them."

But David's face was closed.

A moment later they received the signal that the

225

grave was cosmeticized and ready, and they drove into the cemetery.

Now, beside the flower-draped casket, the priest droned on. He was a good man, thought David, who surely deserved a larger and more attentive audience for his words than he had here today. Although God's ears and Dolores' soul were probably all that were technically required.

Staring into the sun, David saw a car appear. It stopped a short distance away and a man got out, his bald head shining in the yellow haze. It was Sam Ellman.

The agent came up behind the priest, walked around him and stopped a few feet from David. Bowing his head respectfully, he became the second mourner, a short, round man in a tweed coat much too long from him. The priest did not appear to notice his arrival, but his voice rose slightly, to acknowledge the doubling of his congregation. David looked at the agent just once, then lowered his head and gazed at the ground. He refused to trust himself to look at him again. Ellman had said he would try to be there, but David had not really expected him. In this, at least, the man had somehow managed to tell the truth.

The priest's prayers ended, two cemetery workers lowered the casket into the grave, and the first shovelful of earth hit with that most final of all sounds. Goodbye, thought David. Goodbye. But it meant nothing. He had already said his goodbyes. His mind was now on something else.

Ellman approached him. "I'm sorry about being late. There was an accident on the Expressway. It held up traffic for half an hour. I'm really sorry."

David nodded.

"My apologies to you, too, Father," Ellman said. "But I'm afraid it couldn't be helped."

"These things happen," said the priest.

They walked from the grave.

226

"Father," said David, "this is Sam Ellman. He knew Dolores."

The two men shook hands as they walked.

David said, "I wonder if you could get a lift back with the hearse, Father. There are a few things I have to go over with Sam. Would you mind?"

"Not at all."

"I appreciate everything you've done."

The priest half bowed with his head, then got into the front of the hearse beside the driver. They drove off and David held up a shaking hand. "Got time for a fast drink? There's a place just down the road."

The agent nodded.

David led the way in his car and Ellman followed. The tavern was about a mile away, a fake Tudor building with a neon Budweiser sign in the window. There were about a dozen cars and trucks in the dirt parking area and David pulled in among them. Then he got out and waited for Ellman's car. When Ellman had parked, David opened the door of the passenger's side, slid in and shoved the muzzle of his revolver against his ribs.

"Okay. Drive out of here."

"David . . ."

David rammed the gun into his stomach this time. "Just drive."

The agent drove. Sitting close, David watched him carefully. He had him, by God. And with what surprise! Which pleased him as much as anything. The man had been so unsuspecting of his true feelings, that he had actually come to the funeral. Finally he was doing some of the sly-foxing. It had not been easy for him. He had wanted to go after Ellman that same night. For once, though, he had stayed cool and thought it through. He had pretended to accept Dolores' murder as an accident. Ellman had swallowed it whole.

A short distance down the road, David had the agent drive behind a screen of trees. Then he took

227

the keys from the ignition. "Okay, get out. And carefully, because I'm very nervous."

Ellman obeyed. His face was blank and chilled.

"Now take out your gun with two fingers and drop it," David ordered, having seen this particular bit in a hundred TV police dramas. Who said TV wasn't educational?

When the pistol was on the ground, David kicked it to one side. "Now walk straight ahead."

Fifty yards into the brush, David sat Ellman against a tree and took the same position, facing him. Gripping the revolver with both hands, he drew up his knees for support and aimed the weapon at Ellman's head. "Now maybe we can talk," he said and was pleased at the natural quality of his voice. Incredible. The things you could finally get yourself to do.

"Okay if I smoke my pipe?" Ellman asked.

"No."

"That gun is making me very edgy."

"Try sucking your goddamned thumb."

"I don't understand, David. What are you trying to do?"

"It's very simple. I'm trying to discover even one small reason why I shouldn't kill you."

A yellow shaft of sun caught Ellman's face.

"Perhaps that's not true," David said. "Perhaps I just want to enjoy seeing you sweat before I shoot. And do you know where you're going to get it?" David took one hand off the gun and tapped the center of his forehead. "Right here. Right where Dolores got it. Which is what they call poetic justice."

Ellman was silent. He had the look of a man who was thinking very hard and fast and wanted nothing to intrude on his concentration.

"Did you know I was a writer?" David said, then shook his head. "But of course you knew. You know everything about me. Though I guess I'm not really a writer, only a poor slob trying to be one. At least that's what I was doing before you came into my life

228

and turned it upside down. How does it feel to have that kind of power over people's lives? Pretty good?"

"You're the one who has it now. You tell me."

"It's terrific. I wish I'd had it sooner." David looked at the pink, plump, innocuous face over the barrel of his gun and waited for a responsive flood of anger and hate. But for the moment the agent simply looked like his Uncle Louie to him and it was hard to get too worked up about Uncle Louie as a consummate image of evil. "Tell me. Is there a special kick you get in going to the funeral of someone you murdered?"

"I didn't murder Dolores, David. That was just a tragic accident."

"Bullshit! She died because of you. No one else. You promised there'd be no shooting. Or have you forgotten that part?"

"There had to be shooting. Burke was getting away."

"I swear to God; I should give it to you right now."

"You're not going to shoot me, David," Ellman said tiredly. "You may play with me for a while to soothe your own survival guilt, but you're not going to pull that trigger. You're not made that way."

David looked at Ellman and smiled. He was still smiling as he raised the pistol to eye level, took careful aim, and fired. The gun kicked up with the explosion and Ellman slammed against the scrub oak behind him. Then he slowly fell over onto his left side.

David raised his head and sat listening to the echoes. Overhead a flock of crows took off, complaining loudly. Then there was only the faint, irregular hum of traffic from the road.

Ellman squirmed brokenly on the ground.

"You see?" David said quietly. "You don't really know as much about me as you thought. Maybe six months ago I wouldn't have been able to pull that trigger, but I have learned a lot since then. You've been a good teacher. You've made a very practical

229

man out of me, given me an advanced degree in survival. In fact you've taught me so well, you're probably going to die of it."

With much painful effort Ellman managed to work himself up into a sitting position. Blood oozed from a small hole in the left shoulder of his coat. His normally pink face was a pale, jaundiced yellow. If it carried any expression at all, it was one of faint surprise.

"David . . ." The agent's voice was hoarse, unfamiliar. "Whatever I did, it wasn't for myself. There were good reasons."

"There are always good reasons. But you were right about my survival guilt. I blame myself for Dolores almost as much as I blame you. I blame myself for trusting and believing you. You lied about Burke, about his being a double agent, about his having sold out, and I believed you. You lied about just wanting to take him prisoner, and I believed you again. You lied when you said there'd be no shooting and I believed you."

"I never expected the girl to be hurt."

David did not seem to hear him. "You see . . . I've been doing a lot of thinking these past days, and I've decided you're really not a very nice man. Oh, you seem decent enough. You're not openly cruel or brutal. You talk reasonably. You're a Jew, familiar with the tragedy of the Jews. All of which doesn't make you seem like too bad a guy, does it?"

David aimed the gun at Ellman's forehead, then lowered it. "You get the next shot right where Dolores got it."

"I still don't believe you're going to kill me, David."

"You just keep believing that."

"Whatever you've learned, it hasn't been enough to turn you into a murderer."

"What turned you into one?"

"I'm no murderer."

"You want me to dig up Dolores and give you a good look?"

Ellman's mouth twitched and for a moment there was something confused and uncertain in his usually confident face. "I have faith that what I'm doing is . . ."

"I spit on your faith," David cut in harshly. "It scares hell out of me. Have enough faith in anything . . . God, government or the price of tomatoes, and sooner or later somebody's going to be dying of it. I think I'm going to start a new crusade. Not for any God or government . . . but for the greater glory of nonfaith."

David stopped. Ellman was no longer listening. Slumped against the tree, he had quietly passed out.

David sat there, the gun still resting on his knees, still pointing at the agent. The sun felt pleasant on his head and he lifted his face for more of its warmth. He was aware of the treetrunk, rough and hard against his back, and some birds, fluttering in the branches overhead.

"The bastard," he swore softly. But there was little real anger left in him. What animals we are, he thought.

There were rustling sounds behind him in the brush and he turned to see Father Mulcahy running heavily towards him. Red-faced and puffing, the priest looked at the unconscious agent, then at the gun in David's hand, then, with horror, at Ellman once more.

"It's okay, Father," David said. "He's not dead. He just fainted."

The priest stood gasping for breath, his face working. "What an idiot I am. We were ten miles away before I was even able to figure any of it out."

Father Mulcahy bent over Ellman, examined the wound, felt his pulse. "Who is he?"

"A government agent."

The priest shook his head. "We'd better get him to a hospital."

David felt oddly lightheaded and silly, as though he had just come off some sort of high. "Why can't we just leave him here for the crows?"

"It's not funny, David. And for heaven's sake, put that gun away."

"Yes sir, Father!"

With the help of the driver, they carried Ellman to the road and put him in the hearse. Stretched out flat, he slowly revived, opened his eyes and looked around. "Don't I rate a coffin, Father?"

"You don't need one quite yet."

"It's okay. I don't mind waiting." Then seeing David outside the open doors, the agent managed a faint smile. "Well, don't look so damn miserable. You've had your fun."

David turned away. Ah, God, he thought. I hope I haven't made a terrible mistake. I hope I'm not going to regret letting this man live.

22

The offices of the Hemisphere Corporation were located in one of the newer skyscrapers in the Wall Street area, a steel and glass tower whose top was lost in a low-hanging cloud as Pamela and Hank approached. They entered the lobby and took an express elevator to the fiftieth floor.

"Whom would you like to see?" asked the receptionist.

Pamela started to answer, but stopped herself and waited for Hank. "George Reese," he said.

"Do you have an appointment?"

"Yes."

"May I have your names, please?"

"Pamela Bailey and Hank Ryan."

The receptionist spoke softly into a phone, then said, "Mr. Collier will be with you in a few moments. Please have a seat."

They sat down side by side in two straightbacked chairs and stared at the white walls, bare except for two colorprints of Yellowstone National Park. Pamela touched Hank's sleeve. He looked at her, half-smiled, then stared at the walls once more. He'll probably never forgive me, she thought. I've kept him from ruining both our lives, and every time he looks at me it's as though he's seeing me betraying him in bed with three other men.

It was nine days since the telephone ambush and their supposed freedom from threat, and she had not enjoyed a minute of it. Not that there had been any recriminations. Hank had not even mentioned the subject. It was as though Burke and the ambush had never existed. Which meant, of course, that he was thinking of nothing else. Wanting to get it out into the open, hoping to exorcise Burke's ghost with a good, cleansing fight, she had tried baiting Hank.

"What's the matter?" she asked one day. "Is something hurting you? Are you in some kind of terrible pain?"

He shook his head. The effort of talking seemed to have become too much for him.

"Then what's wrong? Why are you walking around with that look on your face?"

"What look?"

"Like someone's been beating on you with a bat."

He said nothing.

"Do you miss the idea of going to jail? Is that what's bugging you?"

"Leave me alone, Pamela."

"No, damn it! I won't leave you alone. For the first time in weeks we're able to walk around without a cloud over our heads and . . ."

"We don't know that," he cut in. "We don't know anything, really. It's been days now and we haven't heard a word from Reese."

"We did our part. We did everything he asked. So what do you expect to hear from him? A singing telegram of congratulations?"

"I don't know. But we should hear something."

She had been worrying about the same thing but was afraid to admit it. "If anything went wrong, we'd have heard fast enough."

He retreated into silence once more.

"Anyway, that's not what's really bothering you," she said. "You're still more concerned about Eric than about us. And that's what infuriates me most."

His eyes were cold. "Get off my back. I went along with it, didn't I? Eric's dead, isn't he? If I can't jump up and down with joy over it, I'm sorry. I apologize. But I didn't know that was part of the contract." Stiffly, he got up and walked out of the room.

Pamela sat looking after him. Some days, she

thought, you can't even get yourself into a decent fight.

When a full week had passed and there was still no word from Reese, Hank had said, "Something's wrong. I think we should call that number he gave us."

"He said it was only for emergencies."

"Well what do you think this is?"

It was Hank who finally put the call through. A woman answered. "Hemisphere Corporation. May I help you?"

"I want to speak to George Reese."

"Who's calling?"

"Hank Ryan."

"One moment please."

There was a click, and a moment later a man's voice said, "Yes?"

"Hello, Reese?"

"Mr. Ryan?"

"Yeah."

"Mr. Reese isn't available right now. Perhaps I can help you."

"Who are you?"

"My name is Collier. Herbert Collier. I'm one of Mr. Reese's associates."

"I've got to talk to Reese himself."

"Could you tell me what it's in reference to?"

"It's personal."

"I see," said Collier. "Would you like to leave a number where Mr. Reese can reach you?"

"He has my number. When will he be in so I can call again?"

"That's hard to say. He's in and out. But if you'd like, I can check his calendar and set up an appointment for you to see him."

"Sure. That'll be great."

"How about tomorrow afternoon at three?"

"That's okay. Where do I go?"

Collier gave him the address of the Hemisphere Corporation in lower Manhattan, said goodbye, and hung up. Hank slowly put down the receiver. "You ever hear of anything called the Hemisphere Corporation?" he asked Pamela.

"No. What is it?"

"I don't know. But we've got an appointment to meet Reese there tomorrow afternoon."

They had been waiting in the reception area for about ten minutes when a tall, thin man came out to greet them. He had a face like a wedge, sharp and intimidating. Then he smiled and was rendered human. "I'm Herbert Collier," he said and shook hands. "And I'm also something of an idiot." He grinned at Hank. "Reese spoke of you a great deal. He was a big fan of yours from way back. And I didn't even realize who you were yesterday until you'd hung up."

Hank shrugged. "That's old history."

"Never mind. Apparently, you were first rate. Among the top few. And a hard line of work. That's something I can respect."

Helplessly Hank felt the same flood of warmth he experienced each time his fight career was remembered by someone. When would he get over it? When would he start getting some of his kicks from now?

Collier led them down a long, bare corridor and into a corner office that overlooked the harbor. From fifty stories up the Statue of Liberty looked very small and insignificant.

"Where's Reese?" Hank asked when they were seated.

Collier considered the question from behind a large, bare desk. "I'm afraid I had to lie to you about Reese. He's not going to be here."

"Why not?"

"Because he's dead."

Pamela and Hank looked at him.

"Unfortunately," said Collier, "things failed to turn out exactly as planned. It wasn't your fault. You did everything that was expected of you. You held Burke on the phone long enough for the call to be traced, and Reese and three other agents were able to move in. We know that from a brief radio message Reese sent from his car. It was the last communication we ever had from him. He and his men were found on a West Side rooftop the following day. They had been shot to death."

Hank felt his ears ringing. It was precisely the same sensation he used to get from a punch to the side of the head. "And what . . . what about Burke?"

"We can only assume he shot them."

"All four of them?" said Pamela.

Collier shrugged. "One man was killed by a single bullet from a .38 caliber revolver that hasn't been found. The other three were shot with a submachine gun that apparently belonged to the first man killed. This weapon was left at the scene. Someone with Burke's training and experience is quite capable of pulling off something like that."

"Then he's still out there somewhere?" asked Hank.

"Very much so."

Hank was afraid to look at Pamela. He had no idea what his face might show. Things were taking place inside him that he wanted to keep private.

"And what about us?" Pamela said. "What sort of position are we in now?"

"A reasonably good one," said Collier. "Unless you're afraid of possible retribution from Burke. If you'd like, we could put you under protective surveillance for awhile."

"Christ no!" said Hank.

"Aren't you going to do that anyway?" Pamela asked. "Or are we actually going to be turned loose?"

Collier smiled. "As far as we're concerned, you're on your own. Since you've exposed yourself to Burke, you're of no further use to us here. And of course we do appreciate your cooperation."

"Hey, come on," said Hank. "Who's kidding who?

I mean Reese had a goddamned gun at our backs. So what's all this crap about cooperation?"

"Would it make you happier if I said we appreciate your forced cooperation?"

"It might not make us any happier," said Pamela, "but it would at least be more accurate." She stared off at the distant lady, lifting her torch in the harbor. "In the meantime," she went on, "I've been fired from my job and have absolutely no chance of getting another."

"Call your former company in a few days," said Collier quietly. "You'll find they've had a change of heart about their need for your services."

"You can do that?"

"We can do that."

"I feel as though I'm going to be sick," Pamela said.

"Would you rather they didn't have a change of heart?"

Pamela left it alone.

"I'm glad you two are here," Collier said. "I know I should have been in touch with you myself, but this wipe-out has had us running in circles. I apologize for that. I can imagine your concern, not hearing anything for so many days. But since Reese was handling your part of things, and orderly recordkeeping was never one of his strong points, I haven't quite caught up yet." He threw in a gratuitous smile. "If any credit is awarded for good intentions, I did intend to call you today or tomorrow."

"What about me?" Hank said abruptly. "Where do I come out in all this?"

"I was getting to that." Collier turned to Pamela. "I wonder if you'd mind waiting in the reception area for a few minutes, Miss Bailey. There's something I'd like to discuss privately with Hank. I'm sure he'll tell you all about it himself, but I'd still like to leave him that option."

When Pamela had left the office, Collier took a manila folder from a drawer, placed it on his desk and leafed through a half-inch of typewritten pages. "This is your personal file, Hank. Everything George Reese knew and thought about you is in here. And as you can see, it's quite a lot."

"I didn't know I was that important," said Hank, certain now that he was about to be set up for something. The only thing in doubt was just how bad it was going to be. He waited while Collier silently read through a few paragraphs. The cancer patient, he thought, waiting for his next tumor.

Collier finished reading. "What do you think of your life these days, Hank?"

"You mean since you guys came into it? Great. I can't wait to get up in the morning."

"No, I mean before Burke started giving you problems. Did you like the way things were going for you then?"

"Why not?"

Collier looked at him.

"Hey, come on," Hank said. "You got my whole goddamned life there in those papers. You know what it is. What are you getting at?"

"Nothing too terrible. I was just wondering if you'd be interested in a change?"

"What kind of change?"

"Like working for us."

Hank frowned. He felt knocked off balance, shaky. "You kidding me or something?"

"No."

"You mean you want me to be a fucking spy?"

Collier laughed. "We're not really spies. At least, not in the accepted sense."

"What the hell are you then?"

"We don't actually have a name. But I guess you could call us middlemen, since we usually operate somewhere between what the government needs to have done and what it can admit doing."

"You mean like killing people?"

"That's very extreme."

"Yeah, but you do it."

"Only when there's no other way."

"Thanks," Hank said. "But I don't think I'd care very much for being a middleman."

Collier smiled patiently. "All right, look at it this way. What if you'd been drafted into the army in 1943 and the government ordered you to kill Germans? Would you have killed them?"

"Sure."

"Why?"

"Because we were at war with Germany."

"Who said we were at war?"

"The government, of course."

"And if the government ordered you to stop killing Germans when the war was over in 1945, you would have stopped, wouldn't you?"

"You sound like a goddamned lawyer."

"I am a goddamned lawyer. Or at least I was, until I got into this. Sometimes it helps. At other times it only gets in the way. When you understand the law too well, you worry too much about having to break it."

Hank gazed off at a departing tanker, faint and small in the grey harbor. Somehow, he was unable to imagine this man being worried about anything.

"What do you want me for?" he asked. "I never even finished high school. What good would I be? Except maybe to bust a few heads here and there."

"That's not what we'd want you for, Hank. And education isn't always important in this work. It was actually George Reese who first mentioned you as a possibility in his reports. He thought you were tough, loyal, intelligent, and had the kind of background that could make you valuable to us in certain ways."

"What certain ways?"

"For several months last year, for example, we could have used you as boxing instructor for the F.B.I. to check on a run of defections. We might also have gotten some help from you in Brazil and Ecuador, where we could have set up a few exhibi-

240

tion bouts to get you in with the locals after three American oil executives were kidnapped and we had no leads. A once popular fighter like yourself is almost universally admired. You'd be trusted as other foreigners would never be. Athletes carry that advantage. They can break down all the usual barriers of nationality difference. Someone like Pele is loved all over the world."

"Thanks, but I'm no Pele."

"Nobody expects you to be. It's enough that you're Hank Ryan, longtime contender for the heavyweight championship of the world."

Hank smiled for the first time in days. "So how come the best I can do is night manager in a pussy parlor?"

"No sponsorship. Fact of life number one. The only thing that matters in this world is who or what's behind you."

"And with you I get sponsorship?"

"The best."

"What's that?"

"Unofficially, the United States of America."

"Do I get a military funeral too? Unofficially?"

"We don't really lose that many people."

"You just lost four last week, and I know of at least three others on this one caper alone."

"An exceptional case."

"Excuse me if I say bullshit."

"That's not what's bothering you."

"Why not? I like living as much as anyone."

"I know. But that's still not it."

Hank was silent. Every instinct told him to get out of there as fast as he could, yet he sat unmoving.

"What's the matter, Hank? Is it that you can't bear the thought of leaving the Orange Lantern?"

"I guess I just don't trust you."

"Have I lied to you?"

"If you have, it's too soon for me to know."

'We're running after you, Hank."

"Why haven't you mentioned anything about that other business?"

"What's that?"

"You know . . ." Even at this point it was hard for him to be specific. "That guy I killed."

"Tom Bishop?"

"Yeah. How come you haven't said anything about him?"

"What do you want me to say?"

"I don't know. But something?"

"Reese told you how we felt about that. What's done is done and we go on from there."

"Then it's forgotten?"

"I didn't say that. I said we go on from there."

"Then it's not forgotten?"

Collier said nothing.

"And maybe," Hank said, needing to get everything clear and out in the open so there would be no remaining doubts, "just maybe, if I decided not to come in with you guys, it could be remembered and hung right up there again, right?"

"We'd rather you came with us because you wanted to, Hank. It would be much easier all around."

"And if I didn't want to?"

Carefully, Collier stubbed out his cigarette. "Then I suppose we'd just have to accept you the hard way."

So there it was, Hank thought, and almost felt relieved. "Jesus, you're a prick."

"Well," said Collier as he stood up. "at least you know we really want you. That's what was bothering you, wasn't it?"

"Not anymore. Now I got other things."

"Who hasn't?" The agent nodded pleasantly. "We'll be in touch, Hank."

Pamela was gone.

The receptionist told Hank, "Miss Bailey said she had something to do and would meet you at home."

The woman smiled. "She said to be sure not to get lost."

"I already am."

23

The irony did not hit Burke quickly or all at once. In fact it came to him rather slowly, in fragments, as he sifted through the events set off by his failure to kill Abu Hamaid. The crazy part was, that if he had carried out his assignment to shoot the Arab leader, he would not have immediately left the Service and would certainly not have changed his appearance. Which further meant, that he would have been readily available when they wanted him—and would now, undoubtedly, be dead.

Sitting against a tree in the early morning damp, he thought: so here I am again.

But it was not really the same. He had no rifle this time, nor did he have any assignment to kill. Still, there was the familiar wait in the rising mists, the tightness in his stomach, and the identical wish that whatever he had to do would be done quickly and without accident or surprise. And again, with the same practicality, he lifted his hands, examined them in the dull, grey light, and was pleased to find they were steady.

He was sitting just off a dirt path that followed a stream through a densely wooded area that might have been anywhere, but was actually less than five miles from the center of downtown Washington. The path ran in a straight line at this point and Burke was able to see north along it for perhaps two hundred yards before it disappeared in the fog. There was a cluster of birch close by and he studied the dark rings on their trunks and wondered, if he were painting them, how many of the markings he would leave out so as not to take too much away from the silver, which was the really beautiful part. When he had first begun to paint, he would have left nothing out. Whatever he saw, he would have painted in, simply because it was the truth. He knew better now, knew that most of art was deception and that truth could often be better expressed through selective lies. A bright thought, but not his. Burke guessed it was Picasso who had first said it, but wished it might have been someone else, someone who had not gone so far off the deep end and spent his last years laughing at the idiots who sanctified every piece of silliness he chose to label with his name.

Burke adjusted his weight, feeling a slight ache in his bad shoulder. It was not quite 6:45 and he had about another fifteen minutes to wait. He hoped nothing went wrong and that this would be the end of it. Yet he knew instantly how foolish any such expectation would be. Even if everything went well, there could be no true end, at least not for him. And there was still always the chance of a real foul-up. His shoulder was better, but far from great, and this could make an important difference in his reaction time. It might have been smarter for him to let the wound heal for another week or two, but he had run out of patience and smartness. And if there was any chance he had not been able to see this for himself, Angela had been worried enough to point it out less than twelve hours before.

"You're still acting like an idiot," she told him. But her voice was quiet, and she was not really angry. Only unhappy.

"Well, once an idiot, always an idiot." He grinned. "Confucius."

"Why can't you at least wait a few days more? You're still half crippled. You wince every time you put your shirt on."

"A few days won't make any difference in my shoulder, and I'm anxious to get this done with."

"Get what done with? Living?"

They were in the room he used as a studio and he was going over some papers at his desk. He did not answer.

"What are you going to do?" she asked.

"Something safe and brilliant. Just have faith."

He reached for her and kissed her. She gripped him hard. "I'm just so damn scared," she whispered. "I don't want to lose you again."

"Nobody's losing anybody."

But later it was necessary to tell her about the money. He had put off the telling until the last possible moment and this was finally it. "Listen," he said gently. "I expect to live to at least a hundred, but we still have to be practical. We still have to get something cleared up for you." He took a valise out of a metal cabinet in his bedroom closet. "There's almost half a million in cash in here. It's good, clean money so you don't have to worry about that part of it." He smiled. "It's sort of my retirement fund, my reward for twenty years of devoted service to my country. What the hell. It's better than a gold watch."

She stared wide-eyed, first at the valise, then at him. "You mean you've been keeping that in the closet all this time?"

"No. It's been in a large safe deposit box until this morning. But I was the only one who could have gotten it out."

Angela frowned slightly, a fine furrow between two delicately arched brows.

"Tomorrow you can take a box under your own name and put the money there. If by some crazy chance you don't hear from me in . . . let's say in two weeks at the outside, you might want to consider some time deposits, or possibly even treasury certificates. If you wish, you can get some advice on that."

Her face was carefully frozen. "To hell with advice. I'm going straight to the nearest track with that bundle. And if there's anything left when I'm through there, I'll try the crap tables in Vegas."

246

"Fine."

"Or maybe," she said "I'll just give it away in a continuing series of Idiot-of-the-Month-Awards in memory of my ex-husband, the super-idiot of all time."

"Anything that will make you happy."

"The only thing that will make me happy," she said with her face intact, "is for us to leave here tomorrow, or the day, or the week, or the month after that, never be apart again for as long as we live, and never come back."

"Don't you think that would make me happy too?"

"Then let's do it, for God's sake!"

"I can't."

"You mean you won't."

"I can't let that man be president."

"My hero!"

"It's not heroics, Angela."

"No? Then what is it? In your own way you're as bad as Ludlow. You both think the fate of the nation lies in your hands."

"I didn't go after this. It was dumped on me."

"It's not your responsibility, damn it!"

"Who else's?"

"There are two hundred million other people in this country."

"None of them know what I know."

"That's not true." Her voice had turned as cold as her face. "You've forgotten Tony and the president. Don't they know as much about Ludlow as you?"

"Yes, but . . ." He was surprised and puzzled. He had expected many things from her, but not this. He needed a moment for regrouping.

She refused to allow it. "But what? But their judgment on the country's needs isn't as good as yours?"

He was silent.

"What makes you think you're in a better position than the president of the United States to decide on the proper qualifications for his successor? If he, the president, thinks Tom Ludlow is the best man around to lead the country during the next four years, who are you to think differently?"

"No one very important," he said softly. "Only Richard Burke. And there's even been some confusion about that lately. But as long as that's who I am, I'm afraid I can't think and make judgments as anyone else. And there's no way under heaven for me to ever make myself believe that someone like Ludlow is the man to be placed within finger-pressing distance of that terrible little black box."

"No way under heaven," she mimicked bitterly. "You're playing God, that's what you're doing. Why can't you just leave it alone?"

"I couldn't live with it, Angela."

"All right, then die with it."

"I'm not planning to die for quite a while yet."

"Of course not. That's why you've just turned your whole goddamned estate over to me," she said and ran from the room.

He slid out of bed at 1:00 A.M. and dressed silently in the dark. Angela seemed to be sleeping. But as he bent to kiss her, she opened her eyes. "I promise you," she whispered fiercely, "I promise you . . . if you don't come back, I swear to Christ I'm going to throw every lousy dollar out the fucking window."

The woods were silent. There was not even a breeze. The only sound Burke heard was an occasional drop of moisture falling from a branch. He watched the path at the place where it disappeared into the mist. No way under heaven, he thought. Remembering his own words, he knew he was not nearly as certain as he had sounded last night. Was he really trying to play God? He had been more strongly affected by the accusation than he cared to admit, but this was an empty, bitter, cynical time. There were no certainties, and he was not about to be swept up in that particular net. He believed in what he was doing. He knew he was the only one who

248

could be counted on to do it. His certainty was that it needed to be done.

Perhaps Angela was right to call it all an ego trip. All motives were suspect, all purity of purpose maligned. Yet it was only ego and vanity that got you out of bed in the morning and kept you from blowing out your brains by dark. They were not dirty words.

The possibility of death was there, of course, but he had lived with it for so long that his defenses were carefully put together. What he had come to feel, rather than fear, was regret—regret at the possible interruption of so many plans, of so much left unfinished. He knew that life would simply go on as though he had never been. So what did it matter? He had seen and felt this clearly enough as he stood outside Angela's window that night and watched her responding to another man. That had been his first true extinction, his first clear awareness that no part of you was really left after you were gone. The soul, of course, was something else, but this was not something to which he had ever given much thought.

He heard the faint sound of someone running. Watching the point where the path disappeared, he heard the sound long before he expected to see the runner. The steady, disciplined beat was as individual as a signature. Burke looked at his watch and saw that it was 7:01. Exactly on schedule. Even in his morning exercise, there was no break in precision. There was a purity to the man that might almost have been beautiful, thought Burke, if it wasn't so frightening.

He rose, stepped onto the path, and stood waiting until he saw the jogger emerge from the mist. Then he started towards him. He walked slowly, almost lethargically, keeping his hands in plain view at his sides. To anyone watching he would not have appeared at all threatening. There was nothing about him to make him look different from any well-dressed area resident out for a casual, early morning stroll. Yet seeing him now, from a distance of almost a hundred yards, the runner abruptly broke stride and cut his pace. Gradually, he slowed until he was no longer running, but walking, a tall, slender, straight-backed man in a dark blue warm-up suit. He still carried himself, Burke thought, as though nothing in God's world could ever bend him.

They were both moving so slowly now that the distance between them hardly seemed to be closing at all. But it was. And they finally came together like two animals of the same species, cautious but not unfriendly, meeting in a quiet mood somewhere in the jungle. They stopped about four feet apart and just stood looking at one another.

It was Ludlow who spoke first. "Richard?" He knew, yet did not know, and had to be sure.

Burke nodded. "Hello, Tom."

"It's a funny thing. At two hundred yards, I felt it was you, and fifty yards closer, I knew it was. When I was close enough to see your face, I had doubts." He smiled, genuinely pleased—an urbane, charming man who might simply have been greeting an old friend after long separation. "It's a good face. I don't think I would ever have known you from your face."

Burke was silent. He was waiting to feel an emotion of some sort. This was, after all, the moment. Yet he felt only the same curious apathy that seemed to come over him during certain periods of great stress.

"The amazing thing is that I wasn't even surprised," said Ludlow, still apparently enjoying the uniqueness of the situation. "It was as though I had been subconsciously expecting it." He smiled almost fondly at Burke. "You know, you've come to play a very important part in my life. Lately, you're the last person I think of before sleep at night, and the first one on my mind when I awake."

"I'm flattered," said Burke. Old working habits had slipped into gear and he was taking automatic inventory. Ludlow's hands, like his own, were in plain sight at his sides; his stance was easy and relaxed.

"Quite honestly, Richard, I underestimated you. I never considered you capable of stirring up this much trouble. It was actually Tony who knew you better." Slowly, carefully, he raised a hand to smooth his hair as a sudden breeze threatened to ruffle it. "Tell me. How were you finally able to trace this to me?"

"What difference does it make?"

"I think I have a small right to be curious. This was a high-priority, top-level operation. Our best talent was involved. I'd like to know who slipped."

"No one really slipped. I suppose I just got lucky. I picked up a lot of loose ends, tied a few together, and bugged your house. I finally heard you talking to the president one night."

Ludlow grimaced in disgust. "Then I was the one. I was stupidly careless. No. I suppose it was really arrogance, which can be even more dangerous."

Grudgingly, Burke admired the man's poise. There was no visible fear, not even concern. Yet he had to know what he faced.

They stood about four feet apart in the mist, but their eyes met and stayed together. It might have been the gaze of lovers. There was that kind of heat.

"Why didn't you just pick me off as I went by?" said Ludlow.

"Is that what you would have done?"

"You know it."

"No I don't. Not really."

"Haven't you noticed?" said Ludlow. "There have been a great many people trying to kill you?"

"Yes, but that was a campaign. Not you personally."

"What's the difference? You would have been just as dead." The pale eyes were puzzled. "I don't understand what you're getting at."

"Eighteen years ago you had me tied to a tree, helpless. Why didn't you kill me then?"

251

"I almost did." Ludlow smiled ruefully. "As it turns out, I should have."

"But you didn't."

Ludlow stared at him. "You mean that's why you didn't put one into me from behind a tree just now?"

"I felt I owed you that much."

"And now?"

"Now I figure we're even."

"Good Lord! You don't really believe that line of nonsense, do you?"

Burke did not answer. His shoulder was starting to ache and he knew he should not be standing there. He hoped Ludlow would declare himself soon.

"I know from way back what a humanist fool you can be," said Ludlow, "but not even you could be that much of a Boy Scout. No. I don't buy that. Not for a minute. And I don't think you do either." He smiled queerly. "You know why?" He laughed. "Because when you cut through all the silly Sunday School sentiment, you know in your heart that I'm exactly what this country needs for survival in our sunny, little, nuclear jungle. And because you do know it, because you do sincerely care about what happens to a couple of hundred million poor, helpless slobs out there, you can never really get yourself to finish me.

"Please, Richard." Ludlow's voice had taken on new urgency. "Too many people have already died in this comedy. Good people, with good motives. And all wanting essentially the same things. It's insane. Don't you know that by now? So let's drop it right here. Let's walk away from this place and one another and call it finished. It's not really all that complicated. Just stay off my back and let things take their course. Promise me that and I'll have Kreuger call off his hounds. His heart was never in this anyway. You know how he feels about you."

"I know. He loves me like a brother."

"It happens to be true. This has torn him apart. He just believed I had something valuable to offer and

252

that you would never allow me to offer it. The man is a true patriot. I know patriots are out of fashion these days, but I thank God we still have a few like Tony."

God and patriotism! thought Burke, rubbing his shoulder.

"What's the matter with your shoulder?"

"A small bite from one of my brother's hounds."

As though in empathy, Ludlow chewed his lip. "Listen, Richard. Finish this thing before it's too late. You've been carrying that load inside you for eighteen years. Isn't that long enough? Whatever we were then, we're not anymore."

Burke did not reply. His hands were in his coat pockets now, his shoulders hunched against the chill.

"All I'm asking is a chance," said Ludlow softly. "Just give me your word on that and this nightmare will be over. No one will bother you again."

"Just my word?"

"Your integrity has never been in doubt."

"What about your word?"

"I'm telling you, Richard. Walk away from here and it's over this minute. What other assurances can I give you? If I don't keep my word, if you see any sign at all of Tony's hounds, you can blow the whistle on me then." He smiled sardonically. "I promise you the *Washington Post* will always be happy to print any horror story you choose to come up with about me."

Burke was still looking at him as though he were far off. Ludlow had been too much for him once. Perhaps he still was. There was only one way to find out.

"All right," he said quietly.

"You'll give me a chance?"

Burke nodded. His mouth was as dry as old leaves, and a sharp sad pain, almost pleasurable in its intensity, was working its way through him.

"You won't regret it, Richard." Ludlow held out

his hand across the four feet between them, across the eighteen years, across the twenty-three dead.

Burke gazed at it for a long moment. Then Burke pulled a hand free of his coat pocket and reached for the one that was waiting.

Ludlow gripped hard, and in a single fluid motion, yanked Burke forward, drove a knee into his groin, and hit him in the neck with his free hand, a chop that dropped him rolling in the dirt. Eyes blurred with pain, Burke barely saw the kick coming and could not have avoided it if he had. It caught him in the side of the head, and it was only because Ludlow was wearing soft running shoes, that his skull was not caved in. He lay on his back.

"You never learn, do you, Richard?"

Ludlow spoke quietly, without elation. Burke stared up at him. Ludlow had taken a small pistol from the back pocket of his warm-up suit and was holding it casually pointed at the ground. He appeared in no hurry to use it. Ludlow was a man who knew how to make the most of life's more glowing moments.

"You were doing so well, Richard. It's too bad it has to end for you like this."

"You're going to shoot me, of course."

Ludlow looked mildly surprised. "Of course. That's what you should have done to me earlier with a rifle. As I told you eighteen years ago, there's no place on this planet for sentiment. It's as obsolete as the dinosaur. And only those who know this will be able to survive."

"I don't think I'd enjoy that sort of survival."

"Have no fear, Richard. You're not going to have that problem." Ludlow shook his head. "You poor, obsolete fool. I really should have you stuffed and mounted in the Capitol rotunda. The nation's own special dinosaur. You'd make a valuable warning to the citizens of the republic."

He started to raise the pistol when Burke fired

three times through his pocket. All of the shots were in the killing zone.

He left the body where it fell.

But driving back to New York, his head and bowels aching, he agreed with Ludlow that shooting from ambush would have been more sensible. Still, needing to be absolutely sure, he'd had no choice. No true, self-respecting dinosaur could have done otherwise.

Epilogue

I

Burke thought of them often during the year, but New Year's Eve was a special reminder of the four.

He and Angela were about to welcome another new year, this one together, in San Francisco, where the light was soft and steady on most days and the limitations on artists were strictly their own. People were, of course, still shooting one another. He supposed they always would. But this no longer had anything to do with him. What he was interested in mostly, was Angela and the substance of their days and years, the ones still ahead. He considered himself ahead on points, and from here on he had the same odds going for him as anyone, the same chances for joy and sorrow. He was pleased to accept them. As was Angela.

She looked younger than he now. She too now had a new face. There had been no choice: if they found her, they found him. But the result was the same. She had been beautiful before, why not now? And she was.

"Maybe I'll have better luck painting this face," he said hopefully, but he didn't. Love still clouded his brush. He continued to do well with her eyes, but of course they were unchanged.

She laughed about it. "Never mind," she said after his latest failure. "It proves you still love me."

So looking at their new faces, they shared an old love. Also, old ghosts. There was no escaping these. Unseen, they still had solidarity. Sometimes they even talked about them. When they did, it was usually Angela who started it. She had less training in silence than he.

"Do you think they're still looking for you?" she said.

"There's no reason anymore."

"That's not what I asked."

"I'm sure Tony still thinks about me."

"That's still no answer."

"It's all I have," he told her.

Which was not entirely true. He also had conjecture. But he saw no reason to involve her in that. Beyond the facts, all he could do was imagine. And the facts were few. One was, of course, that Ludlow was dead, another tragic victim (according to official press releases) of the growing, senselessly violent rash of crime that was sweeping the capital, the country, and the world. Watching the funeral on television, Burke had found it impressive. The President and countless other dignitaries were present. The eulogy was delivered by the Secretary of State, who described Ludlow as an outstanding patriot and one of the truly great men of his time. Burke had never doubted the intensity of Ludlow's patriotism—just its quality. Still, history had been known to honor all sorts of men for all sorts of reasons, and its standards of judgment were not necessarily his own. And if statues were sometimes erected to those so honored, many were later pulled down.

As for Tony, he remained, for Burke, half fact, half conjecture. Walled up behind whatever new cover he had chosen, he was as invisible to Burke as Burke was to him. Having discovered that strong belief could make men willing to deceive and murder even their friends, he undoubtedly was going right on doing whatever his convictions told him to do next. Or so Burke imagined. He also imagined their unlikely but still not altogether impossible meeting. And he had a recurrent dream over which he had no control.

"Well, schmuck," Tony would begin, "you've

257

really done it now. You've buried the next president of the United States."

Unaccountably, Burke would find himself grinning. "The sonofabitch had no integrity. To the last goddamned second of his life, he was making deals, then busting them."

"I know. What a president he would have made. One of our greatest."

"I'm ashamed of you, Tony."

"I just did what I had to. The same as you." He would shake his head here. "Jesus, how did you ever get out of this?"

"It was easy. I just remembered everything you taught me."

"You're better than I ever was. You decimated me."

"He who has right on his side," Burke would quote grandly, "has the strength and wisdom of ten."

"Bullshit! We had the right. You think the world is run with Bible maxims? You've hurt this country, Richard."

"I don't believe that."

"You don't know a damn thing about it. You are a self-righteous fanatic."

"I was trying to stay alive."

"Ha!"

"At first, anyway. Later, when I found out about Ludlow, it became more."

"Lousy virtue-monger."

"I never betrayed and tried to kill a friend."

"I took no pleasure in that."

"And you even tried to use your father."

"If my sainted mother were alive, I'd have tried to use her too." He would take a moment here. "But if it's worth anything to you, Richard, through it all I've never loved you any less."

Because Burke knew the truth would embarrass him, he would say, "You're breaking my heart."

"It's over now. You've won. You can afford to be a little generous."

"Is it really over?"

"I just said it was."

"And I say, 'up yours.'"

Tony would laugh here. "I get the distinct feeling you don't trust me anymore. But there's no practical reason for us to want you now. And you know it's never been anything personal."

"What about leaving loose ends? And you did lose some good people."

"We're not vindictive. Besides, I somehow still think of you as one of our own."

"And my four friends?"

"They weren't all such friends."

"Considering, they stood up damned well."

"Okay. So they're bloodkin. Anyway, if it's over for you, it's over for them." The deep-set eyes would look at him . . . very straight, very sincere. "Listen. I'm unhappy about Ludlow, but not all that sad about you."

"The country picked a better man than Ludlow."

"I don't believe that."

"At least he has human instincts."

"Please, Richard. Just paint nice, love Angela, and keep your sticky, pious hands out of politics."

"You should have drafted your father."

"For what?"

"For president."

"Oh, God!"

"That's some old man. He's one of a kind. I love him."

"So do I, schmuck. But he'd have messed things up almost as fast and thoroughly as you."

"You don't know as much about it as you think."

"And you do?"

"At least I never tried to play God."

Tony would laugh here, loudly, almost uncontrollably. "Christ Almighty! What do you think you've been doing?"

"Following my conscience."

"That can be just as fatal."

259

"What a sad thing to say."

Then they would be silent and just stand there, not quite looking at each other.

"Well, old buddy," Tony would say at last, and hold out his hand. "I'll see you around."

"No you won't," Burke would reply. And ignoring the offered hand, he would turn and walk away.

And this was how the imagined meeting would always end. Burke would sometimes make an effort to change it, would occasionally try to accept the offered hand just to see how it would feel. They had, after all, been friends for more than twenty years, and Tony had said there was nothing personal in his wanting to have him liquidated. But Burke was never quite able to get himself to do it. Taking that hand seemed utterly beyond him. Regardless of how hard he tried, he simply could not imagine anything impersonal about wanting to kill a friend.

II

Three thousand miles away near Kennebunkport, Maine, David Tomschin was also seeing out the old year. It was his first New Year's Eve away from the City, away from the bumper-to-bumper traffic, the rolling tides of people, and the millions of nervously dancing lights. There were times during the past year when he had wondered what he was doing up here (the dark end of the earth, his mother had called it), looking out over rocks and water, watching the gulls, seeing the snow pile up and cover the earth, probably until spring. But generally, he accepted the place and condition of his life without question. He had come up in early April just for the summer and simply stayed on, living alone in a small cabin he had bought near the water. The place had been rundown and needed a lot of work; he had done most of it himself, going into town only for food and supplies. No one bothered him. People minded their own business up here. After a few months, he was even able to start writing again. He had no idea whether the stuff was any good, but at least he was covering pages. Until then, any thought of writing had just made him feel sick. Somehow in his mind the writing had been all tied up with Dolores, and he had needed time to handle that. One corner of his brain was still in mourning. Maybe it always would be. But the rest of him was back among the living.

Before David had left New York, Ellman appeared at his door one day, his arm in a sling. David was not surprised. He had been expecting a visit from him or one of his men ever since the shooting. The only surprise was that it had taken a few weeks in coming.

"What took you so long?" he said. "I was beginning to think you'd either forgotten about me or died."

Ellman settled into a chair with a sigh. "Aren't you even going to ask how I feel?"

"I don't give a damn. Unless it's real lousy."

"It's real lousy."

"Good."

"That's not very charitable."

"Go screw."

Ellman shook his head and struggled to fill his pipe, his fingers working more slowly than usual.

"Look," said David. "If you're going to arrest me, then arrest me, goddamn it. But I hate all this messing around."

"I'm no cop, David. I'm not here to arrest anybody."

"Then what the hell do you want?"

"Not much. Just to give you some information I thought you might want to hear."

"You got cancer?"

The agent looked mildly hurt. "You're a pretty tough kid, huh?"

"Not tough enough. If I was, I'd have put that bullet in your head instead of your shoulder."

"And you're sorry you didn't?"

"Every minute of the day."

Ellman reached inside his jacket, took out a snub-nosed revolver and offered it to David, butt forward. "Okay," he said quietly. "Then do it."

David stared at the gun. "Don't tempt me, damn it."

"I am tempting you."

"You sonofabitch, you're pressing your luck."

"No I'm not. But you'd better know that right now. If you don't, if you keep trying to fool yourself about wanting to kill me, it's going to eat your gut for the next twenty years. And finally, you're the one who'll die of it."

Sweating, David started to reach for the gun. But his hand quit on him and he just sat staring at the floor.

The agent put away his revolver. "Good. At least that's a beginning. In the meantime, I just thought you'd like to know the heat is off on the Burke thing."

"Why?"

"I don't know."

"Did," David was almost afraid to ask, "did they get him?"

"I don't know that either." Ellman chewed at his pipe. "Sometimes I'm astonished at how ridiculously little I do know. But either way, whether Burke's been picked up or not, it's finished as far as you and I are concerned. So if you're smart, you'll just try to forget the whole thing."

"Sure."

"I mean it, David. No one can change what's happened, so don't be foolish. You've got a lot of good years ahead of you. Don't turn them sour by hanging onto this."

David stood up. "You finished?"

"I suppose so."

"Okay," David said. "Then before you get out of here, you'd better understand this. I'm not going to forget a damn thing. Just the opposite. I'm going to make sure I remember. I'm going to remember every trick, every lie, every hurt, every humiliation. I'm going to remember every obscenity committed in the name of our beloved country. And as soon as I'm able, I'm going to start fighting them. I don't know how, but I'm going to do it. Me, David Tomschin, personally."

Looking weary and regretful, Ellman rose. "For your own sake, I wish you didn't feel that way."

"Well, I do."

"David . . ." Ellman began. But he cut himself off and, watching him, David suddenly felt there was something almost frightened in his usually controlled face. Then his jaws tightened on the pipe-stem, his shoulders straightened and he went out.

Big talk, David had decided later. Sometimes you said things without thinking because they sounded good. Afterwards, you thought. So among the trees and rocks, and beside the cold Maine sea, he thought. What and whom was he going to fight? And with what weapons? Even to think about it seemed ridiculous. Yet the sound of his words still echoed like bugles. Me . . . David Tomschin . . . personally. Beautiful. History flowed around him in a rushing stream and he was the rock in the middle. Some rock. He was a skinny, big-city Jew with a damaged face, hiding among the New England *goyem* and mumbling vengeance in his beard. He was a joke and not a very good one at that. In a movie he knew it would have been different. In a movie it would have moved along ritual lines, with Tomschin, the hero, plotting his deeds in valor deep into the night, then marching forth to carry them out. But he was not in a movie. And there were no soft-focus fade-outs or frozen-frame finales to mark any kind of heroic end. What he had, mostly, was his loneliness. The coast of Maine could be a painfully lonely place. And no less so because he had chosen it himself.

Still, he did have his writing, his small flow of words. And he did try to make something of them. It was true that words were not even close to being flesh. They had no real substance, and you could not lie with them in bed. Yet, in a way, you could feel them and they could create feelings in others. They might even attack, destroy, perform heroic deeds. Me . . . David Tomschin . . . personally. And what could be more personal than words? How could you dig deeper than an idea? They lasted. They stayed behind when you went on.

Big deal.

If Sam Ellman knew (which in itself was unlikely), he was not exactly cringing. So David Tomschin was scribbling his small cries of pain and protest in a pine hut somewhere along the coast of Maine. Who cared? Who would see his words? And if they did see, who would believe them? And if they did believe, what could they do about them? This was, after all, America: land of freedom, love, and opportunity.

But David knew better. He had learned a few things about America. He had made discoveries. He had seen dead flies floating in the great pot of American chicken soup. He had discovered history, found out there was injustice in the world, and learned about it first-hand. He had not yet made the other discovery—that to survive, you cultivated a distance from such facts and events. He did not yet understand that kind of retreat. He did not yet know what it meant to settle quietly into the limp acceptance that passed for serenity among certain of the citizens of his country. Or if, subtle and unadmitted, he sometimes did know, he was not yet ready to surrender to it. Maybe he never would be.

In any case, he rarely looked that far ahead. It was enough, for now, that he was alive, that he was in motion, and that the coming year was beginning to look wide open.

III

For Pamela and Hank in New York New Year's Eve was as much a reunion as a celebration. Hank had returned from seven weeks in Brazil only the night before. They gazed at and touched one another and felt young despite their turmoil and their years. They could still make each other feel this. It was a special kind of magic, an answer to the confusing, dangerous times and the horrors of loneliness. Also, they had obligations to one another. They wanted to dive head first into whatever lay ahead. They were in love.

"Tell me about Brazil," she said, when it finally became time for such things as speech, nourishment, and the simple act of breathing slowly.

He lifted his head grandly, brows arched. "I can't."

"Why not?"

"It's classified."

"What's classified? Brazil?"

"I'm classified, ya dumb broad."

She stared at him.

"Listen," he said. "In case you didn't know it, you happen to have just been laid by a very high-class spy."

She hit him with a pillow.

Still, there was a certain truth to it. He had what Herbert Collier was pleased to call sponsorship. He moved in high circles in many different places. He was treated with respect. He heard his name spoken in foreign accents and he loved hearing it. He heard other things, too—bits and pieces, much of which held little significance for him, but which he never-theless remembered and carefully passed on as he had been instructed. And he despised no part of it. What he had started doing reluctantly and under pressure, he gradually came to do willingly and out of conviction. He was, after all, an American and he was working for his country. Life seemed to have joined them in a mutual debt. They both owed and they were both paying. They were surviving together in a hostile world. And it was a hell of a lot better than the Orange Lantern.

But it was more than just that. If Hank was not always able to put it into words, there was always Pamela to help him.

"You're pretty happy about things these days, aren't you?" she said, approaching another year.

"What's happy?"

"Don't be cute. I'm serious."

"So?"

"So you really like what you're doing, don't you?"

But it still seemed to embarrass him to admit it. "Hey, listen . . . it's a lot better than a sharp stick in the eye." The end of the year, which for so many was the time for self-examination, for appraisal, was for him the time to make bad jokes and hide what he truly felt. Perhaps he still carried some of his mother's Old Country superstitions. Why tempt the devil by adding up your blessings? But because he loved Pamela, he tried. "The thing is, I feel like a real person again. You know what I mean?"

Of course she knew. She was no stranger to these things. Her need to be a 'real person' was every bit as great as his, and she remembered what she had felt when she was rehired by her old company. They had done everything but kiss her ass when she came back. And with a little encouragement, the division president himself would have done that, too. But that particular treat was too good for him. The president was as uncomfortable with the rehiring as he had been with the firing, and she did nothing to make it easier for him. "I think the whole thing stinks," she told him when he had finished reciting his prescribed lines. "I think the company's behavior was disgusting, and your treatment of me personally was cruel and inhuman."

He spread his hands. "What else could I have done?"

"You could have at least been honest. I spent a lot of years here. I did a damned good job for you. Don't you think I deserved honesty at least?"

He did not answer.

"What were you so afraid of? It was me they were after, not you."

"The orders came from the top, Pamela. They were very explicit. You were to be let go as part of a general retrenchment. Period."

"And you think that was right?"

"I didn't say it was right. I just said those were my orders."

"Which you would never question?"

"We're all expendable, Pamela. I wasn't looking to be a hero."

"I wasn't looking for you to be a hero either, John. But how nice if you could have at least managed to be a man," she said and walked out.

But any satisfaction she was able to find in this was small and quickly faded. She had betrayed Burke. Under enough pressure, she had proven herself no more noble than John, so who was she to throw stones? Besides, his guilt had been strong enough to get her a senior vice-presidency. Which she undoubtedly deserved, but which would otherwise have been a long time in coming. So she was just as content not to think too much about the past. Brooding about what was over and done was not her nature, even if she sometimes had to concede that things were never really over and done, but just kept making fainter and fainter ripples. Maybe you stopped seeing them after awhile, but that didn't mean they weren't still out there somewhere.

Burke still came to mind, especially at this time of year. She wondered about him—where he was and what he was doing. Considering how things had worked out, she harbored no resentments and hoped he felt the same. Though in his place, she knew she would always feel bitter. But she also knew that given another chance, and all things being equal, she would still act no differently than she had. How could she? She was still Pamela Bailey.

Close to midnight, and as though reading her mind, Hank asked,

"Ever think about Eric?"

"Sometimes. What about you?"

"Almost every day."

"What do you think?"

"Lots of stuff. But mostly, I guess, how he'd probably get a big kick out of knowing what I'm doing."

"You think he knows?"

Hank shook his head. "I don't think he's in the country anymore. I wouldn't be if I was him. I'd have gotten out and stayed out."

But even as he said it, he knew he was probably wrong, for both of them. Months before, Collier had told him they were no longer looking for Burke. No reasons, just the fact of it. It was a crazy business, but he was beginning to know about such things. The first thing he had learned was to accept what he was told and not to ask questions. There was even a certain relief in it. What you didn't know you weren't responsible for. There was also the magic of any functioning system. It was there because it worked, and who was he to second-guess it? So he felt himself in touch with Burke through his new training. Working for your country was a continuum. Probably nothing had changed in two hundred years, other than names, faces and styles. What Burke once had felt, he now felt.

It was mostly out of this feeling that he was able to say, "Hey, I've thought of a terrific way for us to start the New Year."

"How is that?"

"Get married."

She looked at him. He was grinning as though he had just told her a very funny joke and was waiting for her to laugh. Curiously, she just felt like crying.

"Well, what do you think?" he said.

"You don't have to marry me."

"What kind of dumb answer is that from such a smart dame?"

"I'm not so smart."

"You're smart. You're smart. You're so damn smart it scares hell out of me sometimes." He was still grinning, but it was growing a bit forced. "Listen, it's only because I've gotten to be such a big, high-class spy that I've even got the guts to ask you. Or maybe you still think of me as a thick-headed, broken-down pug."

"I've never thought of you that way, you ape." Helplessly, she felt the tears start.

"Hey, what are you crying for? Come on. Cut it out. Okay. Forget the whole thing. I was only kidding anyway."

"Like hell you were," she wailed and grabbed him. "You're not weaseling out that easy. A proposal is a goddamned proposal."

So they had looked past one another's surgically altered faces for a glimpse of what lay beneath and found more than either expected. They had actually changed shape against each other. But the big thing now, was that they finally knew it.

IV

Lilly waited for the New Year under the postcard palms and cerulean skies of Beverly Hills. She awaited it without great joy, although her first film had just been successfully completed and her agent was considering good offers from three major producers. Her luck had been good.

Yet she felt no exultation. Perhaps she had reached a point in life where she no longer soared with the good or plunged with the bad because she knew that either way it wasn't going to last. Wasn't there hurt in even the best of it? She had once read somewhere that those who loved the most had the saddest eyes. Perhaps because they had the most to lose.

Still, when it came to love, she guessed you chose your own poison. Who, but yourself, pushed you? But that was being cynical and she knew she did not want to be that. So what did she want? She was not sure. But it might be nice, she thought, to be able to make a small measure of peace with her own history.

How long had it been? Six months? She was not even sure of that.

"Hello, Lilly," he had said, and turning she saw Burke.

"My God, is it really you?"

He smiled under the streetlight. "Who else?"

"I never thought I'd see you again," she said, and looked furtively up and down the empty California street. "Is it safe?"

"Reasonably."

But she was not reassured and quickly led him into the small bungalow the studio had rented for her. Inside she drew the blinds before she switched on a lamp.

"I didn't know if you were dead or alive," she said. "I swear I'm so excited I'm shaking all over."

He took both her hands in his and sat down beside her on a couch. Looking at her, his eyes were warm. "That's one of the reasons I'm here. I wanted you to know I'm all right. The heat seems to be off. I thought you might be wondering."

"Christ, yes."

"I also wanted to thank you in person."

"Oh, come on."

"I'll never forget what you tried to do for me, what

270

you did do for me. It was much more than I had any right to ask. I'm very grateful, Lilly."

He somehow embarrassed her, made her feel like a child. "Oh, Eric. All I really managed to do was fall in love, make an ass of myself, and stupidly try to suck you into a trap." She saw no point in mentioning that she had also managed to get a strange man in a Mercedes shot full of holes.

"Not many could have shown your kind of heart."

She waved it aside. "What about the others? David, Pam, Hank. I'm sure they did no differently."

"They did the best they could. They were fine, considering the heat. But you were still exceptional."

She stood up and went to the liquor cabinet. "Well, anyway, you're alive and well and here, so let's have a drink to celebrate."

"I've been reading about you." He watched her pour bourbon over ice. "You seem to have taken Lotus-Land by storm."

"Amazing, isn't it? I mean, what bigger tits and a smaller nose can do for a person. Anyway, I'm not kicking. I've been lucky as hell."

"It's a lot more than luck, Lilly."

"Don't kid yourself. It helps." She handed him his drink. "What about you? They're really leaving you alone?"

"As far as I know."

She kissed him. "That's super. You don't know how happy that makes me."

"Yes, I do."

"Have you told the others?"

"No. But I'm sure they've gotten the word."

"How?"

"It doesn't matter."

She knew better than to press it. "So how come you're way out here in Hollywood? You want to get in pictures too?"

"I came here to see you."

"No fooling?"

271

"No fooling." He studied her over his drink. "Have you seen your friend lately?"

"My friend?" She laughed. "Oh. You mean Frank?"

He nodded.

"Not for the past few months. After you turned out to be too smart for him, they shipped him somewhere down in Central America."

"Then it's all over between you?"

She grinned. "Hell, no. When I get my hooks in a guy, they'd have to ship him to another planet to bust him loose. He calls every chance he gets. Crazy, isn't it? I mean we both started out just trying to use each other and look what happened. People can't be too careful can they?"

"I guess not."

"I have a sneaky feeling he's going to surprise me one of these days. Like you just did. He'll probably catch me in curlers and cold cream, looking a mess. I haven't heard from him in about five days and that's longer than usual. I suppose that's why I've got this feeling about him surprising me."

Burke was silent. He seemed to be trying to stare through a solid wall into the next room.

"When you were off on an assignment like that," she said, "did you ever just show up and surprise your wife one day?"

"Once in a while."

She laughed. "I guess it might not always be too smart. You could walk in on a lot more than you bargained for."

"Lilly . . ."

"But I kind of like the idea. It's exciting. I mean, not knowing when he might suddenly turn up. And I'm not worried about getting caught, or anything dumb like that. I haven't done any fooling around at all since we started together. For me, for the way I was, that's saying a lot. I haven't even wanted to. I'd rather just think about him, than have anyone else. I find I . . ."

"Lilly . . ." he cut in, "listen to me a minute."

"Okay, I'm listening," she said and drank her bourbon.

"He isn't going to surprise you."

She looked at him.

"There was an item in the *New York Times* the other day," he said. "Being out here, I didn't think you were likely to see it. It was only a small article. It just said that an American business man, Frank Harkevy, had been in an accident outside of Managua, Nicaragua. His car had apparently gone off the road." Watching her face, Burke took a moment. "I'm afraid he's dead, Lilly."

She sat there for a long time, looking at him. Her face was pale, but otherwise showed nothing. Slowly, very carefully, she finished her drink.

"You okay?"

She nodded.

"I'm sorry," he said. "I had no way of knowing he meant anything to you anymore. I had hoped he didn't. If that was so, I wasn't even going to tell you."

She was still nodding.

"As it was," he went on, "there would have been no way for you to find out. You'd have just never heard from him again. I couldn't let that happen to you."

Dry-eyed, she had stopped nodding. He got up, refilled her glass and handed it to her. Then he watched her as she drank.

"Was it really an accident?" she said at last.

"There's no way to know that, Lilly."

"He was a good driver, very careful. He never even drove up to the speed limit. I used to tease him about driving like an old lady."

Burke was silent.

"They killed him, didn't they?"

"I don't know who you mean."

"Neither do I," she said flatly. "But I know it was no accident."

She knew nothing of the sort, but this was how she preferred to think of it. It was easier for her. Somehow it seemed less of a waste than an accident. Not that reasons changed anything. The result was the same. But the one thing she kept remembering him saying was, "I chose this work, Lilly." All right, you crazy, goddamned spy, she swore silently. You chose it; you got it.

Finally she wept.

Burke stayed with her through the night. They lay together, bodies clothed but pressed close for human touch.

"Do you love someone?" she asked in the dark.

"Yes."

"Who?"

"My wife."

"I didn't even know you were married again."

"I'm not. Not really. We're still divorced. For two years she thought I was dead."

"Why?"

"It was expedient. The Service is a wild business."

"And now you have risen?"

"I have risen. But it took a lot more than three days."

"Maybe?" she whispered.

"Don't even think about it."

"It's just that I feel so damn cheated. We had so little of it."

"You can't measure it that way. Some never have it at all, Lilly."

"I know. But it's so dumb. Managua, Nicaragua, for God's sake! That's not a place; it's a goddamned song."

Her body shook and he tried to stop it with his. Wanting to comfort her, he did not know how.

"It's nice about you and your wife. I'm glad about that. That's really great."

He said nothing.

"Are you going to get married again?"

"We can't. There'd be too many problems. But we don't need that."

"I guess not." She thought about it in the dark. "What's your wife's name?"

"Angela."

"Is she really an angel?"

"Hardly."

"That's good," she said softly.

They held one another.

"Eric?" She used the name that was not really his, but which she would not have felt comfortable about changing now.

"Yes?"

"Do you think Angela would mind very much if you made love to me tonight?"

It took him by surprise.

"It would be better than sending flowers," she whispered.

Her face wet and tight against his, she felt him smile.

"Well, maybe if I don't enjoy it too much."

They did not come together as lovers. They were not that. The act was tender for him, a trifle desperate for her. Still, from a purely practical standpoint, she was right. It was better than flowers.

"You're really a very kind man," she said afterward.

"It wasn't that difficult. Believe me."

"Probably a lot kinder than Frank ever was."

"We are all pretty much alike."

"I have to tell you something," she said, and told him about the shooting of the stranger in the parking lot. "Frank never gave him a chance. The poor guy never even knew what hit him. And that could have been you."

275

"I'm glad it wasn't. But Frank was just following an accepted Service procedure. It even has a special name. It's called to terminate with extreme prejudice." He smiled in the dark. "It has a ring, doesn't it? So condemn his job if you have to, but not him."

"Would you have done something like that?"

"I have, Lilly."

She stared off into the dark. There was still a lot of anger in her. "God, I'll never understand any part of that."

"Not many can."

"But how could you?"

"It was never easy. Finally, as you know, I couldn't. But even now, I do know this." It took him a long moment to drag loose the admission. "Someone has to."

Six months, and in that time she had been up and she had travelled down. At times she had even hung somewhere in the middle and irrationally refused to accept the fact of Frank's death. Had she, after all, seen his body? Burke had told her he was dead, but they had also told Burke's wife that he was dead. So obviously anything was possible in that loony world in which these curious men had chosen to operate. Burke had told her not to think about it, but who could stop her? Whatever happened once could happen again.

She was not religious, but felt certain the world could not run without some design. Her rage, her pain, her fear hung on to what she remembered of the past, and rejected what she did not want of the future. With a controlled will and a small private angel you could do anything, she told herself. So one day, she knew it would happen. One day she knew she would hear a familiar voice in a strange, new face say, "Hello, Lilly," And she would turn and smile and say, without surprise, speaking directly to his eyes because the eyes were always the same and she would know them instantly, "Ah, love . . . what took you so long?"

About the Author

Norman Garbo is the author of CONFRONTATION (with Howard Goodkind), which won the Harper Find Award. His other novels are THE MOVEMENT, THE ARTIST, CABAL, and TURNER'S WIFE. In addition to being a novelist, he has also been a syndicated columnist and a painter whose work has been shown at the Metropolitan Museum of Art, the Chicago Art Institute, and the Philadelphia Museum.